MW01125096

CRY OF
THE HEART

RLYNN JOHNSON

MILSPEAK BOOKS

An imprint of MilSpeak Foundation, Inc.

© 2021 MilSpeak Foundation, Inc.

All rights reserved, including the right of reproduction in whole or in part in any form except in the case of brief quotations embodied in critical articles or reviews. For permission, contact publisher at the following email address: info@milspeakfoundation.org.

DISCLAIMER: Cry of the Heart is fictional, as are all the characters that inhabit its pages. Although many of the places and events portrayed in this work exist or happened in the real world, the characters' participation in them is purely the product of the author's imagination.

Manufactured in the United States of America

Library of Congress Cataloging-in-Publication Data

Johnson, RLynn

Library of Congress Control Number: 2021947281
ISBN 978-1-7378676-1-6 (paperback)
ISBN 978-1-7378676-5-4 (epub)

Editing by: Ann Wicker
Cover art by: www.BoldBookCovers.com
Formatting by: www.BoldBookCovers.com

MilSpeak Foundation, Inc.
5097 York Martin Road
Liberty, NC 27298
www.MilSpeakFoundation.org

For mothers and daughters, especially Barbara and Caroline

PROLOGUE

The woman at the counter was drowning Pauline just as surely as if the woman were holding Pauline's head under water. Pauline had asked her whether it was possible to trade an aisle seat for a window, expecting in response a word (*yes* or *no*), or possibly a phrase or short sentence (*I'm sorry, there are no window seats available.*). Instead, Pauline was flooded with information about the plane being completely booked and an earlier flight that had been canceled and passengers from that flight being rebooked on this one and Monday being Columbus Day and therefore this the start of a three-day weekend and therefore an exceptionally busy travel day. *Yes or no.* In the weeks before the Alpha Weekend, two people had not asked Pauline an infinitely more important question, with infinitely more ramifications and yet the choice of responses was the same. Yes or no. The answer to the question posed to the woman at the counter would determine if Pauline would have a place to rest her head or if she would be crawled over by someone on the way to the lavatory. The answer to the question that had not been posed to Pauline would mean the difference between a future of sailing and one of dog paddling. The difficulty was that Pauline wasn't sure which answer was the sailing response.

She was glad that the Alphas weekend was in the autumn this year. For a time, they had fallen into the pattern of getting together in February. In Minnesota. Up north in Minnesota. She had to smile when she thought about it: one would think that four reasonably intelligent, overly educated women could do better for their annual no-husbands-no-kids weekend than northern Minnesota in February. At least this year Pauline's "warm" clothes might be adequate for mid-October up there. It was good to gather in autumn this year, their twentieth of such gatherings, since the first Alpha Weekend all those years ago had been in the fall.

Twenty years ago they had all just graduated from law school in St. Paul, taken and passed the bar exam, and were gliding off to Life in the Real World. Arden and Jeanne were going to work in law firms in the Twin Cities. Angela was going to change the world as an assistant district attorney in one of the outlying suburbs. Pauline was on her way to Fort Ord, in Monterey, California, as a first lieutenant in the Army Judge Advocate General's Corps. That first year, the four, who didn't yet think of themselves as Alphas, borrowed the keys to Arden's in-laws' cabin, persuaded some husbands that they needed a little girl time, and headed north with sleeping bags, cigarettes, and boxed wine. As the years marched by, incomes grew and locations and accommodations improved in proportion. The dates of the annual weekends shifted in the calendar to accommodate pregnancies, family responsibilities, and work schedules. Over time, the flow of wine and clouds of cigarette smoke that filled these weekends diminished as their lives expanded with children, jobs becoming careers, and dreams of the future becoming either present realities or tender regrets.

Now, instead of Arden's in-laws' cabin, they would be at Arden's cabin on the lake. So many life-important decisions pondered, so many joys and heartaches shared, and so many of the world's problems solved during these weekends! During one of the gatherings, at a chilly 2:00 a.m., Angela and Pauline solved global warming, halted the spread of AIDs, and brought peace to the Middle East. All that was required for solving those sorts of dilemmas was a river of wine and a fair amount of sleep deprivation. More important matters were tackled during the weekends too, like the year Arden arrived with her heart being pulled toward an extramarital affair and she barely spoke a dozen words together all weekend. Yet she knew that the other three loved her and although they did not deluge her with advice, they hoped in their hearts that she would make a true decision, which she did. Partnerships in law firms, promotions, the deaths of parents, children leaving the nest—all their individual milestones during the year were marked and honored together over one weekend. This year, Pauline would be pondering a life-altering decision and she was glad to be on her way to The Weekend.

CHAPTER 1

The summer of 1987 was but a distant memory when she arrived at Fort Ord in the autumn of that same year. Pauline and the other Alphas had graduated from law school and spent a hellish couple of months studying for the bar exam. In July, they and six hundred of their closest friends sat for the Minnesota bar exam on the floor of the St. Paul Civic Center. Jeanne made some waves when she refused to sit at the same table as a guy who had graduated from law school a year before the Alphas and had already taken the bar unsuccessfully twice. "Nothing personal," Pauline heard her tell the proctor, "but seriously bad karma." In the interest of preserving the peace, the proctor moved Jeanne to another table. Apparently, the karma was better there because Jeanne and all the Alphas passed the bar and put their student and test-taking days happily behind them.

During the agonizing months between taking the bar and getting the exam results, Arden and Jeanne worked at the law firms at which they had conditional offers–conditional on passing the bar. Angela continued to clerk at the District Attorney's office. Pauline, who had a conditional offer from the Army JAG Corps, planned her suicide. Like the others' job offers, her suicide was conditional. She would only have to kill herself if she failed the bar. She simply couldn't face another season of stressing out over a preposterous test upon which the rest of her life depended; youth and the Socratic method will do that to one's perspective. Fortunately, there was, as always, construction on 35W that summer. In the event that she failed the bar, Pauline had planned to crash her 1973 Plymouth Duster, that the Alphas called "Doug," into a reinforced concrete overhead support on the freeway. She figured that if she ended it all that way, her family could take comfort in the belief that it was just a tragic accident.

Pauline almost believed that for her mother, the wife of an air force officer, death was probably preferable to a daughter in the army. Pauline knew that when she had decided to go to law school in the Twin Cities, her mother had visions of the *Mary Tyler Moore Show* that Pauline grew up watching: her daughter, like the TV Mary, having a fabulous job in a fabulous office, living in a darling apartment, striding around a charming snow-covered lake, throwing her chic beret in the air. She knew her decision to join the army was a great disappointment to her family, but the Army JAG recruiter had promised Pauline that she would be in the courtroom her first day on the job, and Pauline had believed him.

The Weekends had started that first year after their graduation. Waiting the three months between taking the bar and getting the Life and Death results was too much for them. Pauline would miss subsequent weekends because of circumstances she could not then imagine, but she was there in 1987, the Inaugural Weekend. That year, they all needed a break and the weekend before the bar results were to be published, Arden got the keys to the cabin, and they were off to the north woods. After a weekend of too much wine, too many cigarettes, and almost enough sleep, on Monday morning they met on the steps outside the Minnesota Supreme Court, said a little prayer, and found the posted results. The results–simply *pass* or *fail*–were posted by exam number, and as they scrolled down the list, looking for theirs, Jeanne gave up.

"I think I'm going to be sick–Vickers, you have to look for me," she said and retreated to the steps, where she sat down and put her head between her knees.

After significant scuffling in the scrum of lawyer wannabes crowded around the board with the posted results, Pauline, Arden, and Angela found the only four numbers that mattered and the magic word, "pass." Pauline grabbed the man next to her, Bad Karma, and almost hugged the life out of him. Turns out his karma was not bad that day, and he took Pauline, Angela, Arden, and even Jeanne to the nearest bar and bought the first round of many that night.

Four days later, after being sworn into the bar at a special session of the Minnesota Supreme Court and being sworn into the U.S. Army by her Air Force officer father, First Lieutenant Pauline Vickers drove Doug to Fort Ord in Monterey, California.

Timothy Francis William Kennedy was the best friend a girl ever had. Pauline didn't know that when she first met him on her first day of her first real job at her first duty station at Fort Ord. Tim was a captain in the Office of the Staff Judge Advocate and, in Pauline's eyes, an experienced prosecutor and brilliant brigade legal advisor. He had arrived at Fort Ord eight months before Pauline and it seemed to Pauline that in those eight months Tim had amassed an ocean of experience that made him the wisest, most soldierly JAG she would ever know. She was wrong about other things too.

It was truly tragic that Pauline didn't appreciate it at the time, but she would look back at her first years at Fort Ord and judge them to be the best of her twenty-year career in the army. Best in the sheer funness of the work that she did, best in the friendship and camaraderie that she would find with her fellow junior officers, best social life she would ever again experience. Pauline arrived at Fort Ord with another JAG who had been in her Officers'

Basic Course at the JAG School in Charlottesville, Virginia. Unlike Pauline, who went to Ord to be a trial counsel, that is, a prosecutor and brigade legal advisor, First Lieutenant Richard Gerard was assigned as a defense counsel and spent his first tour of duty defending soldiers at courts-martial. With Pauline's arrival, there were a total of five trial counsel at Ord, including Tim Kennedy, and an equal number of defense counsel, including Richard. Pauline was the only woman among them. This did not cause any problems for her–other than when the boys took to calling her the "JAG Girl." Pauline told them that if they didn't stop calling her that, she would report it as sexual harassment. Tim told her that if she reported them for sexual harassment, they would call her "Shithead," and the choice was hers: JAG Girl or Shithead. Pauline got used to JAG Girl. She also learned to love to run in formation–nothing was more humiliating than falling out of an office formation run and, as the only woman, Pauline felt a certain obligation to keep up for her gender.

Fort Ord was a good place to be a military criminal attorney in the late 1980s. The 7th Infantry Division was there, and an infantry division meant lots of infantry soldiers, and lots of infantry soldiers meant lots of courts-martial. In addition to a sea of criminal trial work, Pauline, Tim, and the other trial counsel served as general legal advisors to the brigades at the 7th. Pauline was assigned as the trial counsel for 2nd Brigade, nicknamed the Cold Steel Brigade. That meant that she spent as much time down in the brigade with commanders and "real" soldiers as she did in the courtroom. And she spent a lot of time in the courtroom. It was a dream for a freshly licensed young attorney. Pauline tried cases ranging from murder to abuse of a public animal. In fact, her case against Richard for abuse of a public animal may have been the first such case in the history of modern courts-martial.

US v. Malone. Article 134 of the Uniform Code of Military Justice, the so-called "general article," articulates an offense called Abuse of a Public

4

Animal. The offense finds its roots in historic times when animals were used to transport people and supplies, and were otherwise put into military service and considered military equipment. In the case of Malone, the roots of the crime were planted in a Field Artillery Battalion, and a mutt of a dog called Fascam. On the eve of a division run, in which the Division Commanding General would lead the entire division formation in a run around the installation, Infantryman Private First Class Peter Malone and an unknown number of his fellow hooligans dognapped Fascam, the artillerymen's beloved mascot. While holding the dog captive, Malone and his unnamed co-dognappers dyed Fascam's coat a brilliant shade of Infantry blue.

Of course, such conduct should not have resulted in a criminal trial, and in a grown up world it wouldn't have. But the nature of the soldier and the workings of military justice system can sometimes combine for unexpected results. Fascam was returned to his unit, blue but otherwise unmolested. He missed the run–it was unthinkable that the mascot of a field artillery unit, whose heraldic color is red, would make a public appearance while the color of Monterey Bay on a sunny day. The night after the division run, a brawl broke out at the enlisted members' club. Half a dozen artillerymen and infantrymen were apprehended by the MPs and released the following morning back to their units, three of them injured to the extent that they were unable to report for duty for a number of days. Pauline met with the infantry unit commander and advised him to administer nonjudicial punishment under Article 15 of the UCMJ to Malone and the other dognappers, should they be identified, in order to make peace and put the matter to rest. Article 15 allows commanders to administer minor punishment against soldiers for minor offenses under the Code, without having to go to a trial by court-martial. Pauline called it "teenager punishment"–Restriction, aka, being grounded; Extra Duty, aka, additional chores; Forfeitures of Pay, aka, no allowance; and Reduction in Grade, aka, "you must earn back my trust." The

UCMJ also permits the accused soldier to refuse punishment under Article 15 and demand trial by court-martial. The commander did as she advised and offered Malone an Article 15. His cohorts were never identified and Malone refused to rat them out. However, acting on Richard's advice, Malone turned down the Article 15 and demanded trial by court-martial as was his right. The issue at the subsequent trial was whether dying a dog blue constituted "abuse" under the law.

There was evidence offered on both sides of the issue. In the past, Fascam always ran alongside the battalion commander in division runs, and indeed, there was testimony that running alongside the commander at the head of the formation was Fascam's greatest delight. There was further testimony of Fascam being off his feed since his ordeal and his demonstrating other signs of canine psychological distress. On the other hand, a veterinarian testified for the defense that Fascam suffered no physical injuries as a result of being dyed blue and that it appeared that his captors had taken care to protect his eyes and ears from exposure to, and to prevent his ingestion of, the dye. The matter was also muddied by the fact that upon his return, the field artillery soldiers shaved Fascam to eliminate the humiliating hue. Even without the benefit of expert testimony from a Dog Whisperer, Richard was able to cast reasonable doubt as to whether the dog's alleged depression was a result of being blue or of being bald. Richard had a way with words. At the close of evidence, the military judge, demonstrating sound judicial temperament, granted Richard's motion for a directed verdict of "not guilty," much to Pauline's relief.

Most of their cases, however, were of significantly more consequence. Richard had practiced in the private sector as a criminal defense attorney before joining the army and because of this experience, he was often detailed to represent those soldiers accused of the most serious crimes. When Pauline prosecuted soldiers accused of murder, rape, or child abuse, more often than not Richard was seated at the defense table with the accused. Although adversaries before the bar, Pauline and Richard enjoyed a generally cordial relationship outside the courtroom. The only case that ever threatened their ability to get along outside the courthouse was not the most serious, or even the most contentious case that they tried from opposite tables. It was a case of bad language. *US v. Kiefer*. Specialist Clark Kiefer was charged with Failing to Obey Lawful Orders, Disrespect Toward a Superior Commissioned Officer, and Indecent Language. In short, Specialist Kiefer, a communications specialist, had gone off on his female company commander. He called her every obscene word that he knew to describe women and various parts of the female anatomy. When Pauline reviewed the witness statements as she was preparing the charge sheet, she had to ask Tim what some of the words meant or to what body part they referred. As dictated in the Rules for Courts-Martial, which require a certain amount of specificity in charging documents, all of the language had to be included in the Indecent Language charge on the charge sheet.

At court-martial, procedure requires that the trial counsel in the case read the charges into the record. In practice, the accused, through his counsel, always waives reading of the charges. Always. Except in the case of *U.S. v. Kiefer*. At the appropriate time during the arraignment, newly promoted Captain Vickers asked, "Does the accused waive the reading of the charges?" And newly promoted Captain Gerard replied, "The accused does not." As a result, in open court, on the record, and in front of God and everybody, including all the other trial and defense counsel because they had been tipped off to Richard's plan, Pauline used every dirty word that she knew and some that she didn't. It was a long time before Pauline had anything nice to say to Richard, in or outside the courtroom.

Richard and Tim did not enjoy the same cordiality, even in the best of times. Tim never fully appreciated Richard's zealousness on behalf of his clients, nor Richard's talent for not using ten words when one was sufficient. Following Captain Kennedy's fifteen-minute opening statement in a case about an elaborate LSD distribution ring involving several soldiers, late night runs to a lab in Santa Cruz, drop spots in seedy hotels, and coded telephone messages, Captain Gerard's opening for the defense was slightly less elaborate: "Sir, Members of the Panel: Entrapment. Thank you." Richard's understated eloquence often had the effect of throwing Tim off his courtroom battle rhythm. However, it was Richard's performance in the case of *US v. Moneymaker* that indelibly scarred relations between the two.

Pauline had been sitting in the back row of the courtroom during the Moneymaker case. Moneymaker was accused of taking pre-approved credit card offers from his neighbors' mailboxes and opening accounts using their names and rented post office boxes in Monterey. Following a months-long investigation, Moneymaker was apprehended by Criminal Investigation Division agents while emptying a post office box rented under the name of Moneymaker's across-the-street neighbor. Moneymaker was prosecuted by Tim on a number of theft and fraud charges. During the trial, Tim called a Bank of America employee to testify about how Moneymaker was able to open a Bank of America Visa card account in the name of the soldier living across the street. Following a series of questions and responses, Tim offered the credit card statements into evidence. Richard objected: "foundation, your Honor." The military judge sustained the objection. Tim asked another series of questions intended to lay the proper foundation for admission of the documents and offered them again into evidence.

Richard objected, "Foundation."

The judge sustained.

Tim asked further questions and again offered the documents.

Richard, "Objection, foundation."

Judge, "Sustained."

Finally, mercifully, the judge put the court in recess to give Captain Kennedy time to collect his thoughts and seek advice from Tim's boss, Major Mark Nightingale. During the recess, Richard, who knew Mark would know how to get the documents admitted, approached Tim and offered to stipulate to the admission of the documents in exchange for the government reducing the theft charges to wrongful appropriation and limiting the amount of prison time Moneymaker would face. Tim agreed, Moneymaker was convicted of fraud and wrongful appropriation, the theft charges were dropped pursuant to their agreement, and Moneymaker was sentenced to a greatly shortened period of confinement. That evening, in the Fort Ord Officers' Club bar, Tim asked Richard what element of the evidentiary foundation he had been missing during the trial. Richard replied, "I have no idea. Actually, your foundation sounded pretty good to me, but it never hurts to object. I figured the judge would know. And when he sustained my first objection, I decided to run with it."

Tim was furious. He did not appreciate a military defense counsel's two-part mission: 1. Zealously represent the client. 2. Screw with the government.

The week often ended for these courtroom warriors at the Fort Ord Officers' Club. The Officers' Club was the place to be for young officers after work on a Friday night. Oh, the romances born at the O Club on a Friday night! It was there that Richard met Jill, Pauline met Oakley, and Tim met, well, he didn't actually remember most of their names.

Richard met Jill Monroe, the daughter of the Commanding General, at the O Club on a Friday night when she was staying with her parents while she was working on her thesis for her masters in modern semantics. Tim called a master's in modern semantics an "Mrs" degree for girls who under-graduated from college with a BA or BS, but no husband.

Courting the general's daughter was a time-honored military tradition, and the keepers of military tradition would have approved of Richard's courting tactics. Buying Jill Monroe a wine spritzer that Friday night at the O Club. Asking her to go dancing later at the Naval Postgraduate School Officers' Club where they had a dance floor, a DJ, and doormen who carded men to ensure they were officers and women to ensure they were over twenty-one. The next Sunday morning sitting near, but not too near, General Monroe and his family in the pews at the generic nondenominational Protestant worship service in the post chapel, and then "bumping into them" afterward at brunch at the O Club. It was hard to know who fell in love with Richard first–Jill or her parents. Like many generals' children, Jill had been something of a wild child in high school, dating enlisted soldiers and drinking beer at night on the post golf course, and then going off to college and running around with purple hair and a boyfriend in a new wave band. Her parents were only too happy to welcome a nice, well-pedigreed officer-lawyer into their home and hearts –just as Pauline's mother would have been.

Pauline was not surprised how Richard embraced all military tradition. Richard was older than the average new lieutenant JAG. Unlike most JAGs who go straight from law school to the bar exam to commission in the Corps, Richard practiced law for a couple of years in the old family firm before applying for active duty in the JAG Corps, making him a couple years older than most of his new lieutenant peers. Indeed, he was probably born older than most JAG lieutenants.

The Gerards were among the Brahmins of Providence. Richard was a second son; his older brother was Robert Elliot Gerard, III. Following in Father's business wake was the duty and right of the eldest son. The second son's name, sans postnoms, seemed to be an extraneous "Gerard" on the firm letterhead. Besides, the secretaries never quite figured out how to refer to Richard when "the younger Mr. Gerard" was already taken. As a result although Richard dutifully went to law school and gamely gave a stint in the family firm a try, he never aspired to seeing his portrait hanging on the wall in the firm conference room. He joined the army partly because military service was a time-honored vocation for a second son, and partly because Richard, as all Gerards at least in theory, believed in public service. Pauline, when she met Richard in Charlottesville, assumed he would serve his three-year commitment then go home to Rhode Island and run for office, military service being a required entry on a candidate's vitae in the Reagan years. Pauline and the other lieutenants in their JAG basic course were giddy with graduating from law school and passing their respective bar exams. They were intent on taking advantage of a couple of months of fun in the town Mr. Jefferson created and on the grounds of his University. Richard, on the other hand, spent his evenings preparing for the next day's classes and reading military histories. Pauline, later to her shame, would not even know who Sun Tzu was until she was at the Command and General Staff College, some ten years later. The military turned out to be an institution that Richard could relate to–it breathed of such things as honor, integrity, discipline, and selfless service. He loved the military and over time it became not just a part of his life, but it seemed to become his entire life. Pauline knew her mother would have loved him.

Richard was ready to get married. It was the next marker in every successful officer's career. Like nature abhors a vacuum, the military abhors a single officer. Richard was already starting to fill the void in him with the army; the other JAGs joked that he bled green. Richard clearly loved the institution, its traditions, its order and dress-right-dress, and its Soldiers. He even he used the upper case "S" long before the Chief of Staff of the Army decided to capitalize "Soldiers" like the Marines capitalize "Marines." Abandoning the Brahmins and that life left a hole in Richard–or maybe the hole was there in Providence too. The army filled it. He loved the discipline. He loved the haircuts, the uniforms, the shiny boots and unit Physical Training. He loved going to the field and being cold and uncomfortable and sleep-deprived. He loved the Soldiers that he defended and the commanders who brought the charges. He loved the mandatory fun events meant to build camaraderie and encourage devotion—Pauline added "blind"—to the institution. He loved Jill, a product of that institution. She knew what "PT" stood for and would happily host officers' wives' coffees, just as her mother had done. She would wait for him when he went to the field, and if he were lucky, when he went to war. She would bear his children and make homes of institutional army quarters with eggshell white walls and linoleum tile floors. Richard loved Jill and everything that she was.

Tim loved women. He loved women in as many different ways as there were grains of sand on the beach. Tim loved his mother and his four sisters. He had loved the girl who sat next to him in ninth grade Algebra as only young hearts can love: open and unjaded. For years afterward, when Tim remembered that girl from the ninth grade, he was still sad she had gone to the homecoming dance with someone else. He loved Gloria Nightingale, Mark's wife, who brought home-cooked meals to the office when they were working late on a trial and made breakfast for them after division runs. He loved the motherly real estate agent who lived in the apartment next to his, who kept an eye on his place when he was in the field, and whom he'd taught to change the oil in her car because she needed an oil change and he was her neighbor. Tim knew how to love women; he listened to them when they spoke, cared about their opinions, and treated them like people, not ornaments or objects or servants.

In his way, Tim loved Pauline too. Tim recognized that Pauline was a better prosecutor than he and a little smarter. He knew that she would have been able to lay the foundation for the documents in the Moneymaker case. Unlike some men who might, Tim did not begrudge Pauline her capabilities. He used to wander into her office, splash down in a chair, and ask her, "Vickers, why is it that you walk on water around here and I doggy paddle?"

He did not hesitate to ask for her help when preparing for trial, or for her opinion about how to advise a commander on a sticky matter. There were no romantic feelings between them. Pauline would think, *How could I be romantically interested in such a loveable knucklehead?* and Tim, *How could I ever fall for a woman who could kick my ass daily?* That didn't mean that he didn't think that Pauline was a good catch for someone. When the trial counsel decided that they needed business cards, they all went to the Post Exchange and ordered cards with the JAG Corps logo, the division emblem, and their names with "Judge Advocate General's Corps" printed beneath in fine letters. Tim would go into Pauline's office, dig through her desk, and take stacks of her cards, provoking a "How many times have I told you to stay out of my drawers, Kennedy?" He would take the cards down to his brigade or to the O Club or to the post barbershop and hand them out to all the single officers he met and tell them that she was a great gal and they should give her a call. He probably circulated more of Pauline's cards than his own, and certainly more than Pauline did herself. It was not uncommon for Pauline to get a call out of the blue from an unmet lieutenant or captain, asking her if he could buy her a drink at the Club on Friday night.

Pauline didn't mind too much. Most of the guys who called were nice enough guys. Some of the infantrymen were a little too "the army is really a man's job, but since you're just a lawyer, that's okay." Some were intimidated by her education and her unwillingness to pretend they were smarter than she was. Some of the service support guys were too eager to prove they were just as manly as their combat arms brethren. But whatever their specialty—infantry, engineer, intelligence, logistics—she could always count on them to pick up the tab, and dinner and a movie was worth occasionally having to listen to some well-intentioned "this is man's work" BS. It was during this time, when Tim was handing out her cards and she was living in the midst of a division of about 10,000 men, Pauline adopted the Three Date Rule. She determined that a woman could go out with a guy three times before he had any reasonable expectations of anything more than a proper goodnight kiss at the end of the third date. After three dates, if Pauline didn't think the guy was Officer Right or if she had had enough of the BS, that was it. A kiss goodnight was a kiss goodbye. Only once did the quality of a goodbye kiss turn it into a goodnight kiss, and she dated that officer a few more times until the BS became so intolerable that even a good kisser just couldn't overcome it. Pauline became a pro at turning down fourth dates:

"It's really busy in the office right now. I'll give you a call when things lighten up."

"I'm going to the field and I'm not sure when we'll be back in."

"The General will be selecting new court-martial members soon and he can pick anyone in the division, including you. Since it would be bad if I were dating a panel member, we'd better not see each other off duty anymore."

And every now and then she would overhear Tim's side of a telephone conversation:

"You think she's giving you the brush?"

"Uh-huh."

"Uh-huh."

"How many times did you guys go out?" . . . "Oh, I see. Well, here's the thing . . ."

Tim had a different rule for dating. His rule could be called the Anyone Who Says Yes Rule. Tim's weekends began on Friday nights at the O Club, drinking beer and telling lies with all the other young officers and local women who gathered there. All the military types went to the club straight from work, so all the officers would still be in uniform. Pauline found it to be an interesting dynamic—being in a bar where everyone, at least all the men and some of the women, were wearing nametags and their military rank. Even the civilian women knew that a "butter bar" —a second lieutenant—was fresh

14

out of college or the Academy, and a guy wearing an eagle was a colonel. And everyone knew a colonel was too old to be there, and consequently either (a) had recently been left by a woman for a good reason or (b) was married and soon to be left by a woman for a very good reason. The nametags proved especially useful for Pauline who was often meeting someone she had made plans with over the phone, sight unseen.

Tim was absolutely in his element at the O Club. He loved telling exaggerated courtroom war stories to his non-lawyer peers and talking about "sending fire down range" and "popping smoke" with them as if he too were a trained killer. Then he'd leave the club with some woman and have exaggerated stories of bedroom frolics to regale the other trial counsel with on Monday morning.

And so went the first two years of Pauline's JAG military career. Lots of great work, lots of camaraderie, and lots of nights out. She missed the Alphas weekend the first year because she was on a Team Spirit military exercise in Korea that October, but she was too young to miss it as she should have. She missed the weekend the second year for different reasons, but by then she knew to miss it as she should.

CHAPTER 2

"There's a beer out there calling your name, Perry Mason. Let's hit it," Tim said to Pauline, one Friday night.

"Perry Mason was a defense attorney. I'm beat. I'm going home," Pauline replied.

"Yeah, but not even you can remember the DA's name and he was a loser anyway," Tim said, continuing to prod her. "Look, I know you're wiped out, but come have one beer with us, we'll pat you on the back, and I'll put you in your POS and point it in the direction of your apartment."

"All right, but one beer and I'm done," Pauline said, relenting.

It had been a long week, a long trial, and Pauline was ready to go home, go for a run, take a hot shower, and go to bed. She really didn't feel like going to the Officers' Club and listening to a bunch of Joes' bar talk. But, on the other hand, it had been a long trial and the government had gotten a really good result, and a beer might taste pretty good. Besides, it was easier to acquiesce a "yes" to Tim, than to argue a "no."

The club bar was full of junior officers and women there to meet junior officers by the time Pauline, Tim, and the other trial counsel arrived. Some of the officers from the court-martial were playing pool, a couple of them still in their Class A "pickle suit" uniforms from having testified for Pauline at the trial earlier that day. Tim was particularly happy to see them because Pauline's success at trial would mean that the JAGs would drink free; Tim was not above basking in Pauline's glory, especially if it meant free beer. Someone dragged a stool over to the pool table and Pauline sat and listened to Tim's trash talk about how she had handed the defense counsel his ass in the courtroom in the case of *U.S v. Waters*. In fact, it had been a pretty grueling trial. Sergeant Thomas Waters was a cocaine dealer. He was caught in a Criminal Investigation Division sting operation. Richard had argued his favorite drug dealer defense–entrapment–and what should have been an easy "win" for Pauline had turned into a four-day dogfight. Pauline was glad it was over. Pauline zoned out through most of Tim's malarkey, that is, until he said something that brought her back.

"This weekend?" she heard him say. "Vickers and I are going up to Berkeley for the weekend."

Which was technically true. Their boss, Major Nightingale, had been selected for the JAG Corps Masters of Law degree program. That meant that the army was paying for him to go to law school at UC-Berkeley to get a masters in criminal law. He had started the fall semester several weeks earlier. He and Gloria were renting a place in Berkeley in a complex with tennis courts, racquetball courts, sauna, and a pool. Tim and Pauline had already been to visit them once at "Club Nightingale" and had planned to drive up the next morning to go to the UC-Berkeley–Washington State football game and hang out with the Nightingales.

"Tim," Pauline said, "quit telling everyone that you and I are going away together for the weekend. I don't want people thinking you and I are doing something that we aren't."

"Well, first of all," Tim said, "we *are* going away for the weekend together, and second, since they think you're quality, it's good for my rep if these guys think whatever."

"If you're going to be a jerk," Pauline responded, "I'm not going to Berkeley with you tomorrow. You're not going to trash my rep to prop up your own. I'm going home."

Tim followed her out of the pool room and through the bar, carping. Pauline put on her blinders and pushed through the crowd to the door.

But Tim would not let it go: "We told Mark and Gloria that we were coming," as they left the pool room. "We've got tickets to the game. And what do you mean, it's trashing your rep if people think you are with me? That really hurts, Paul. Besides, you're just tired—you won't feel like such a bitch in the morning."

"Is this captain bothering you, ma'am?"

That stopped them both. As Pauline and Tim were approaching the door on Pauline's way out, a trio of Marine lieutenants pushed in. They looked a little rough, as if they had been in the field for a while and had prioritized a cold beer above a hot shower.

"Yes, as a matter of fact he is," Pauline said to the tallest of the trio.

"Sir," Tall Marine said to Tim, "why don't we step outside and discuss this. Ma'am, are you trying to leave? If you'd like to wait here, I'd be happy to walk you to your car when we're done."

"Oh, for the love of St. Francis," Tim, said, exasperated, "Paul, I leave you to Lieutenant Galahad here. Give me a call if you change your mind and want to do Berkeley tomorrow."

That's how Army Captain Pauline Vickers met Marine First Lieutenant Oakley Bannon at the Fort Ord Officers' Club on a Friday night. Pauline didn't know at the time he would be like a stone dropped in the pond that was her life, and she would feel the ripple for a long time to come. All she knew at the time was that he was tall and cute as a button and he'd given Tim a hard time when Tim had deserved it. She decided she didn't need to leave right that minute. She let Oak buy her a wine spritzer and they found some stools at the bar. Oak and the other Marines explained that they were part of an advance party from a Marine unit at Twenty-nine Palms Marine Corps Base near Palm Springs. They were at Ord to make preparations for their battalion that was coming up the following week for an exercise in the post's east garrison. They had been out at east garrison all week making the necessary arrangements and had come onto main post to stay in the Bachelor Officers Quarters over the weekend, before the rest of the battalion started rolling in on Monday. Once these explanations were made, Oak's compatriots honored the time-honored code among men hitting on women and made themselves scarce.

It had been a long week, a long trial, and Pauline was ready to go home. Charming as Oak was, in a not-quite-real-fairy-tale-Prince-Charming kind of way, all she wanted to do was to go home, to hell with a run, take a hot shower, and go to bed.

"I'd like to offer to see you home, ma'am," Oak said, "but I don't have a vehicle here."

"Well, Marine," Pauline replied, "I have a vehicle here, and I'd be happy to let you use it to see me home if you stop calling me 'ma'am.'"

"Then may I see you home, Pauline?"

And so began the nicest weekend Pauline ever had. They both had hot showers that night and they both slept like the dead. On Saturday, they drove up to Santa Cruz and spent the day at Santa Cruz beach. They walked on the boardwalk. They rode the world's highest rollercoaster made entirely of wood. They played miniature golf. They scammed the Marine recruiters on the beach who were giving USMC T-shirts to any man who could do ten pull-ups and any woman who could do fifty sit-ups. They both did more than the minimum as a matter of pride. They ate the best seafood in the world with plastic forks off of paper plates. Oak won a humungous stuffed seal at the shooting gallery. They bought Oak a tie. Later, they drove back to Monterey and down to Pacific Grove and had dinner at Pasta Mia, Pauline's favorite restaurant, where they waited for a table on the front stoop with a glass of red wine and chatted with other waiting patrons. After dinner they wandered through a little cemetery nearby where deer roamed among the tombstones and where peace settled down like a fog swallowing the place up. Later, they bought a bottle of wine and plastic glasses at a convenience store and sat on the beach on a poncho liner they found in Pauline's trunk and watched the stars over the bay.

Pauline was in love but not in love. She knew that she was not in love with Oak. No, that's not true. She loved Oak, so far he was a part of the world that she had fallen in love with that day. She loved the day that they shared and the beauty of the place and the happiness of their lives and brightness of their futures and the romance of their meeting. That night they made love and that was lovely too. The next morning they went to church at the Naval Postgraduate School chapel, brunch at the Officers' Club—tie required—and then Pauline took Oak back to the BOQ. They kissed and it was goodbye.

CHAPTER 3

During those first years at Fort Ord, Pauline knew real joy. Her life was full of meaningful, exciting work, light romances, good friends, and the paradise that was Monterey Bay. Her joy had crested that morning when she kissed Oak goodbye. At that moment, her heart was full of love for all creation, and she could feel that all creation loved her in return. It was a long time before she would feel joy like that again. Maybe if she had made the Alpha Weekend that was to come that fall, the Alphas might have thrown her a lifeline and she might have come up for air sooner. As it was, she missed the second annual weekend as she had the first.

After Pauline missed the first post-Real Life weekend a year earlier, there was concern among the other Alphas that they had lost her to the army and the Real World. She had returned from a military exercise in Korea to find a blinking answering machine.

"Paul, Jeanne here. What—you afraid if you come back we'll ply you with cheap booze and make you give up military secrets? Like we care. See you next year—or else!"

"Hey, Pauline, this is Arden. We missed you! We'll come to you next year if we have to —California in the fall—that wouldn't be too bad! Keep in touch, my friend."

"Vickers, Martelli. You know I'm not above tracking you down and dragging your sorry ass back here for a weekend once a year. Seriously, we are a lot harder to dump than you think. Better see your face soon!"

In return:

"This is Pauline. I love you all too. It sucks that I had to miss The Weekend. If it makes you feel better, I spent the month sleeping in a musty, moth-eaten tent and slogging through three inches of cold mud to go to the latrine. Going to the field in Korea sucks! If they ask me, I'll tell them to tell the North Koreans that they can have it, but that if they take it, they can't give it back. I'll see you all next time, without fail."

Pauline was wrong about other things too.

A couple of weeks after the Oak Weekend, Pauline took a test very different from the bar exam, and much more significant. The results of this test so shocked her that, for several minutes, she could not function. Always in the back of her mind, she imagined someday she would get married and have seven children. She imagined coming home from the doctor's office and telling her husband she was pregnant with their first child and the two of them exploding with joy. Pregnant. Now the word filled her with indescribable sadness. It was as if she were mourning for a lost future that was unknown and unknowable. She knew that she would never know the joy of that moment when she would find out that she was filled with a new life. Forty years from now in some parallel world, if she were to look back on her life and know she had never experienced such a moment, she may feel sadness or some regret. But it was unbearable to know now that moment would never be hers to rejoice in. It would never happen because in this world she hadn't planned and hoped and prayed with someone she loved to get this test result, but she got it anyway. She had lived that weekend with Oak in paradise; for that time she had only been there, in those moments.

Now those moments were gone and they were replaced by a single wonderful and anguishing word.

She was paralyzed. Up until that moment, Pauline had always known how to move forward. When she was waiting for the bar results, she knew the way ahead: pass and head out to Charlottesville, or fail and crash Doug into a concrete support on the highway. Now, she didn't know what to do and she couldn't move. Maybe this was punishment for living for the moment, all those moments of the weekend with Oak. She should have known spontaneity was not to be indulged. She'd studied for the bar, hadn't she? She didn't just decide to walk into the St. Paul Civic Center one morning and take a test. She prepared for trial before walking into court, didn't she? She never asked a witness a question she didn't already know the answer to. Didn't she always refuse to ride to the Club on Fridays with Tim because she had to be prepared to get herself home when he picked up some floozy and abandoned her there? But this. Feeling unprepared for this was insufficient; this was like a tsunami in the middle of the Mojave–she could not have conceived of preparing for the inconceivable. And she didn't even have a cat to tell her troubles to.

Pauline considered calling her mother. Unthinkable. She knew her mother would not abide an unwed pregnant daughter. Pauline remembered the year she went home from law school for Christmas and her mother found her tampons in the medicine cabinet. "You really should not use these until you are married," her mother had told her. And she had meant it.

Pauline couldn't call any of the Alphas. Jeanne would be happy for her. Unbearable. Angela would give her a hard time for not being smarter. Unnecessary. Arden would be understanding, let her cry, and tell her everything would work out fine. Undeserved.

The next Monday morning, Pauline had pulled herself together, and went to Tim's office, shut the door, and told him her news.

"Tim, I think I'm pregnant," Pauline told the best friend a girl could ever have.

"They can test for that now, you know," Tim told her. "Should I go find a rabbit?"

"No, when I say 'I think I'm pregnant' I mean, 'I'm pregnant,'" Pauline said.

"Galahad?" he asked.

"Yes," was her simple reply.

"He shouldn't be too hard to find. We know his name and his unit," Tim was all business.

"No," Pauline said, "That weekend he *was* Galahad, not some poor dumb lieutenant that I can dump this on." Pauline paced the floor in front of Tim's desk. "This just isn't real. He isn't real. What we did isn't real. It was like something out of a cheap romance novel. We spent two completely unreal days together, acting out roles in some sappy chick flick. You say he would be easy to find, but the guy that I was with is not at Twenty-nine Palms. He's some place not here—someplace in my heart like Captain Wentworth or Colonel Brandon. I can't change the unreality of that weekend and hope he turns out to be a real-life Galahad just because I have to deal with this reality."

"Clearly your brain cells have already turned to hormonal mush," Tim said. "I don't know Wentworth or Brandon—are they in 2nd Brigade?—and I'm certainly not going to force a Marine on you. He'd probably insist on marrying you, taking away your shoes, knocking you up every twelve months, and you'd be stuck with the jarhead for life. I'll go to the county courthouse over lunch and get a license. How fast do you think your mom can put together a wedding? My mom had to do it for one of my sisters and it only took a week."

"Tim, firstly, Mrs. Major General Vickers does not do quickie weddings for knocked up daughters," Pauline said. "Secondly, you know that I love you like a not-particularly-close cousin, but I am not going to marry you. Besides, I'd never get along with all your girlfriends."

"Let's spend the weekend at Club Nightingale," Tim said, "like we should have done a few weeks ago. We'll deal with this when we get back."

"Thanks for that," Pauline replied, "I'll cancel my flight to Minneapolis."

And that's how Pauline missed the second Weekend.

Pauline didn't sleep for a week. During the days, she worked on cases, advised commanders, and mentored junior JAGs. She did more PT that week than she did in the previous month, trying to wear her mind down. Every night, she got back to her apartment exhausted, took a hot shower, and climbed into bed. And the moment her head hit the pillow, her situation exploded in her brain and her thoughts raced.

How can this be? Why has God let this happen? I can't be pregnant. How can I have a baby? I'm in the army. I'm single. I work eighteen hour days, go to the field, deploy? What if we go to war? I can't even have a dog with this life—how can I have a baby? Like they would even let me stay in the army as a single mother anyway. I don't think they can kick me out for just being pregnant, but they'll surely try. Make me so miserable I quit. How can I face the SJA? My brigade commander? He doesn't like women in the army to begin with. But a pregnant single officer? I've never even heard of such a thing. They give enlisted women hell for getting pregnant—married or not—what will they do with me? This can't be happening! How can I tell Mother? Her son comes out and her unmarried daughter gets knocked up? It will break her heart—she must have one. She'll give me hell, or worse— or maybe better?—never want to see me again. But what about Dad? He'll still love me, right? What if I don't have the baby? No one will ever know. The army won't hate me. My family won't hate me. I can still have a career I love. No one will know. I can always have a family later, when I'm ready, when I have someone to have a family with. It will be all right. Maybe this is just a test. No one will ever know. It could be just like it never happened. It will be all right. Everything will be all right.

"You're never going to believe it—we're pregnant!" Gloria said as Tim and Pauline got out of Tim's jeep in the driveway of Club Nightingale.

Of course she was. Gloria had never looked more glorious. The same word that drained the last drop of joy out of Pauline, bathed Gloria with radiance. Gloria was so swallowed up by her and Mark's happiness that she hadn't waited for Pauline and Tim to cross the threshold of their apartment before she shared their happy news.

It was surprisingly easy for Pauline to keep her own news inside herself. She was genuinely happy for the Nightingales, even though their happiness accentuated her own distress. While she celebrated their joy, her capacity for joy was disappearing, like a black hole grows darker by consuming stellar energy. As the evening went on, the shadow in Pauline's heart grew deeper, from the restaurant on the wharf where they ate the best seafood in the world, to the club on the bay where Mark, Tim, and Pauline drank champagne like water and toasted Little Vanna or Little Elvis. During this evening of revelry Pauline retreated into her heart and made a decision that would be like a star imploding within her. By the time they returned to Club Nightingale, she was already starting to collapse in on herself.

That night Tim and Pauline had to share the hide-a-bed in the living room because within ten days of a positive pregnancy test, Mark and Gloria had dismantled the guest room to convert it to a nursery. It was very quiet in the apartment that night. Mark and Gloria slept with the exhaustion that follows in the wake of such exhilaration. Tim slept with the confidence that the morning would bring another day with the same possibilities for happiness this one had found, certain he could convince Pauline to take joy in her pregnancy as the Nightingales had in theirs. He was wrong about other things too.

Pauline lay awake, feeling the specter of Mark and Gloria's happiness hovering over the apartment like a fog. It was so quiet it should have been peaceful, but it was not. Pauline was amazed that a space could be crowded with so many conflicting spirits and yet could be so still. She felt the black hole in her soul would devour the Nightingales' happiness that was seeping through the walls of the apartment. She dreamt that when they woke up in the morning, she and Tim would find nothing but dry bones in the master bedroom. Instead, she woke to find her pillow damp and Tim's arm around her.

"I was going to say that even if you won't marry me, you can put my name on the birth certificate. But you've decided that that won't be necessary, haven't you?" he said quietly.

CHAPTER 4

The summer of 1990 witnessed the break-up of the Fort Ord posse. Nine months after that weekend at Club Nightingale, Gloria gave birth to a perfect baby boy. A month after that, Mark was awarded his masters in criminal law, received orders to Fort Lewis, Washington, loaded the family into the new minivan, and drove 700 miles north. As it turned out, Gloria proved to be the glue that held them together across the world and the years. She was the one who mailed Christmas cards on Thanksgiving Saturday every year, filling in everyone on Mark's rise in the Corps and the growing number of Nightingales inhabiting the earth. She always had an updated address book and always knew how to put people in touch with one another. By the time Mark retired from the army more than twenty-five years later, her Christmas card list had more than 300 names on it.

Richard married Jill in June, moved to Fort Bragg, North Carolina in July, and in August deployed to southwest Asia as part of Operation Desert Shield. In January 1991, his every soldier's dream came true when he invaded Iraq as part of the Desert Storm invasion force. For her part, Jill dutifully hosted coffees for the other officers' wives, made their dreary military quarters a home, and, while she waited for Richard to come home from war, prepared for the birth of a most perfect baby girl.

In July, Tim took his Jeep to the port at Oakland and boarded a flight to Frankfurt, Germany, via JFK. Two weeks before Tim left, Pauline walked into his office to say her final farewells.

It was both easier and more difficult to say goodbye to Tim than Pauline had expected it to be. They were both looking forward to their follow-on assignments. They both joined the army in part to see the world and were looking forward to their next assignments. Besides, at the time, Pauline's parents lived in Colorado Springs and her brother lived in Atlanta and she had said goodbye to them many times in her life. It ought to have been easy to say goodbye to a man she had known for only two-plus years.

But it wasn't. Pauline had come alive at Fort Ord and Tim was a large part of her life there. He was her best friend, but she didn't love him like she loved one of the Alphas. She didn't loved him like a brother, because her love for him was nothing like her love for her brother. She had male cousins on her dad's side that she loved, but she didn't love Tim like them either. She thought she knew romantic love, but she didn't love Tim like that either. But just as she had come alive at Ord, part of Pauline had died there, and Tim was part of that too. After Tim had offered her his name on a piece of paper, they never talked about that again. The silence they shared was also part of how she loved him. When she stopped by his office as part of their exodus from Fort Ord, she and Tim kissed and it wasn't "I love you" or goodbye. It just was.

In August, Pauline left Monterey for Fairbanks, Alaska, to be the Chief of Military Justice at quiet little Fort Wainwright. It was nothing compared to Ord. Where Monterey was Eden, Fairbanks was Hades. Where Monterey had the bay, wonderful restaurants, and a vibrant, young, growing population, Fairbanks had perpetual permafrost, permanent dusk, and a dying population of aging hippies and fugitives from the law from the Lower 48. Where Fort Ord had a mission and acted like it, Fort Wainwright was pretending to wait for the Russians to come screaming across the Bering Strait, or the North Korean hordes to flood south. When discussing her follow-on assignment to Fort Ord, Pauline had been misled by the assignments officer who had described the job at Wainwright as the "Chief of Justice at a Division." Where they had five trial counsel at Ord, they had one and a half at Wainwright—one full time and one part-timer who reviewed administrative investigations and wrote ethics opinions the other half of his time. In the year before Pauline moved there, fewer than a fifth of the number of cases were tried at Wainwright as had been at Ord.

Later that fall, when Angela called Pauline about The Weekend, Pauline's Justice shop had two whole cases pending: an adultery/ maltreatment of subordinates case (a married major sleeping with one admin clerk and sexually harassing a couple of others) and a case of bad checks ("just because you have checks in your check book, soldier, doesn't mean you have money in your account to cover them"). By October, permanent darkness was descending on Fairbanks. It was the perfect time to escape this hell on earth.

"Here's the plan," said Angela, "Don't tell anyone else you're coming. You fly into Minneapolis. I'll beg off driving up with the others, pick you up at the airport, and you and I will drive Barbie up to the cabin on Mille Lacs Lake and surprise the hell out of the others."

When Angela had received her first Real Job paycheck, she had traded in her old junker car and bought an almost new 1988 Jeep Cherokee. It was pearlized bubblegum pink, 'specially ordered—not by her—and rejected by the orderer. The dealer had been happy to get it off the lot and Angela got a great deal on it. The Alphas named it "Barbie." Pauline thought it was perfect that she would go from being driven around the frozen tundra in an olive-drab Humvee to being driven to an all-girls weekend in a pink Cherokee. When she and Angela arrived at the cabin at Brady's Ski and Golf Resort at Mille Lacs, the others really were surprised as hell.

Pauline felt a spark of light in her heart when she saw Arden and Jeanne, in flannels and sweats, drinking wine, around the coffee table in the front room of the cabin. They had graduated from Arden's in-laws' place, where they had escaped during law school and had rented a very deliberately rustic cabin at a golf (June, July and August) and cross-country ski (the other nine months of the year) resort on Mille Lacs Lake in central Minnesota.

"Why haven't you babes got a fire going?" Angela said, when the hugging and "oh my God's" were finished.

"They charge extra for wood," Jeanne told her.

"Oh no, they do not!" Angela said. "That is just sick and wrong. No worries. As luck would have it, Vickers and I passed around the back of the lodge while we were looking for the cabin and they have a great stack of wood back there. Since I see you ladies didn't wait for us to unscrew the wine, G.I. Jane and I will take Barbie, load her up, and be back in a flash."

Angela and Pauline put their jackets back on and under the cover of darkness, Angela drove Barbie to the back of the resort lodge, headlights off, of course, backed her up, and relieved the resort of some fire wood.

"Ange, don't you prosecute people for doing stuff like this?"

"I figure with you along, it's more of a military operation than an unconsented taking. Besides, at the rates they charge here, they have no business charging extra for firewood. We ought to sue their asses. They're lucky we don't break up the furniture and burn that. And besides, I only prosecute people who get caught, so keep your voice down."

Angela and Pauline made it back to the cabin, they thought undetected, and proceeded to unload the wood from Barbie's backside. As they were doing so, two middle-aged women walked passed.

"I wish we could have a fire our cabin," one of the women said.

"It's crazy that they charge for wood, isn't it? We brought this wood in the back of our truck," said Angela, careful not to make eye contact with Pauline.

"It's not that," the woman said. "The fireplace in our cabin doesn't work."

The women further explained they were staying in a neighboring cabin with their husbands. The fireplace in their cabin was "broken," they explained, and they could not light a fire in it. Angela and Pauline traded raised eyebrows and offered to walk the women back to their cabin and see if they might be able to "fix" their fireplace. The women were delighted, but skeptical, and took Angela and Pauline to their cabin. Their husbands were sitting in easy chairs, drinking beer, and talking about the football games they were missing that weekend at the deliberately rustic cabin with no TV and a broken fireplace. Pauline, explaining she had significant experience in fixing fireplaces, knelt down, reached up the fireplace, and muscled open the flue.

"That should do it," she said, dusting off the knees of her jeans.

The women were thrilled, the men embarrassed. On their way out the door, Angela turned to Pauline and almost whispered, "I bet they're impotent too."

When they got back to their own cabin, Arden had a fire going and Jeanne was holding court from a winged-back chair near the hearth. Jeanne was a second career lawyer. Her first career was Wife and Mother. She had started law school when her twin son and daughter started high school. Jeanne and her social worker husband had decided Jeanne would put off law school until the kids were in high school, when she would have more time on her hands, and so that she could help pay for their college when the time came. She graduated second in their law school class and accepted a position in the firm for which she had clerked while a student.

Jeanne continued her diatribe as Pauline and Angela poured themselves some wine and settled in.

". . . and I don't understand why she just can't see the irony of financially ruining her parents and amassing oceans of debt while studying the 'politics of poverty' at an overpriced, elitist college. Her father is a social worker, for heaven's sake, and I had relied on Fifty Ways to Serve Hamburger to keep red meat on the menu through her childhood. I cut off my wedding dress and dyed it peach to wear to her First Communion, for crying out loud. I cut her and her brother's hair until they started high school, and I still cut mine and her father's. So, why do I get my head snapped off for merely suggesting she can study being poor just as effectively at a fine state school like the University of Minnesota as at Bennington bloody College? She might even get to observe some real poor people living on the streets in Minneapolis and not just read about them from some ivory tower!"

The Alphas knew Jeanne adored and admired her daughter. Pauline had to laugh with the rest of them, but her laughter was not so light as the others. She wondered if she would ever love a child enough to be driven mad by the child's youth or whether she would ever know what it was to be happy only if that child were. Jeanne had her twins. Arden had given birth to her daughter the summer between college and law school and seemed happy to be the mother of an only child. Angela seemed content being a party of one. Pauline wondered if her future would include that kind of mother love or, in the alternative, Angela's kind of contentment.

Pauline's soul felt removed as the conversation continued. Probably because of Jeanne's remarks, that night they talked about health insurance coverage, maternity leave policies, and the cost of raising children in today's world. Arden made them laugh with a story about how she had been on birth control when she conceived and her husband's shocked reaction to her announcement.

And so the conversation went. By about one a.m., Jeanne and Angela drifted off to claim their beds leaving Arden and Pauline by the fire, filling in the gaps between three years of hurried letters and sporadic phone calls. Through law school, Pauline had at different times felt closest to each of the Alphas. Arden was physically the most beautiful woman that Pauline knew, and now and then Pauline was distracted from the beauty of Arden's heart by the beauty of her countenance. Arden saw things differently, and usually more clearly, and Pauline appreciated that about her. In the autumn of their second year of law school, they had participated in a moot court exercise. The "case" given to them involved a student who was suing a university for failing to provide him with a sufficient education to secure gainful employment upon graduation. The students were instructed to address the case as a tort; that is, to make the case that the university had acted negligently in the course of the student's education. While their classmates were researching the standard of care expected of an institution of higher education in the education of its students, Arden approached the matter as a breach of contract. Arden argued the three elements of a contract: Offer–the university offered to provide an education with the understanding that such education would result in enhanced employability; Acceptance–the student accepted the offer by matriculating at said university; and Consideration–the payment of tuition. It was a much simpler, more straightforward, truer to the facts, legally logical approach. The moot court "judges"–third year students, play-acting in black robes–were not expecting such an argument and consequently, of course, they graded her poorly.

As Arden and Pauline tucked themselves in to the hide-a-bed they were sharing in the front room, Arden unknowingly asked, "So, my friend, when are you going to find some upstanding, clean cut, soldier boy, get married, and settle down to an itinerant military life?"

Pauline answered her question with a question of her own. "Arden, all the talk tonight got me thinking, do you think being pregnant or having children changes a person's view on abortion?"

Although they had never talked about it, Pauline assumed that the other Alphas were pro-choice.

"Where did that come from?" Arden asked. But when Pauline didn't respond, she continued. "I don't think being pregnant or having a baby changed my view concerning whether abortions should be safely available or legally protected, but becoming pregnant certainly influenced my opinion about whether it was an option for me. The Man and I didn't plan to start law school with a new baby, but once I got pregnant, starting law school not with a new baby didn't seem like an option to either of us. That doesn't mean I think abortion should be illegal, but getting pregnant took it from being a legal argument to a reality for me. So, I ask again, where did that come from?"

Pauline was quiet for a long time before she answered. "I don't know. I completely agree that a woman's sovereignty over her own body must be legally protected, and that includes our right to decide if we have children. I don't think I want to live in a country where anyone's religious beliefs are legislated for the rest of us. I guess I've just been thinking about whether what is–and should be–legal, would necessarily be the right choice for everyone."

"Anything you want to tell me, Pauline?" Arden asked softly.

"Not tonight."

The Alpha Weekend at Mille Lacs Lake was also Columbus Day weekend. And like any respectable small town in the upper Midwest, this one had a parade. The Alphas weren't thinking about that until they drove into town at lunchtime the following day in search of a hot breakfast and discovered that the one street with a stoplight had been closed to traffic. They parked on a side street, possibly legally, and found Carmella's Diner, a perfect place for breakfast at lunchtime on the parade route. Eggs, potatoes, sausage, toast and leave the coffee pot on the table, please. Lots of water too. The waitress provided parade commentary as the people marched and floats pulled by pick-up trucks passed by the windows of the diner. The mayor and his wife in a convertible. Local Boy Scout Troop color guard. Midget majorettes from the elementary school. Fire truck from the local volunteer fire department, complete with dog.

"They don't have a Dalmatian," the waitress told them, "Too high strung for all the bells and whistles. Lucy, the Lab mix riding shotgun, has the right temperament for the work."

A gorilla band–a drummer, a couple of guitars, and a bass player in gorilla suits–from the local bank. "The bank manager is on the drums," she told them.

A marching formation of veterans. A county beauty queen. A few pickup trucks pulling advertisements for local businesses on flatbeds. A motorcycle cop bringing up the rear.

Back at the cabin, they lit another fire. Jeanne, who had bartended her way through law school, made a pitcher of brandy old-fashions. Arden, Angela, and Pauline settled on the sofa with a stack of home and garden and scandal magazines. There were lots of "I'm going to try that in my house" comments, and "Is that girl an orphan? Where was her mother when she left the house?" commentary. After a couple of old-fashions, Angela made herself comfortable in the winged-back chair by the hearth and took off, much as Jeanne had the night before.

"You know what really pisses me off?" Angela said. "Everyone assuming I'm a lesbian because I'm almost thirty, a kick-ass prosecutor, single, and happy. Is it any of their business? What difference would it make to them anyway? Some of the cops that I deal with are complete dicks and I know they call me 'Dike' behind my back. Which makes me want to kick their asses, but that would just confirm in their pea brains that I'm a dike. Last week, a judge told me that he preferred women appearing in his courtroom wear skirts instead of trousers, unless that was 'against my beliefs.' What the hell? You must deal with this crap every day, Paul."

"Not so much at Ord, apart from that JAG Girl thing," Pauline answered, "but I have to say, the guy I'm working for now put the 'I's' in 'sexist idiot.'"

"No, no, no! You must be in the chair before you launch," Arden stopped her.

"What are you talking about?" Pauline asked.

"The chair," said Arden. "Haven't you noticed? Every time one of us sits in that chair, she becomes the Alpha Bitch. So, if you're going to bitch about something, you have to sit in the Alpha Bitch chair. Move it or lose it, Martelli."

Angela and Pauline switched places. Arden put her arm around Angela's shoulders and told her, "I think you're the best, even if you do turn out to be a lesbo!"

"You are such a jerk," Angela said, teasing her back.

"Within the first two minutes of our first meeting," Pauline continued, "I knew that he'd gone to West Point, that he drove a Corvette, that his wife was a stay at home mom, and that he played tennis with the Chief of Staff. He's very macho—just ask him. When we were talking in his office, he sat there with the soles of his feet on the edge of his desk and his knees spread like he was trying to give birth to a basketball. He's too smart to do anything that would get him court-martialed, so no grab-ass business, but he does this kind of stuff: we have a legal assistance attorney, a captain, who has about a million—or four—little kids. One morning he came in and announced that he was taking that afternoon off to go to one of his kid's T-ball league meetings. That day happened to be walk-in day in legal assistance, when people can just walk and see a lawyer without an appointment. It is by far the busiest day of the week. Since this captain took off, we had people waiting for over an hour to see someone and, finally, I had to send one of my prosecutors to help with the overload. The Idiot's response: 'Isn't Captain T-Ball a great dad? Putting his family first. What a great guy.' Fast forward two days and my Non-Commissioned Officer-In-Charge, a single mom, got a call from her day care provider who told her that her son was running a fever and my soldier needed to pick him up. This was late in the afternoon, we had nothing going on, and plenty of people there to cover all that nothing, so I told her to go. As the Idiot was leaving for the day, he came through the justice shop and asked where my NCOIC was. I told him, and then had to listen to a five-minute lecture about how lucky she was we are so understanding, and that I can't let her think that she can just take off any time that she wants, and that since she chose to be a single mom she really needs to do a better job getting reliable child care. I could have punched him in the face. He is such an idiot. The captain is a great dad because he screws the office to go a T-ball meeting and my NCOIC is a bad soldier because she isn't even missed when she goes home to take care of a sick kid."

"Right now," Pauline continued. "I'm prosecuting a married major for sexually harassing the young female soldiers who work for him and sleeping with one of them, and the Idiot wants to know why I'm not prosecuting the single gal he slept with. Never mind that the major was the one who was violating his vows and had all the power. I swear, that Idiot's insidious kind of chauvinism is as damaging as the ass-grabbing kind, and a lot more prevalent in the army. It makes me insane."

"Who do you blow steam off with up there?" asked Arden.

The question slapped Pauline in the face like a bucket of cold water. At Ord, Pauline had the camaraderie of Tim and the other trial counsel. At Wainwright, she was the only single officer in the Staff Judge Advocate's office, except for the captains who worked for her. In Monterey, she had a reason for the Three Date Rule; in Fairbanks, she hadn't met anyone she could imagine dating even once, let alone three times. When she went out in

Monterey–downtown, to the wharf, or running along the Bay–people were out and alive. When she went out in Fairbanks, the town was gray and gloomy and the only people she met were trying to get away–from the weather, the dying economy, each other. The loneliness of her worldly situation sadly suited her internal loneliness. Every now and then, she became aware she was guilty of basking in her loneliness and she knew it wasn't right, but she couldn't seem to pull herself away from it. She was finding it increasingly easy, and sickly satisfying, to collapse in on herself and settle in her loneliness.

CHAPTER 5

T he years after Fort Ord rolled over Pauline like waves on the beach. When she looked back on those years, she had only vague memories of working on this case or that, or mentoring this young officer or that one. It was all very fuzzy, like looking through the windshield of a car during a rainstorm without turning on the windshield wipers.

JAG Corps officers are migrant workers. Every two or three years they pack their bags, load their furniture on moving trucks, and drive off with "Welcome to Fort . . ." signs in their rear view mirrors. Pauline had felt profoundly sad when she drove away from Monterey. She felt nothing when she drove away from Fairbanks a year after that Columbus Day Weekend. Someone in the JAG assignments office decided that she needed more "face time" with the senior JAG Corps leadership, so she traded the ALCAN Highway for the Washington, DC, beltway and spent two years working in the Army JAGC Litigation Division.

Pauline was not thrilled to be assigned at the Pentagon after Wainwright, away from the troops and what she thought of as the "real Army." And "Litigation Division" was a bit of a misnomer; none of the JAGs assigned there ever actually did any litigation; they mostly did all the legwork for the Assistant U.S. Attorneys who walked the JAG-prepped cases into trial in

Federal District Courts. For two years, Pauline worked on cases of either military personnel suing the army to get out, or military personnel suing the army for wrongful discharge. Every now and then, she got a different kind of case to work on that sparked just enough of an interest to keep her in the Corps.

Like the Dr. Dopesmoker case. Dopesmoker was a surgeon whom the army paid to go to medical school in exchange for his commitment to serve on active duty for a million—or eight— years. At his first duty station after completing his residency at Walter Reed Army Medical Center, Dopesmoker tested positive for marijuana during a routine health and welfare inspection. He received an Article 15 and then was ordered to "show cause" why he should be permitted to remain on active duty. At his show cause hearing, Dopesmoker stated that he was not a habitual drug user but he had been at a party, had too much to drink, and must have taken a drag on a marijuana cigarette without knowing what it was. The Show Cause Board was not impressed and voted to kick him out of the army. He appealed and lost and was subsequently discharged. Then the army got really ugly: it went after Dopesmoker for the cost of his medical school education on the grounds that he had failed to fulfill his obligation to serve. He counter-sued the army on the grounds that he did not fulfill his obligation because the army kicked him out. Pauline enjoyed writing the brief for the case, explaining that he would not have been kicked out if he had he not smoked pot; the army, as Pauline explained to the Assistant U.S. Attorney on the case, frowns on drug use, especially among those who fire weapons or cut people open.

In another case, she was exasperated she had to explain to another doctor's lawyer that the years the doctor spent in medical school at army expense did not count against the obligation to serve that he had incurred while he did his undergrad at West Point, also at great taxpayer expense. Then there was the trio of doctors who sued the army for the right to moonlight.

They planned to close the orthopedic clinic on Fort Lewis two afternoons a week for "training;" such training to consist of treating civilians in a boutique clinic in Seattle at exorbitant rates (after all, they could advertise as specialists in treating catastrophic war injuries).

In her time at Lit Div, Pauline was amazed at the number of doctors who, after the army had paid them to go to medical school and paid their medical school tuition and expenses, came to the surprising self-realization that they were gay and should be discharged. It seemed that all the doctors she became familiar with while working at the Lit Div were passionate about one thing, and it wasn't serving their country or mending broken soldiers. These doctors were passionate about money. It would be a long time before Pauline met a doctor whose passions ran to more noble pursuits.

Although Pauline worked on a number of doctor cases, she increasingly found that she was being assigned the wrongful discharge cases brought by gay soldiers. Working to ensure doctors who claimed to be gay fulfilled their obligations to serve, and at the same time enforcing the army policy of discharging gay soldiers who wanted to serve was a large part of Pauline's schizophrenic legal practice during that time. The other JAGs in Lit Div started calling her "the Homosexual JAG," which pretty accurately summed up what she did during the latter two thirds of her time there. She reluctantly became the army expert on the law and policy concerning gays in the military and regardless of whether she agreed with that law and policy, she became a pro at articulating it and applying it to the facts of her cases. She personally thought the law and policy were the knee-jerk reactions of old, out-of-touch, homophobic white guys. However, because of her expertise in the area, and her more mature perspective compared to some of her peers, Pauline was often asked to brief the army leadership on the litigation surrounding the policy, and she wrote a number of articles for various military and non-military legal and non-legal publications on the subject. If someone thought she needed "face time" with the JAG Corps and army leadership, being the Homosexual JAG punched that ticket.

At the end of her time at Lit Div, she figured she had enough face time and was ready to move on. From the Litigation Division, Pauline went to the Army JAG School to attend the Graduate Course, where she earned a master's in Military Law. From there, she was detailed to Aberdeen Proving Ground in Maryland to oversee and coordinate the prosecutions of the rape and sexual harassment cases there, and to try to minimize their negative fall-out.

In the mid-1990s, a dozen officers and non-commissioned officers were charged with rape and maltreatment of subordinates in connection with soldier training at Aberdeen Proving Ground. These would not be the first such cases nor were such cases limited to the training facility at APG. But, as "Tailhook" became synonymous with sexual harassment in the Navy, "Aberdeen" became synonymous with sexual harassment in the Army. Pauline and her team did not create the concept of rape by constructive force to address the sexual exploitation of junior enlisted women by their superior officers and non-commissioned officers, but the Aberdeen cases put the concept on the military justice map. Following Aberdeen, the Uniform Code of Military Justice was revised to better address the crime of rape by constructive force. It did not escape Pauline's attention that, in typical army fashion, the working group tasked to recommend revisions to the Code did not talk to her or any of the members of her prosecution team when developing those revisions.

Pauline tried many of these cases herself because she was so outraged by them: drill sergeants abusing trainees whose well-being was entrusted to them; drill sergeants, selected for that duty in part because of their physical stature and prowess; drill sergeants, whose responsibilities include instilling unquestioning obedience to orders in new recruits—when to get up in the morning, when to eat, when to stand in formation, how to polish their boots, how far to run, how many push-ups to do, and when to go to bed; drill sergeants, commanding recruits to "drop and give me twenty," and those recruits never thinking to refuse—not being able to even think of refusing; drill sergeants ordering young women to report to their offices, knowing those women would comply with those orders; drill sergeants shutting the office doors and forcing those women to the floor or pinning them up against the wall; drill sergeants knowing that those women had no one to whom to call for help. Other drill sergeants? Drill sergeants who were their attackers' friends, who would believe their attackers, who maybe were assailants themselves? These drill sergeants didn't just assault these young women, they violated the honor of every other soldier and officer who wears the uniform. Including Pauline, and it made her want to spit nails.

Until Aberdeen, Army courts-martial had generally been civilized affairs in which counsel for both sides worked zealously within the law, the rules of evidence, and the rules of civility in the prosecution of accused soldiers. Aberdeen changed all that. For the first time, publicity-seeking civilian lawyers solicited military clients in large numbers. Aberdeen introduced the army to the concept of trying cases in the media. Civilian lawyers who knew a potential headline when they saw one flooded Aberdeen. Pauline would leave pre-trial hearings and conferences with these lawyers and tell her legal specialist to "break out the lizard cream–I've been slimed." News agencies, likewise, knew the makings of a good scandal and the resulting increases in circulation and ratings when they saw one. Nothing sold better than sex. Pauline and the other military lawyers were in unfamiliar territory when it came to the courtroom of the mass media. They were slow to learn that responding to a question from the press about a case by telling them that they would not comment on evidence until it had been admitted at trial was all too easily characterized as a "dodge" or "cover-up." Pauline's experience at

Aberdeen was eye-opening. Until Aberdeen, Pauline had loved doing trial work and had become very good at it. Aberdeen killed any desire Pauline had to continue to practice criminal law.

As detestable as the work was, the notoriety Pauline received in large part resulted to her selection to attend the Army's Command and General Staff College at Fort Leavenworth, Kansas. From JAG Girl to the Homosexual JAG to Sexual Harassment JAG. The not-quite-mainstream JAG career of Pauline Vickers. At least at the Command and Staff College, she thought, she could get her career back on track.

CHAPTER 6

Through these years in Fairbanks, Washington, and Aberdeen, Pauline kept in sporadic touch with the people she met along the way and with those she loved from the old days at Ord. She could always count on Gloria Nightingale's early Christmas cards, informing her of the Nightingale's latest assignment, Mark's most recent success, and the children's accomplishments. Pauline noticed that in every Christmas card she received, her friends' children were accomplished–like at Lake Wobegon, they were all "above average." Receiving Gloria's card always sparked her to reach out and touch her friends whom she only reached out and touched seasonally in December. She and Tim, and less frequently she and Richard, traded occasional phone calls and emails as the army went from Enable to WordPerfect to becoming subjects of the Microsoft empire.

Microsoft Outlook: the genesis of the Skirtnet.

While Pauline was at Aberdeen, she received an email from a friend who had attached an email from a young female JAG who was looking for some guidance. The friend had forwarded the request to Pauline and three other female JAGs, all of whom had deployed either to Panama, like Pauline, or to Iraq in Desert Storm. The request from the young JAG was straightforward: she was a trial counsel assigned to a unit that was going to deploy to Bosnia for six months. What advice, the young JAG asked, did women with deployment experience have that she wouldn't find in army field manuals or training circulars?

Pauline replied: "Get on birth control, not so you don't get pregnant, which you wouldn't anyway, but to stop your periods while you are deployed. Take plenty of underwear and socks as laundry opportunities may be pretty lean. Take industrial strength flip-flops. Take a couple of jars of peanut butter—you'll get sick of MREs and peanut butter will last forever and you can eat it with your finger if you have to. Take a bunch of baby wipes—you will feel dirty all the time. Take a long-reading paperback book."

Pauline not only responded to the young JAG and the three others who received the original electronic missive, but copied any other women JAGs whom she thought might have something useful to add or who might benefit from the advice. By the time all the emails had landed, there were about thirty female JAGs, ranging in rank and experience from captain to lieutenant colonel in the net. And so was born the "Skirtnet."

The Skirtnet became a valuable resource for all its members. Want advice on how to charge an offense under the General Article, Article 134 of the Uniform Code of Military Justice? Someone on the Skirtnet would know. Need to counsel a subordinate who has failed the Army Physical Fitness Test, to motivate the individual without destroying his morale? Someone on the Skirtnet will have some guidance. Moving to a new post and looking for information about childcare in the area? Ask on the Skirtnet. The Skirtnet became the official unofficial source of information, serious and silly, for all the JAGs in the net. On an apparently slow workday for one member, she asked a whimsical question: "I wonder who the patron saint of female JAGs should be?" It drew responses ranging from Joan of Arc (too martyred), to Saint Jude, Patron of Lost Causes (too pessimistic), to Raphael, Patron of Travelers and Friendships Restored (Pauline's contribution).

The annual "Top Three People I Would Never Work For Again" list that went around at the start of the annual assignment season, with each member adding her own top three, was an especially popular email stream, except among those who found themselves on it. One woman put her own name on the list–"I would not want to work for a bitch like me"–and meant it. There were no rules to restrict Skirtnet subject matter, except the "Article 88 Rule." Article 88 of the Uniform Code of Military Justice made it a crime for any commissioned officer to use "contemptuous words" against the President, the Vice President, the Secretary of Defense, the Secretaries of the Military Services, and a number of other public officials. There had not been a question of a Skirtnet violation of Article 88 until the Secretary of Defense's wife began referring to herself as the First Lady of the Pentagon, which the Skirtnet members at the Pentagon promptly acronym-ed to FLOP. Was referring to the SecDef's wife as "the FLOP" contemptuous toward her? And if so, was that contempt impugned to the SecDef and therefore punishable under Article 88? Weighty legal questions, indeed. Such weighty questions arose again until some years later when members of the Skirtnet began referring to President George W. Bush as "the Decider." Was calling the President "the Decider" contemptuous? After all, he called himself The Decider. Could the President be contemptuous toward himself? And if so, as the Commander in Chief, was he subject to the Uniform Code? Such silliness was a light in Pauline's dark years.

There were no rules about who could be included in the Skirtnet. Men could be included, in theory, if they didn't mind being called members of the Skirtnet and if they didn't say anything stupid in the judgment of the skirted members of the Skirtnet. On the other hand, some women were tossed out of the net. A female lieutenant colonel who opined that calling themselves the "Skirtnet" was self-demeaning and injurious to all the women of the Corps was dropped from the Skirtnet rolls for taking herself too seriously.

The most senior officer ever to be a member of the Skirtnet, a colonel, was likewise dropped from the rolls, not for being too uptight, but for being clueless. The colonel was married to an Infantry colonel. They had waited to have children until they were both lieutenant colonels. In response to a very young, very junior JAG's inquiry about childcare, the colonel had responded, "just get a live-in nanny like I have." She and her husband made more than twice what the younger officer made, and she had family money to boot. They could afford a live-in nanny's salary, a house big enough to house a live-in nanny, car insurance coverage for the live-in nanny, and airfare for the nanny to travel home to Guatemala every year for a holiday. She had no clue that her advice to the young JAG was not just unhelpful, it was out-of-touch.

Tim was the only man to maintain a long-term relationship with the Skirtnet. He never commented on the term "Skirtnet." He only weighed in when he had something useful to say. He never started an email with "if I were you . . ." which might have been interpreted as, "if I were a woman . . ." And he never patronized a member of Skirtnet. If a member asked for advice about how to deal with a sexist commander, Tim did not weigh in with an electronic "there, there . . ." or an "I'm sure you've misunderstood his intent," as some men might have done. If a member asked a female-specific question, Tim did not pretend to be able to provide a female-specific response. (Except in connection with a discussion about whether plain black pumps that showed toe cleavage were a uniform violation—he couldn't help himself.) He never took offense at the occasional poke at men: "A blonde was driving home on the Beltway when his cell phone rang. "Honey," the blonde's wife exclaimed, "be careful out there. There's a knucklehead driving on the wrong side of the road on the Beltway." "A knucklehead?" the blonde replied, "there are hundreds of them!" Or, "three guys walked into a bar. The girl ducked." Occasionally, Pauline would forward Richard a Skirtnet message containing a criminal law inquiry because she knew that he would provide a comprehensive and practical response. However, Richard never aspired to Skirtnet status and advised Pauline on separate occasions, off-line, to disengage from FLOP, the Decider, and other borderline disrespectful conversations.

During those years as she grew up in the army, Pauline went to Alpha Weekends and found temporary respite from disgruntled doctors, angry gays, arrogant assistant U.S. attorneys, unctuous civilian attorneys, and scandal-mongering reporters. Those weekends, aside from an occasional entertaining Skirtnet exchange and increasingly infrequent holidays with her family, were the only color in her otherwise gray world. When she looked back on the years after leaving Ord, it was like watching the tide erase footprints on the beach that show people have passed by. As the years passed by, time seemed to erase the imprint of people and events that touched Pauline's life, leaving only blurry outlines or nothing at all.

Pauline and Tim saw each other only once in the eight years following their departure from Fort Ord. They both attended a weeklong seminar at the JAG School a couple of years after they had been transferred from Fort Ord. The subject of the seminar was "Legal Operations in a Combat Environment." Tim was invited to attend based on his experience in Desert Storm. Pauline was invited because she had deployed to Panama with an Infantry Brigade during Operation Just Cause—not as Tim opined, just because they wanted a girl in the seminar photo. True, she was the only woman in attendance. And they did push her, literally, into the front row of the picture, even though there were several guys there who were much shorter than she was.

It was the first post-combat operations legal After Action Review held at the JAG School. It was a good AAR. Many of the junior officers were quite candid in their comments—describing shortfalls in rules of engagement training, lack of familiarity with contingency contracting procedures, inadequate pre-deployment weapons training, considerable equipment failures. The senior officers also provided comments: superior planning at higher headquarters, swift responses from higher to requests for assistance from the field, outstanding communications flow from higher to subordinate commands. Pauline finally understood the Soldiers' Curse: during operations, company commanders are frequently heard exclaiming in times of frustration, "it's those bastards at battalion." Likewise, at battalion, "it's those bastards at brigade," and at brigade, "it's those bastards at division." The junior officers at the AAR were frank in their feedback and the senior officers were equally frank in their surprise at the junior officers' feedback. At the AAR, Pauline realized that those jerks at division weren't really just being jerks —they really did think they were providing superior planning, swift responses, and outstanding communications and were genuinely taken aback that the Joes in the field didn't think so too.

Pauline was as candid as any of her peers during the AAR. She did, however, leave out the part about how she thought her Brigade Commander might have been crazy.

She didn't think he was crazy at first. She probably missed the first indicator that occurred when she was riding through the jungle on the border with Colombia in the Commander's Humvee. The driver and the Commander were in the front, she and the Commander's Spanish-speaking soldier/translator were in back. As they were blazing a trail on the jungle floor, the Commander looked over his shoulder and said to Pauline, "this reminds me a lot of 'Nam." The Commander had served in Vietnam and his heroics at Hamburger Hill were legendary in the Brigade. Pauline and the translator exchanged concerned glances. A couple of seconds later, the Commander looked back at her and finished his thought: "Of course, we would have napalmed it to hell." Later incidents made it clearer to Pauline that he may have been a little battle stressed.

Pauline didn't tell the JAGs at the AAR about the time the Commander discovered one of his lieutenants had brought a local prostitute into his company area. The Commander had called the lieutenant to his tent at two in the morning, put the lieutenant at attention, and told him exactly what he thought of the lieutenant's honor, discipline, moral character, and parentage. He then took the lieutenant's bayonet and cut the young man's rank and Infantry insignia off the collar of his battle dress uniform. After the Commander was done with him, Pauline walked the lieutenant out of the tent. The lieutenant was as white as new snow.

"I thought he was going to cut my throat, Captain Vickers."

"So did I, L-T."

Pauline also failed to tell the AAR about the time when the other JAG with the Brigade, a defense counsel, bolted. The Commander was so angry he almost struck Pauline when she told him that the defense counsel had hitched a ride on a Blackhawk helicopter back to the Task Force headquarters in Panama City, and then got himself on a C-130 aircraft back to California. At the time, Pauline was convinced that her gender saved her a fat lip–no matter how angry, the Commander never would have struck a girl. Unfortunately for the Brigade logistics officer, the logistics officer was not a girl. But when it came to the Commander's attention that he had sent a supply convoy out with inadequate security, the logistics officer might have wished he were. Had he been, the Commander likely would not have, as Pauline later described it to the investigating officer, "pushed him with a closed fist."

"So, you're not going to tell them about that wacko Colonel Woodburn? If I had stories like that, I'd write a book!" Tim had told her.

"Well, Tim, dear, Woodburn did all right by me, taking me–a girl–to war and all. Besides, I'm never going to write a book. Most of this stuff nobody would believe anyway."

CHAPTER 7

The U.S. Army Command and General Staff College at Fort Leavenworth, Kansas, was the epitome of institutionalized tradition. Every year, approximately twelve hundred mid-grade officers, mostly majors and some junior lieutenant colonels, were selected to attend CGSC. Those selected to attend tout themselves as the "top fifty percent of the Army," very purposefully failing to ask themselves if they are part of the top one percent or only breaking into the top forty-nine. About eighty foreign officers also attend every year in the interest of coalition building. The twelve hundred officers are divided into eighteen sections and each section into four staff groups. Each staff group has a mix of military specialties represented–combat arms, combat support, combat service support. Each staff group gets one, sometimes two women; one, sometimes two, international officers; and one, sometimes two, Black officers. Sometimes a staff group gets a twofer with a Black woman. Back in the day, officers came to Fort Leavenworth to read great military works, study great battles, and gather in staff groups to discuss and share insightful insights. In the late 1990s when Pauline was in residence, officers came to Leavenworth to read their assignments ("it's only a lot of reading if you do it") listen to endless lectures ("there I was . . ."), and do group practical exercises ("a 'B' at 1700 hours is better than an 'A' at 1800").

Each year, sixteen JAGs are competitively selected to attend CGSC. In 1997, Major Pauline Vickers and Major Richard Gerard were two of those JAG students. Major Tim Kennedy was not selected to attend. However, as life would have it, in 1997, Tim was serving as the JAG at the Disciplinary Barracks at Fort Leavenworth when Pauline and the Gerards arrived in Kansas. He had not changed appreciably in the ten years since they were at Ord together.

"How are you loving the great Midwest, Tim?" Pauline said after they had finished hugging hello at a cocktail party hosted by the senior JAG at Leavenworth to welcome the incoming JAG students.

"As long as I am on the friendly side of the wall of the Big House, I am good to go," Tim replied. "Lawrence is the bomb. Farm girl coeds go crazy for a war hero. And KC is almost a real city."

"You're not a little old for that?" Pauline said, laughing.

"What—did you go under for the third time somewhere between California and Kansas?" Tim replied, laughing back.

Tim still loved life. He had loved Germany and doing what earned him a Bronze Star in Desert Storm. He'd loved Fort Campbell, Kentucky ("southern girls – sweet!") and Fort Drum, New York ("sub-zero degree field exercises make men out of boys, that's for sure") where he'd been stationed following his assignment in Germany. He loved being the Disciplinary Barracks JAG. Certainly not everything had been goodness and light for Tim between California and Kansas. He had seen Iraqi soldiers bulldozed over in the desert in Iraq and had defended soldiers accused of truly heinous crimes in tragic situations. But in the ten years since they had shared paradise on earth in Monterey, nothing had dulled Tim's natural inclination to view life as mostly good. Although he could have felt slighted that he had not been selected to attend CGSC as Richard and Pauline had, he didn't. Tim had the gift of being happy for a friend's good fortune, even when it passed him by.

As relieved as he was to see his own name on the list, Richard had been surprised to see Pauline's name on it. Pauline had gone to the Grad Course in Charlottesville the year after Richard, during his first year on the faculty. The Grad Course was considered the flagship of the JAG School and there were many senior JAG officers with puffed chests over the fact that a couple of years before Richard had been a student, the JAG School had been accredited by the American Bar Association to award Masters of Law degrees to graduates of its advanced course called the "Graduate Course." However, in her end-of-the-course evaluation, Pauline had written that, in her opinion, the Grad Course should return to its roots as a JAG Advanced Course, like any other branch officers' advanced course; cut its length from ten months to twelve weeks like any other officers' advanced course; and get the JAGs out of the schoolhouse and promptly back to the field to do the government's business. She had expressed scorn for the title "professor" that the JAG School bestowed upon the officers assigned to teach there, and suggested that it was academically deceptive to compare a junior major with no scholarly credentials assigned to teach at the JAG School to a tenured professor at a real law school. And she may have even gone so far as to say that with a masters in military law and three bucks, she could get an overpriced cup of coffee. Richard had inadvertently overheard the Commandant of the JAG School's reaction when the Commandant read Pauline's evaluation. He hadn't been eavesdropping–everyone within a 100-foot blast zone had heard it. Richard's ears still burned. He could not understand how Pauline could break ranks as she did and still expect to have a successful career in the army. Yet, here she was, attending CGSC, just as he was.

Just as Tim had not changed, Richard was consistent in his essentials as well. His circumstances, however, had changed unimaginably. By the time he was at CGSC, he had Nadia, the sweetest little daughter Pauline had ever met and Jill was confined to a wheelchair. Shortly after Nadia's birth and Richard's return from Gulf War I, Jill began experiencing symptoms of something: fatigue, reduced dexterity in her hands, blurred vision. Her health care providers initially diagnosed "Wait and See." None of the lab tests they ordered confirmed or ruled out any of the possible or likely causes of her problems. The physician's assistant referred her to a general practitioner who referred her to a physical therapist who finally referred her to a neurologist. After more tests and an MRI, the neurologist changed Jill's diagnosis from "Wait and See" to multiple sclerosis. The stress of her condition lived in Richard's eyes. And although his essentials remained unchanged, such circumstances had smoothed Richard around his edges, and his perspective had diffracted like rays of light bend differently through a crystal after it has been sanded around its edges. Just as his soul had been the oldest among the students in the JAG Basic Course all those years ago, it was the oldest among the CGSC students. His hair had not grayed and he still did a sub-thirteen minute two-mile run, but his spirit had aged.

Although saddened by some of the circumstances that had caused it, Pauline thought the mellowing of Richard's "the army is my life" mind-set brought about by Nadia's birth and Jill's illness was for the better. Richard's face glowed as he told her about Nadia's accomplishments– scoring a goal for her pee-wee soccer team, doing her first swan dive, having a speaking part in the school production of *Charlotte's Web*–and her sweet nature–her gentleness with animals, her fond relationship with her grandparents, and her efforts to help care for her mother. His eyes darkened when he told Pauline about Jill's battle with MS. Jill's frustration with her disability had been evident in flashes at the cocktail party. She had snapped at Richard when he inadvertently set a glass a couple of inches beyond her reach, and she was short with anyone who offered to help her negotiate her wheelchair in the house. Pauline thought Richard had a romanticized view of "lady invalids"– he had seen *Camille* one too many times. Pauline tried to tell him without telling him, that it was unrealistic and unfair for him to expect Jill to always act with the grace of the play-acting Greta Garbo. Grace is harder in the real world. Richard had a hard time accepting that. In his perfect world, Pauline thought, with his perfect career and the perfect daughter, he struggled to forgive Jill for not being the perfect invalid.

At the JAG cocktail party, Tim convinced Pauline and Richard that a Fort Ord reunion was in order and the three met that Friday night at pub in Weston, a charming little prairie town not far from Fort Leavenworth.

Although Tim offered her a ride, Pauline drove herself–one never knew if Tim would be good for a ride home on a Friday night. And, God bless him, it turned out that she'd made the right call. While Richard and Pauline were catching up, Tim went to the bar to get a round of drinks. Richard had gone from Ord to Bragg to the JAG School to attend the Grad Course. He had taken a position on the faculty at the JAG School after he finished the Grad Course so that Jill could continue to receive treatment and physical therapy at the University of Virginia medical center. He had worried that his decision to homestead in Charlottesville might have hurt his chances at advancement in the Corps. He had been tremendously relieved to attend CGSC, a well-recognized indication that a JAG was still a comer.

Tim returned to the table to ask Pauline if she could give Richard a ride back to Leavenworth; Tim was going to hang around and see one of the barmaids home. Richard had ridden out to Weston with Tim. *Some people never learn*, thought Pauline. Pauline and Richard told Tim stories all the way back to Leavenworth, and both wondered whether he would ever join the adult world and, for that matter, if they even wanted him to. There was something reassuring about the unchanging current of Tim's life. Tim knew how to be happy. Pauline experienced infrequent moments of true happiness. She tried to acknowledge those moments as they were happening and live in them and appreciate them. She realized that the moment those pebbles of happiness dropped into her life, they began to ripple away until her spirit was once again still, as if it had never been disturbed. Sometimes she experienced endless dry spells, when she thought that she would never feel a drizzle of joy again. She loved Tim because of the constant flow of his happiness with life that flooded the banks of his spirit and nourished the lives of the people around him. People like Pauline and Richard.

CHAPTER 8

"We have to push the weekend back to January or February. Arden's knocked up again." Jeanne's voice was blunt across the telephone line.

The Alphas had had to push the weekend back to February before. Three years earlier, Arden, who had both gone through in vitro treatments the winter before, was pregnant in the fall, so they waited and celebrated the birth of her daughter, the newest junior Alpha the following February. This time, when Jeanne told Pauline of the plan to meet in February, Pauline told Jeanne that she couldn't face Minnesota in the dead of winter. Fortunately, someone told Pauline about some cabins at an army recreational facility on the Gulf Coast in Destin, Florida. So on Presidents' Day weekend Friday, the Alphas flew into Pensacola and spent a couple of days in an army cabin in Destin. Definitely not rustic or charming. Metal bedframes and thin mattresses, linoleum floors, and leftover institutional furniture. But they could sit on the screened porch and look at the gulf, walk on the fine sand beach, and put their toes in the too-cold surf.

Although they pushed the weekend to accommodate Arden's pregnancy, as it turned out Arden wasn't recovering from childbirth in February; she was recovering from a miscarriage. It had been an unplanned pregnancy. Arden, her husband, and her daughter were a happy family of three. They had not planned on another child, nonetheless, they had been happy at the prospect of becoming a family of four.

"It's such an odd feeling to lose an unborn baby," Arden told Pauline, the first day they arrived at the cabin. "We were sad when I lost the baby, but not devastated like I imagine we would be if we lost our daughter. It's more a feeling of regret—we couldn't grieve for something we never knew, but we were, for a time, overwhelmed by regret that we would never know what she might have been. It made us wonder what God was thinking—we hadn't planned or tried to have another baby—when I missed my period I thought I was starting menopause. It didn't even occur to me that I might be pregnant— so why would God let me get pregnant for no reason and then take the baby away? I don't get it. Maybe our lives were too happy and God felt like He had to step in to remind us how to feel something other than contentment."

"You really think God had a hand in it?" asked Pauline, even though she was afraid to go to that place in her heart.

"I think He has a hand in everything. 'There's a divinity that shapes our ends, rough-hew them how we will,'" Arden responded.

"John Donne?" asked Pauline.

"Hamlet."

"But, doesn't that make you sad? To believe in an omniscient, omnipotent God and know that He would, if not cause, certainly permit, you to get pregnant and then lose the baby?" Pauline asked, continuing to push.

"There are more things in heaven and earth, my dear Pauline, than are dreamt of in your philosophy." Arden replied.

"What's with all the Shakespeare?"

"Shakespeare was a very spiritual guy. Besides, you're asking me to explain the ways of God, for heavens' sakes. What do you want me to say?"

Arden and Pauline were unpacking their suitcases in their shared room with two miserable twin beds, florescent lights, and a WWII era military hospital dresser. Jeanne had been granted the "master bedroom" with a miserable full-sized bed, a dresser with a mirror, and a three-quarter bath en suite. Jeanne was the Alpha Queen this weekend because she had picked up the tab for all of their airfares. She had been on the trial team of one the numerous firms that had represented the hundreds of fishermen who had sued the Exxon Corporation after the Exxon Valdez went aground and spilled nearly fifty million gallons of crude oil into the cool, clear water of Prince William Sound. Three years after the case had been tried and a jury in Anchorage, Alaska, awarded the plaintiffs more than five billion dollars, Jeanne treated the Alphas to first class tickets to Pensacola. "If I can't earn a bucket of money so my posse and I can go first class, what's the point?" On their way to the cabin in their rented SUV, they stopped at a Burger King and Jeanne, the Alpha Queen, got to wear the paper crown. They had to stop at Burger King because when asked what she wanted Arden to bring her back from Florida, her daughter requested either "a real live alligator or a kids' meal toy." The Alphas were only too happy to have kids' meals for lunch to accommodate a junior Alpha.

"Five billion dollars? Honey! My head can't even hold that many zeroes," Arden said in the ride to the cabin.

"Well, the jury did what it thought was right," Jeanne said. "The jury found that Exxon was reckless, its recklessness had caused a shit-ton of economic and environmental damaged, and they let Exxon know it was not amused."

"Yeah, Jeanne, but five billion?" Arden still couldn't seem to believe it.

"Well, don't you worry about Exxon," Jeanne told her. "Twenty years from now those bastards will still be the biggest oil robber-barons in the world, gouging us at the pumps every chance that they get."

Pauline saw the irony of the tragedy at Prince William Sound paying for their first class airfare to the Gulf of Mexico. It was the perfect time to be on the gulf. It was cold by Florida standards, heavenly by Minnesota's. They dropped their suitcases and the shopping bags from the supermarket and from the liquor store, where they stopped after Burger King, at the cabin. They unpacked their essentials, but did not linger there very long. Instead, they drove down to an Air Force facility on the beach. Access to the beach facility was a dirt road off the main road, through a gate in a chain link fence. By the time the Alphas got there that evening, the gate was closed and padlocked for the night. Fortunately, the shoulder was wide enough to accommodate the SUV. They parked to consider the situation.

"Are they allowed to lock this gate?" Angela asked. "Doesn't government property belong to the taxpayers? I don't think they should be allowed to lock us out."

"This fence looks perfectly climb-overable," said Jeanne. "I didn't come all the way down here to stand around on the side of the road. Let's do it. G.I. Jane's got a military ID card if anyone tries to make trouble, and Martelli's a judge, so what can happen?"

"Let's see…I could be court-martialed and Angela could be impeached," Pauline said.

"Only if we get caught, baby," Angela said. "We're going over. If anyone sees us, scatter and run like hell, and we'll regroup at the cabin."

As always, the weight that they carried as grown-ups in the Real World was lifted during the Alpha Weekends. Pauline felt like a juvenile delinquent as she climbed over the fence. It was a beautiful feeling. It was beautiful on the beach. The sand was that fine sugary sand that they have on the panhandle beaches. The sky and the water were so blue that they blended together and it seemed to the Alphas that a woman, if strong enough, could swim into the heavens. The facility was deserted and the only people they saw on the beach were an ant-sized distance away. Arden pulled a grocery bag out of her jacket pocket and filled it with sand.

"What are you doing, Arden?" Pauline asked.

"I'm taking some sand home for the daughter," Arden replied.

"A shopping bag full?"

"Why? Won't they let me take this much?"

"No, I don't think they care, but why do you want so much?"

"I want her to be able to put her feet in it."

They spent The Weekend walking on the beach, dining in trendy restaurants, breakfasting in local joints found on the recommendations of the wait staff at trendy restaurants, and drinking daiquiris on the screened porch in the evenings. One year, they had forgotten a corkscrew and had to pound corks into wine bottles with the heel of a butter knife. Every year since, they had four corkscrews among them, and they always had a featured cocktail. In college, Jeanne had worked as a bartender, and she was happy to revive that role during The Weekends. One year, she experimented with the drinks their mothers had drunk: Sidecars, White Russians, Sloe Gin Fizzes. The year after Arden had her daughter, they celebrated with Kir Royales. One year when they had an early cold spell—"northern Minnesota *is* an early cold spell," Pauline had commented to Jeanne as she tried to warm things up with mango margaritas. This year it was daiquiris. "Since we're in Florida, I thought we should go Buffett, but not too Buffett," Jeanne had explained.

"I've quit the law biz," Arden said.

The Alphas had gone for a walk on the beach and stopped at one of the bars overlooking the gulf. They sat on the patio even though it was too cold to sit outside, even with the bar's patio heater roaring. The Alphas were the only people sitting outside, unwilling to put a sheet of glass between themselves and creation, and proud to show off their thick Minnesota blood. Pauline had been the first Alpha to invade another country, Jeanne had been the first to make partner in her firm, Angela was the first to be a judge, and now Arden would be the first to leave the law.

Arden went on to explain that her firm was involved in the defense of the tobacco industry in cases brought in Minnesota and Washington. The tobacco litigation was probably the largest and most complex litigation in the history of American jurisprudence. Billions of dollars were at stake and the precedent established by these cases would have effects worldwide. Arden had attended a settlement conference shortly before the Alpha Weekend.

"And then I heard one of my law partners say, in the course of the discussions, 'only if you believe smoking cigarettes causes cancer,'" Arden continued. "And all of a sudden, I couldn't believe that I was sitting there, nodding my head and playing high powered lawyer. It was like a light bulb suddenly came on in my brain. This was not what the law should be and it is not what I should be doing. Can you imagine? 'If you believe smoking cigarettes causes cancer?' I was busting my ass to bill hours, dropping my youngest kid off at daycare at six o'clock in the morning, missing meals with my husband, so I could hear my side say 'if you believe smoking cigarettes causes cancer.' At that moment I decided that it wasn't how I want to live my life. So, I quit. It wasn't even all that hard. I mulled it over a little, talked to The Husband, mulled it over some more, and when I finally said 'I quit' out loud, it was like the weight of the world had been lifted off my shoulders. I didn't even know how it was weighing me down until I felt it gone. There is such relief in making a decision and knowing that it has been made."

"What are you going to do now?" Angela asked.

"I don't know," Arden answered. "Be a mom. Live off my husband. Hang out with my girlfriends. During the coffee hour at church last Sunday, one of the church ladies mentioned that they were looking for someone to head up Vacation Bible School for this summer, and I volunteered. It is so cool to be able to do something that I want to do and have the time to do it—I could actually commit to Vacation Bible School without having to check my PDA first! Maybe when I'm done with that, I'll write a book about four women who went to law school together and get together for a long weekend every year. One of us should."

"Just remember two little words when you're writing the great American novel about us: *tall* and *thin*," Angela told her, not altogether jokingly.

Pauline knew the after-feeling of making an important decision. But for her, making the decision had not lifted any weight; it had crushed her. For ten years, she had felt her decision sucking the life out of her. Listening to Arden, she realized that she should have felt more relief at the decision being made and done, like Arden did. The ramifications of Arden's decision were significant. She had been made a partner in her firm the year before. Her firm was well established and respected in the Cities, and partners don't leave such firms because "it's not how they want to live their lives." The financial effects of her decision were considerable. Her husband was a lawyer in a small firm that specialized in representing non-profit corporations. Arden used to say, "my husband saves the world and I pay the bills," and it was only a little funny because it was mostly true. Both Pauline and Arden had made no-turning-back decisions. But while Arden felt an after-glow, Pauline felt darkness. She realized that she had to figure out how to come to grips with her decision, let it go, and find her way back into the light.

Later, sitting on the porch at the cabin with the Alphas, Pauline felt the vacuum in her soul cracking and felt the first ripple of serenity starting to seep in. Maybe she could, she thought, accept her decision and its consequences and move on. Maybe she could look ahead and look for the possibilities of the future. She looked out to the waters of the gulf. The water was bluish-gray and rough, and the sky was grayish-blue and windy. It was still too cold to be outside, but they felt like they had to be. Pauline could feel peacefulness settle in around them like a cloud. Photo albums were being circulated. The mandatory Weekend home and garden and gossip magazines were being perused. "I could do that in the garden by my back patio" and "Someone needs to give that girl a good shake and some panties." Angela suggested that they break up the coffee table inside, dig a hole in the sand, and 'voila!' a fire pit. Arden pointed out that the coffee table was probably not real wood. Pauline smiled at how much she loved them. She only saw them once a year when she could, and they traded occasional notes or emails when the spirit moved them. So little contact, yet the bonds remained and strengthened. The intervening years of life had changed all of them in some way or another. While life had soothed some of Angela's rough edges, practicing law had toughened up the Arden's tender core. Jeanne was a little bit mellowed by finally having some money in her pocket. Pauline was amazed that she should love the Alphas, collectively and each of them individually and uniquely as she did too.

"What are you thinking about, Paul?" Arden asked, seeing that Pauline's mind was miles away.

"Just about how much I love you guys."

"Hey, Ange! It's Vickers who's the lesbo, not you!" Jeanne said, lightening the moment.

Angela replied in kind, "Jeanne, you ignorant slut."

Pauline was happy to be sharing a room with Arden. She felt like she could empathize with Arden's loss by the miscarriage even if Arden was unaware of the source of Pauline's empathy.

"I really am sorry for your loss, Arden," she said as they were settled into their twin beds. She took a breath and make a decision.

"I think I know how you feel," she said.

"What do you mean?" Arden asked.

Pauline took another deep breath.

"You know how I missed the second post-law school Weekend?" Pauline said.

"Yeah."

"Well, I never told you all *how* I missed that weekend."

"Go on."

And Pauline told Arden everything. The weekend with Oak. Finding out she was pregnant. Tim's reaction. Her distress. The Army. Her Mother. The weekend at Club Nightingale and her decision. Her pregnancy terminated. The hole it left in her soul.

Pauline finished her story and she and Arden lay in their adjacent beds, staring at the ceiling in the sky's light coming in through the window between them.

"Then why did you do it?" Arden finally asked.

"What?"

"Then why did you do it?" Arden repeated. "If it caused you so much angst, why did you do it?"

"I told you – I wasn't ready to start a family alone. I didn't want to lose my job, my family."

"So you were scared," Arden said.

"Yeah, I guess I was scared and unprepared and overwhelmed."

"So, you were scared so you took a life, or at least, the potential of a life," Arden said.

"Arden, I don't understand . . ." Pauline began.

"I don't understand how you can think that you know how I feel," Arden said. "I *lost* a baby, you took one. You made a decision and have had to live with the consequences. I understand that you might regret it, or feel sad about it, or wish you'd made a different call. But how can you think my losing a baby is the same thing?"

"I didn't say it was the same thing. I didn't mean to diminish your loss. I thought you would understand," Pauline said, her voice cracking with tears.

"No, Pauline," Arden said. "I do not understand. You made a decision because you were a coward and you compare that to my loss. My heart was broken and you showed no heart at all. I do not understand. Good night."

Arden rolled over and turned her back on Pauline.

The next morning, the Alphas packed up the SUV and drove to the airport in Pensacola. If Jeanne and Angela sensed the tension between Arden and Pauline, they didn't say anything directly. They must have felt something however, because as they were approaching the airport Jeanne joked, but not really joking, that Exxon was going to put a pool in her backyard and that they were all going to have to come over for a barbeque. As they did every Alpha Sunday, the women from the Cities promised that they would get together for lunch or drinks soon, and noted they didn't have to wait for The Weekend to get together. Pauline, as usual, talked about going to the Cities to attend a course or seminar and pick up some Minnesota Continuing Legal Education credits and how they could all get together then, but this time she didn't sound like she meant it. As they were unloading the SUV at the rental car return, Pauline found half a dozen cans of diet soda rolling around in the back.

"Anyone want a diet soda for the trip?" she asked.

"Yeah, I'll take one," answered Arden, not meeting Pauline's eyes.

"Me, too," said Jeanne.

"Hand 'em around, Vickers," Angela said. "Where's that bottle of rum, Jeanne?"

"In my carry-on, why?" Jeanne said.

"You can't take a bottle of rum in your carry-on, knucklehead," Angela said. "Hand it over."

They each popped a can of diet soda, took a swig, and Angela topped off the cans with generous glugs of rum. Pauline hadn't planned to open a bar in the back of a rented SUV, but she was flexible. And Jeanne's carry-on was appreciably lighter when she handed it to the flight attendant in first class.

"It's the only way to travel," Angela whispered to Jeanne as she found her seat.

CHAPTER 9

T he end of the Command and Staff College academic year was fast approaching. They were down to the culminating exercise in which every student played a part in play-fighting a war that they were not allowed to call Korea, even though the political situation, terrain, and force alignments were strikingly similar to those on a peninsula off northwest China in the early 1950s. Twelve hundred mid-grade U.S. and multinational officers playing war. Long-retired general officers staged their own invasion of Leavenworth as they flew in to observe the exercise, mentor the younger officers, and feel important again. Pauline was assigned as the legal advisor for the Special Operations Command. Richard was the JAG for their higher headquarters and admitted that he liked the idea of being Pauline's boss.

"I'll be issuing lots of rules of engagement orders and will expect end-of-the-day reports from you, Major Vickers," Richard told her, with a note of self-importance.

"I'll be advising bored steely-eyed killers who will gladly simulate killing you in your sleep for a simulated case of beer, so don't screw with me, Major Gerard."

"That's what I love about you, Pauline—your ladylike demeanor in the face of battle."

The members of the faculty served as Observers/Controllers for the exercise. That is, they played the opposing forces and fought the enemy battle; they made up battle results and reported numbers of killed, casualties, equipment losses, and terrain gained and lost; they injected tasks and unexpected events into the scenario; and they monitored and evaluated the students' performances. Faculty members also served as escort officers for the horde of retired Generals who descended on Leavenworth during the exercise. Tim, on loan from the Disciplinary Barracks legal office, was tasked to be an escort officer. It was the perfect job for him. He loved the dress-right-dress performance and standing slightly behind the General while the General received briefings, gave advice, and told war stories of real wars. Although unchanged in his essentials, Tim had grown up since Fort Ord. As he escorted Generals from one Tactical Operations Center to another, he queried the Generals about their relationships with their JAGs when they had been serving. He heard stories about JAGs "saving my butt" when a General did this or that, and about JAGs filling in voids left by wounded, killed, or relieved line officers. Inevitably, when the general arrived at the next Tactical Operations Center, Tim asked the pretend commanders about their JAGs. In this way, Tim was training line officers to value their lawyers, but the bullet on his Officer Efficiency Report would only say "Served as escort officer." Tim was not the dog paddler that he pretended to be and, unfairly, was believed to be by some of the JAG leadership.

The first morning of the exercise, Pauline went to a classroom, now the Special Forces Command Tactical Operations Center, and found that although in uniform, none of the Special Forces officers had shaved that morning.

"What's up with the seven o'clock shadow, gentlemen?" she asked.

"We train like we fight, ma'am," was the response.

"What the heck does that mean?" she asked again.

"When SF go to war, we have to blend in with the local populace. We have to live in the shadows, be just another man in the crowd. We have relaxed grooming standards in the field so we'll fade into the background– we grow our hair out and grow beards. Standard SF procedure," one of the guys told her.

"Well, that's not going to fly when they run the pachyderms through; I'm thinking a retired four star isn't going to appreciate relaxed grooming standards in the classroom. You guys need to shave. ASAP," said Pauline, the mansplaining prompting her to assert her personality.

"We don't have razors here," the SF officer said, pushing back.

"You're 'special'–use your bayonets."

Such mansplaining aside, Pauline enjoyed being the Special Forces JAG. The SF officers were able to focus on their mission and get the job done, without lighting their too-long hair on fire, and without taking themselves too seriously. Early in the exercise, after the planning was completed, the best course of action selected, and the "war" had begun, the Special Forces Commander received a report from the exercise Observers/Controllers that a prisoner of war had died while in Special Forces' custody. The Commander tasked his JAG, Pauline, to investigate. The prisoner had been captured by a multinational forces unit. Pauline found the French Special Forces officer playing the role of liaison officer between the multinational forces and the Americans.

"Major LeFevre, we have a report that an enemy prisoner of war died in coalition custody," Pauline said, playing the game.

"C'est la guerre, ma chere," The French officer responded, not playing at all.

"Work with me, Major," Pauline said.

"He died of his wounds," LeFevre said, in heavily accented English. "C'est bon? Allez, come have a café au lait before you return to the field of combat."

72

On the afternoon of the fourth day of the exercise, Richard found Pauline to tell her that a pretend Corps Commander had relieved a pretend Operations Officer on the first day of the exercise. The Ops Officer had not been seen since. After four days, his absence was noticed by a faculty member. The pretend Commander (a real life major) explained that the pretend Ops Officer (another real life major) had been insubordinate and that he had relieved the Ops Officer and sent him home. Sure enough, reported Richard, when a faculty member went to the Ops Officer's quarters, there he was, in workout clothes watching golf on the twenty-four hour sports channel. The faculty member was not amused. They decided that it was time for someone to have a "come to Jesus" talk with the pretend Commander and pretend Ops Officer. Richard was tasked to be the pretend Jesus. Richard had to tell them: 1. It's an exercise; nobody's really invading not-Korea and no soldiers are really going to die. 2. No one has the authority to relieve anyone else. 3. Everyone has to come to work every day, even if a pretend commander pretends to relieve one. 4. Can everyone spell AWOL?

"What the hell were they thinking, Pauline?" Richard asked Pauline.

"You know ten years ago, that commander would have been you, don't you?" Pauline told him. "Besides, I heard last year two guys had a fist fight over courses of action. A Patton-wannabe and a loafer seem pretty mild in comparison."

After the "war" (the students won as they were predestined—a couple of years earlier, the administration discovered that no one would play and take it seriously if they lost), all that was left to do were the course evaluations and the graduation ceremony. In addition to tactics and operations, logistics, intelligence, and branch specialty courses, the coursework at the Command and General Staff College included military history. Every week, every staff group met to discuss military history from Sun Tzu's *The Art of War* to Thucydides' *History of the Peloponnesian Wars* to the Army-approved account of the Gulf War's "left hook." Pauline's instructor had served at Fort Bragg with Richard, so when the instructor read Pauline's evaluation of the history course, he approached Richard and suggested he have a "come to Jesus" talk with his friend. (The expression "come to Jesus" were buzz words the year Pauline and Richard were at the Command and Staff College. So were "challenge the paradigm" and "there's no 'I' in "team."")

"Do you not want to make lieutenant colonel, Pauline?" Richard asked.

"Don't say any more, Richard," Pauline said. "I know where you are going with this, but if they ask for candor on the evaluations, they should expect to get it. Besides, I thought the evals were confidential—where do they get off showing mine to you?"

It was like Pauline's Grad Course evaluation all over again. But instead of poking her finger in the eye of the JAG Corps leadership, this time she was poking her finger in the eye of every army historian and army historian wannabe, including the Command and Staff College Commandant. Among army historians and wannabes, the Civil War *is* U.S. military history. Manassas, Gettysburg, Vicksburg. Lee, Longstreet, Stewart. They consider *The Killer Angels* great literature and every year twelve hundred majors are required to write twelve hundred book reports on it. Most present day army officers glorify the Civil War South—the glorious leadership, the brilliant strategy, the glorious honor in defeat (of course, two-thirds of present day army officers are from the South). They talk about General Lee as if they personally served with him and Stonewall Jackson as if he were about to enter the room. They re-fight Gettysburg until the Confederates win the battle. "Never mind," Pauline had quipped in class one day, "that it was an immoral war and they lost." The Civil War is such an important watermark for army historians that they spend nearly half the academic year talking about it in the Command and General Staff history curriculum.

"You just had to say that we should spend one week studying the Civil War and eleven studying Vietnam, instead of the reverse as they do now?" Richard said, not to be deterred. "You had to say that they should retire *The Killer Angels* and require us to read and write on McMasters' *Dereliction of Duty*? I don't understand you, Pauline. You know that they are not going to follow your recommendations and all you do is mark yourself as a troublemaker. You just have to make waves, don't you?"

"That's not fair, Richard. I really thought about the eval before I wrote it," Pauline told him. "The leadership is all the time telling us that we "can't be afraid to tell the boss bad news," and that we have to 'think outside the box.' I really believe that we need to spend more time studying Vietnam than the Civil War if we want to learn lessons that will serve us in future wars. What are we more likely to do in the future—fight another conventional civil war or involve ourselves in an ugly, protracted counterinsurgency of questionable legitimacy? I'm not trying to make waves, I'm just telling them what I think because they asked me what I thought. I'm hardly throwing my career away. Besides, I got here after the Grad Course, didn't I? Thanks for worrying about me, but I'm just going to have to do what I think is right and live with it. I couldn't live with it if I didn't. I've tried and it doesn't work."

"I think I'll get married tomorrow," Tim said.

"Have you got someone in mind or are you just going to play that by ear?" Pauline asked, thinking Tim was just being Tim.

"Actually, when I say 'I think I'll get married tomorrow,' what I mean is, 'I'm getting married tomorrow,'" Tim said.

Tim had cajoled Pauline and Richard into a final Fort Ord group hug the Friday before the Saturday that Pauline and Richard were to graduate. The year had sailed by—it seemed that they had just met in the pub in Weston the day before. This time, however, they all arrived in separate cars.

"You remember Mandy?" Tim continued. "You met her that night we first met here. She was working behind the bar. She's getting her Masters in Islamic Art at KU. We're madly in love and we're getting married tomorrow. Sorry you guys can't make it with your graduation and all, but that's how it goes sometimes."

Pauline was stunned into silence. It had never occurred to her that Tim would ever get married. It just wasn't his way. Yet here he was, telling Richard that after meeting the girl at the first Ord reunion, he and Mandy had seen each other (*translation: slept together,* she thought) off and on over the past ten months. She half listened to Tim tell Richard that he was almost thirty-six years old and that it was time he take the plunge. "I don't want to wind up dried out and lonely like Vickers here." She faintly heard Richard ask Tim when he had decided to get married and why hadn't he told them sooner, sent invitations, and planned it for a day when Pauline and he would be able to attend. Some part of her brain heard Tim tell Richard that he and Mandy weren't into the whole big show, everyone-go-broke-for-a-twenty-minute-ceremony sort of wedding hoopla. Quick and easy with the Disciplinary Barracks chaplain presiding.

"Who needs a big to-do to prove that we have true love?" Tim said, ending the questioning.

They finished their beers, toasted the ghost of Fort Ord, and for the first time in their history, Pauline, Richard, and Tim left a bar at the same time, alone in their own vehicles. As Tim hugged Pauline to him—not like a sister or a girlfriend or a lover—he asked her, "Why are you so surprised? Don't you think I'm capable of loving a woman? Besides, you turned me down once and I can hardly wait until all my vital juices are dried up for you to come to your senses." They kissed. It wasn't goodnight and it couldn't be goodbye. It just was.

Pauline lost her best friend when Tim married the next morning. As many ways as there are for a man and a woman to love each other, a married man cannot be a single woman's best friend. Tim was wrong if he thought they could be. Pauline knew they couldn't.

The morning Pauline lost her best friend, she and Richard graduated. The Gerards were pre-packed and Richard threw his class-A uniform jacket into the back of the truck and they headed for I70 west to Fort Carson, Colorado. Pauline threw her class-A uniform jacket into the trunk of her car and headed southeast for MacDill Air Force Base where she would serve at U.S. Special Operations Command. And Timothy Francis William Kennedy married a woman he didn't know how to love as a wife.

CHAPTER 10

It's a long, ugly, eighteen-hour drive down I75 south from Kansas City to Tampa. It suited Pauline. There is no more alone place to be than in an aging muscle car called Doug on a soulless, unending highway. She had lost something of Tim and she had lost Arden. Maybe, she feared, she had lost all the Alphas. Arden's reaction shocked her those months ago and Pauline was still absorbing and processing Arden's words. Alone in Doug, driving the mindless interstate, Pauline replayed the scene that night over and over. She hadn't expected to be judged by an Alpha and as the shock and pain of it absorbed into her heart, she felt it turning to anger.

Where does she get off calling me a coward? Pauline thought. *I'm in the damn army. I uproot my life every two years and move to a new post and job and people. I didn't stay safely tucked away in Minnesota with a husband and a safe job and a little house with a white freaking picket fence. I went to war, God damn it! And she called me a coward.*

Anger felt better than pain and Pauline clung to it. She had left Leavenworth after mid-day and had originally thought she would try to drive as far as Georgia, get a hotel room for the night, and then finish the trip into Tampa the next day. But as she drove, Pain and Anger were like the Two Wolves Within from Native American folklore. Pauline fed Anger and it grew, and the adrenaline required to feed Anger kept Pauline alert.

78

She drove "with a purpose" as her father would say, and only stopped when she needed to feed Doug gas. She drove through Tennessee without seeing it, and when she came to the Georgia border, she was wide awake. *Well,* she thought, *I'll go as far as the Florida line and then find a place to crash.* She continued driving. She and Doug had the freeway almost to themselves in the darkness right before the dawn and Pauline was high on Anger's adrenaline. There was construction on I75, as always, and as she neared the first of the Gainesville exits, lanes were blocked and what had been six lanes narrowed to two, with orange cones separating vehicles from oncoming traffic. Pauline blinked hard at the oncoming headlights, and then blinked again.

She woke up.

"Where am I?" Pauline asked.

"It's all right," a voice said. "You're in the hospital. You've been in an accident, but you're all right now."

Pauline forced her eyes open. The room was blurry and fractured, like she was looking through a cracked window. She blinked her eyes hard several times and things started to slowly come into focus. The face that produced the voice became clear, and Pauline became confused.

"What are you doing here?" Pauline asked her mother.

"That's a fine thing to ask your mother," her mother said. "Where else would I be when my daughter has been in a car accident and winds up in the hospital?"

"Where's dad?" Pauline asked.

"He's in Yakota, of course," Pauline's mother answered, referring to the U.S. air base from where Pauline's father commanded U.S. forces in Japan. "He has obligations, Pauline. But don't worry, I'm here and you're going to be fine."

Pauline closed her eyes and must have dozed off because when she opened them again, her mother was gone and a doctor was standing next to her bed, holding a clipboard, and looking down at her.

"How do you feel?" he asked.

"I don't know," Pauline said. "I don't understand. What happened? How did I get here? Did I talk to my mother? Is she here?"

"Do you know what day it is?" the doctor asked.

"Friday? Saturday?" Pauline said. "I don't know. Am I in Tampa?"

The doctor rolled a stool to her bedside and sat down.

"Today is Tuesday. You're in the UF Shands Trauma Center. You were in an accident on I75. There's construction and you apparently fell asleep at the wheel and hit an elevated exit ramp support head-on. You were air evac-ed here from the scene. You suffered several injuries, most notably a broken pelvis. We operated yesterday. Essentially, we opened you up, re-aligned the bones in your pelvis, and put in some metal plates to keep them in place.

"You also suffered some cracked ribs and other minor internal injuries. No discernable head injuries, but short term loss of memory after a trauma such as you experienced is not uncommon. It's a miracle, really, that you weren't hurt more badly."

"And Doug?" Pauline asked.

"I understood you were alone in the vehicle," the doctor answered.

"Doug *is* the vehicle."

"Oh. Totaled, I imagine. I did say it's a miracle that you weren't hurt more badly," the doctor answered, and then permitted himself a smile. "If it makes you feel any better, he probably saved your life. He must be built like a tank."

"And is my mother here?"

"Yes, she arrived Sunday afternoon. She's been very, uh, *engaged* with your care."

It was Pauline's turn to try to smile. "Yes," she said. "I imagine she has."

The doctor leaned in toward Pauline and, in a stage whisper, said, "Did you know she's a general's wife and that you're a general's daughter?"

"I have heard something like that," Pauline replied.

"You try to get some sleep and I'll tell the general's wife that you need some rest."

"Thank you, doctor."

"Pauline, wake up."

Pauline again forced her eyes open. Her mother was sitting in a chair next to her bed, looking at her. Hard.

"Mother," Pauline started.

"Pauline," her mother interrupted. "I've been talking to the doctor. He just told me that your injuries would not affect your ability to have more children."

"What?" Pauline asked.

"He said your injuries would not affect your ability to have more children."

"Why is the doctor talking to you about the effect of my injuries? I'm an adult. There are privacy laws."

"Pauline, don't test me," her mother said. "I'm your mother—of course he talked to me about your injuries. And given the nature of your internal injuries and your brother's 'condition,' it's only natural I would want to know whether I would be able to have grandchildren."

"But, Mother," Pauline began again.

"Pauline, he said your ability to have more children. *More* children. What was he talking about, Pauline? What have you done?"

"Mother . . ."

"He says that you will be discharged tomorrow and ambulanced to Walter Reed until you can be released for further rehab and physical therapy. I'll stay until then."

The headquarters of a Combatant Command, like U.S. Special Operations Command, was a good assignment to facilitate Pauline's recovery. Generally regular hours, no deployments, plenty of time for physical therapy. Her JAG friends routinely checked in on her via the Skirtnet and she received occasional emails from Tim and Richard. She didn't hear from Arden, and seven months into her tour of duty there, she had not heard about any plans for the next Weekend. Her fear that she had lost the Alphas seemed to be realized. She wanted to call Jeanne or Angela, but she was afraid of what they might say. Pauline fed Fear rather than Hope and didn't make the call.

Just as she was feeling fully physically recovered, Pauline received a call from now Colonel Mark Nightingale. Mark was working in the JAG Corps assignments branch, and he told her that an officer in the Joint Chiefs of Staff Legal Office was being relieved and that he wanted to put her in for that job.

"After your accident, Pauline," he told her, "it's important that the leadership see you're fully recovered and squared away. The RUMINT is that you're not yourself anymore and might be PTSD-ing down there in Tampa," he said, referring to "Rumor Intelligence."

"I'm fine," Pauline said, "and I've only been here a year."

"I know that," Mark said, "but this is a great opportunity and you've got to take care of your third file."

"Third file?" Pauline asked.

"Yeah—you know everyone has their official permanent file with efficiency reports, awards, and stuff like that at Human Resources Command. Then we all have a local file, wherever we are assigned with local counselings, letters of commendation, and that kind of stuff. And then there's our third file. That's all the unwritten stuff—your reputation, who you know, who knows you. Arguably the most important file. You need to get up here and show leadership that you are physically fit and mentally good to go."

So just a year after arriving at SOCOM, Pauline packed up her new used Volvo rag top convertible named Sven and drove north.

CHAPTER 11

T hey had closed Fort Ord in September 1994. The other JAGs in the course couldn't understand why Pauline would want to drive almost five hundred miles up the coast to visit a post that had been closed for more than ten years. It was the end of a week-long Special Operations Legal Seminar held at the Navy base in San Diego. Pauline had been invited to present at the seminar because of her experience in Panama, at Special Operations Command, and in her current position in the Joint Chiefs of Staff Legal Office in the Pentagon. Many of the attendees were making plans to enjoy all things San Diego before returning home to their camps, posts, and stations in such garden spots as Fort Bragg, North Carolina and Fort Drum, New York. Pauline had decided to take a couple of days leave and drive up Highway 1 to Monterey and the remains of Fort Ord. Her heart was telling her that the writer was right, that she could not go home again, but the sirens' calls to the Bay were too compelling to ignore.

She didn't arrive until well after dark and the B&B where she had a reservation was harder to find than she had expected it to be. It was disconcerting that she didn't know her way around the Monterey peninsula like she was sure that she did. Things were not where they were supposed to be. The next morning, she found that the front gate to Fort Ord was further north than it was supposed to be, and she couldn't find the back gate that led into old training areas at all. There were no MPs at the front gate–anyone at all could drive right on in and Pauline thought that surely wasn't right. The PX and commissary were where they were supposed to be, but the courthouse was two blocks wrong and the street in front of it was not supposed to be one-way. The old post headquarters was too small and the building that had housed the legal office too empty. The flagpole was flagless. Pauline remembered when she had been dating the Commanding General's aide de camp and had mentioned to him at PT that the flagpole was all beat up and rusty from the riggings banging on it. Two days later, it sported a fresh coat of white paint. That resulted in a fourth date; it was Pauline's first taste of power and she laughed at herself when she remembered feeling it–*I caused the flagpole to be painted with an off-the-cuff remark to the General's aide.* She remembered forming up for PT with the rest of the General's staff on the parade grounds in front of the flagpole at zero-dark-thirty. The taped reveille would play, the cannon would fire, and if it was especially foggy, all the car alarms in the vicinity would go off. She remembered how Tim used to keep a PT uniform in the back of his Jeep in case he didn't get home the night before.

As she drove around the post, looking for places that had been misplaced, she was unsettled by all the longhaired young people she saw. When it was closed, most of Fort Ord had been given to the state of California, which turned it into California State University, Monterey Bay. Pauline could not bear seeing longhaired, disheveled, aimless twenty-somethings strolling the grounds where squared-away, fit, purposeful soldiers had marched years earlier. She had to consciously restrain herself from yelling out the rental car window, "get a haircut!" and "get a job!" The thought made her smile, but it did not make her happy.

There were many places that she couldn't go, and some places she oughtn't to have. Beach Range Road and most of the east garrison were off limits due to left-over military munitions and ordnance contamination. Pauline drove around the unit areas and found the old 2nd Brigade headquarters. It was good that was where it was supposed to be because she might not have found it otherwise. All the unit identifiers and emblems had been pulled off the building, and all that were left were their ghosts on the paint where it had been protected from the elements. The outline of the bayonet above the main entrance made her smile again, but not like she had smiled at the longhaired twenty-somethings. She looked for something, a unit crest or insignia–anything that she could pry off the building so that she could take some of the Brigade back to DC with her. She found nothing; previous memory seekers had stripped the building of all its identity. She hesitated to drive up to the Officers' Club, but she couldn't help herself. She felt like she was testing herself to see how far she could go without crying out loud. She parked in the parking lot of the Club and sat in the car. She remembered the night, after a grueling trial, that she had met the other trial counsel for a beer and then sat in her car before driving home. She had been brutally tired. She had put her arms on the steering wheel and lay her head down for just a moment. At least, it had meant to be for only a moment; she didn't know how long she had been hugging the steering wheel when an MP tapped on the window and asked her for her keys and whether she had been drinking. In that moment she saw her short career flash in front of her eyes. Fortunately, the MP recognized her as the JAG Girl who had called him as a witness in an assault case and exercised what he called "professional courtesy" and let her off with a stern warning. "If you'd flashed him some skin, Vickers, he would have given you a ride home," Tim told her the next day.

What had been the Officers' Club when alive was now a dark, hollow place that had that "after-the-party" spent look. She walked around to the Bay side of the building and stood in the tall weeds in front of the picture windows that vacantly looked out over the water. She expected to hear echoes of music and laughter. The crack of a cue on a billiard ball. Tim telling outrageous stories. The field artillerymen who, on the night of the Artillery Ball, had challenged her to find out if their underwear was red like their socks. *If this were a movie,* she thought, *she would see all their faces in brilliant Technicolor and hear all their voices in stereo.*

But it wasn't a movie, and she saw only the abandoned building, the sky, and the Bay. All she heard was the wind, the seagulls, and sea lions in the distance, demanding food from the tourists on the wharf. As she stood looking out over the Bay, she knew that she should have felt as empty as the building behind her. Fort Ord was gone. Her friends and adversaries, scattered to the seven seas. Her youth and the exhilaration that had been her life–the trial work, the deployments, Club Nightingale, the Three Date Rule– were faded cellophane. Life as she had known it there was gone, and she felt like she had not been truly living since.

But instead of drowning in emptiness, she felt the sky and the scruff and the Bay filling her up. She was very still. Everything was so sharp and so clear. She didn't just see the gray sky, she felt the gray on her skin and seeping into her soul. She felt the wind in her hair and heard it in her ears and she felt it blow right through her being. She smelled the sea and felt the blue water of the Bay flowing in her–not suffocating and drowning her, but swelling up in her until she felt like it would flow out of her and give life to the tangle of dry weeds around her feet. She didn't think she could move and she was afraid to try–she was afraid that if she did, the moment would be gone. In that moment she was part of creation again. She didn't just remember how she had felt that night sitting on a poncho liner eighteen years ago, she felt it again. And just as she had felt her soul emptying that night in Tim's arms at Club Nightingale, she felt it filling up again. Life returned to her. Creation reclaimed her and Pauline submitted.

CHAPTER 12

Life in DC was different when Pauline returned from the past. It was easier to find a parking space on the street by her Dupont Circle apartment, or she no longer noticed driving in endless circles around the block looking for one. The light flowing in her apartment windows was pure and peaceful and no longer carried with it the humidity of the Potomac or the noise of the traffic. There was always room on the metro during rush hour and she no longer felt herself being swept on board and crushed by the wave of people on the platform. Her work in the Pentagon was interesting, challenging, meaningful. Living was once again more than just existing. She had the glimmer of a feeling that her life had reached its fullness and that there was no room left in her for anything else. She was wrong about other things too.

Tim was divorced and in Iraq. Tim did divorce like no one Pauline knew. He and Mandy ran out of bedroom adventures and motivation to stay married less than two years after they wed. Nonetheless, when he was transferred from Leavenworth to Fort Bliss, Texas, Mandy followed but did not live with him. When he transferred from Bliss to Fort Stewart, Georgia, she moved to nearby Savannah. It was crazy to Pauline that Mandy and Tim dated each other (*translation: slept together*), but dated other people too (*ditto*).

When Tim deployed to Iraq for a year or longer, he gave up the lease on his apartment and left all his property, the little that he had not already given to her when they split, with Mandy.

"When did you actually get divorced?" Pauline asked Tim during a phone call while he was deployed.

"Right after we moved to Georgia," he replied.

"What finally brought it on?"

"Well," Tim said, "I had picked up a copy of *Curious George* for one of my nephews. I had left it on the table and when she was at the apartment one morning, she picked it up, paged through it, and said, 'this is really good.' I said something like 'yeah, the illustrations are fantastic,' and she said, 'yeah, but the plot is really interesting.' I realized it's one thing to shag a woman who reads children's books and finds them really interesting, but do I want to be married to one? I knew it was time to cut bait and move on."

Pauline and Tim had more routine contact while she was in DC and he was in Iraq than they'd had since they had both been assigned at Fort Leavenworth. Tim was a JAG in Iraq in the Green Zone and Pauline worked the same issues as Tim, only in the Pentagon. They communicated lawyer to lawyer almost daily and friend to friend nearly as often.

Iraq sobered Tim. His tone changed and he seemed to take things—life—more seriously. Much of his time was spent working detainee issues for the command. Coalition forces held anywhere between twenty- and twenty-five thousand detainees in Iraq. Every day, he dealt with issues of conditions of confinement, overcrowding, misconduct by prisoners and guards, interrogation, American citizens captured while fighting with al Qaeda in Iraq, the International Committee for the Red Cross. Fortunately for Tim, he arrived in Iraq nearly four years after Abu Ghraib. Nonetheless, the issues surrounding detainees were difficult, legally complicated, and of high visibility, and the taint of Abu Ghraib lingered. No matter what the question,

CRY OF THE HEART

the answer was never "right" to everyone. And the guy on the ground–Tim– was made only too aware of how "wrong" his advice was considered by whoever disagreed with it. Pauline, and all the uniforms in Pentagon, did what they could to protect the guys on the ground from the politics of Washington and the outside interest groups. But on such high visibility issues like detention, there was no adequate flak jacket to protect the men and women in Iraq, living and dealing with the issues, from all the Beltway shrapnel.

Pauline could tell in his emails that the goodness and light had faded a little for Tim. He was changing, joining the grown-up world. She knew this in part because, at least in his emails, there were no women in the Green Zone. Pauline expected Tim's emails to be full of information about hot female officers, Coalition officers with sexy accents, and aid workers with hearts of gold. But nothing. It was so unlike the Tim that she knew. She could hardly ask him about it in official communications, but she was a little worried. When she mentioned it to Richard, Richard speculated that either Tim's past escapades had finally caught up with him and something important fell off, or Tim had come to his senses and was saving what was left of himself for a woman of quality. Pauline worried even more when, as Tim's time for his mid-tour leave approached, he began talking about spending it in DC, rather than at home in Georgia.

Between Leavenworth and Washington, both Pauline and Tim had made lieutenant colonel–Tim to Tim's surprise, Pauline to Richard's. Richard was also a lieutenant colonel. And he, too, was in DC. He and Nadia lived in the Gucci suburb of McLean. "Brahmin money is good for something," he had admitted.

Jill did not live in McLean. She was buried at Arlington National Cemetery, her name and dates on the back of a small white cross which one day would bear Richard's on the front. Pauline had flinched inwardly but said nothing when Richard told her that Jill was to be buried there. It seemed to

Pauline that burying his wife in a military cemetery was taking "the army is my life" too far. She inwardly accused Richard of seeking the perfect military end to a disappointingly imperfect military marriage.

The night before Jill's funeral, Pauline had gone to Richard's house to help him get his in-laws and Nadia fed and settled in. After they had picked at the dinner Pauline had prepared, the Monroes and Nadia retired to their rooms to try to get some sleep. Richard helped Pauline tidy the kitchen before she left for her apartment.

"I know the in-laws think I failed her and them," Richard said, as he dried the serving dishes Pauline handed to him after she washed and rinsed them. "It's so unfair. I did everything for her. Passed up plum assignments to homestead close to the best medical facilities for her. Worked ten hours a day at the office, to come home and play Mr. Mom until Nadia went to bed and then work a few more hours at home, all in order to maintain a "normal" family life for her and Nadia. Busted my ass hosting family holidays and office parties at our house so she could feel like a good Army wife. Dodged a tour in Afghanistan so I could stay home and take care of her. But nothing I did was enough. Nothing I did helped her accept her condition and make peace with the world. And now her parents are upstairs thinking I'm a failure as a husband and a father. How are Nadia and I going to get through this?"

"I don't know, Richard, but you will," Pauline answered. "It will be all right."

At Jill's funeral the following morning, the chaplain had talked for too long and said too many words:

"Jill had been taken from a husband who had loved her and a daughter who needed her." *No kidding*, Pauline thought.

"Her death was a tragedy." *Newsflash.*

"Only in rare cases is MS terminal." *Does rarity make it more or less tragic? Do you think that matters to Richard and Nadia?*

"She would have wanted her family and friends to go on living." *Really? You don't think she wanted everyone else to die too? Thanks, Sherlock.*

Maybe some found comfort in his words; Pauline felt herself being smothered, and she felt like she should throw Richard and Nadia a lifeline to save them from being suffocated by his platitudes. At the graveside, Richard and Nadia barely spoke. How can one give words to a broken heart?

After the graveside service, Pauline wandered the cemetery, reading the markers. The perfect peacefulness of the hill on the river overwhelmed her. The hillsides that are Arlington National Cemetery are covered with markers, uniform and standing in formation, like the men and women they mark had stood during their lives. Here and there, more elaborate crosses and tombs, effigies and obelisks, break ranks with the little white markers. Some of the more elaborate markers were erected before the rules about the size and shape of markers were adopted. Some mark the famous, as if fame matters at this place, or particularly historic deaths like those of the Desert One and Challenger catastrophes. The elaborate fountain and deliberate site of Bobby Kennedy's grave almost mock his reported humble desire to be buried on a hillside near a waterfall, marked with a simple white cross. But mostly the hillsides are flowered with ranks and files of little white crosses or other religious symbols, facing east to hear Gabriel's horn. On the front of the markers, the man or woman's name, rank, dates, and wars served. Sometimes the words "Medal of Honor" or "Silver Star." On the back of some markers, the names and dates of spouses or children. Their simplicity spoke eloquently and completely. Nothing more was required.

Maybe Richard was right to bury Jill here on this hillside, marked with a simple white cross, Pauline inwardly conceded.

CHAPTER 13

Pauline was minding her own business in her cubicle in the Chairman's legal office when her phone rang.

"Pauline, this is Colonel Nightingale. Do you have a couple of minutes?" a voice from the past asked over the line.

Pauline knew it must be serious. Mark was a couple of years senior to her and had been promoted to colonel a couple of years before. However, when it was just the two of them, or just the old Ord gang together, they were still on a first name basis. Mark was still in DC, working in the JAG officers' records branch.

"Of course, sir," Pauline responded. "Shall I walk down to your office?"

"That would be great. See you in a few."

Getting from one point in the Pentagon to another never took just "a few." Five floors, five rings, and ten corridors. A person could get lost for days. The ubiquitous "they" probably thought it made perfect sense; room 3B740, where Pauline would find Mark, was on the third floor, B ring, seventh corridor. Easy. Except the corridors are so wide that there are unnumbered corridors between the numbered corridors, so 3B740 is not actually on the seventh corridor, but on an unmarked corridor between corridors seven and eight. And it's not actually on the B ring, but through a door on corridor seven and a half, between the A and B rings. Easy.

Fortunately, Pauline had been to 3B740 before, so she didn't keep Mark waiting. If it was going to be a conversation with Colonel Nightingale, and not just Mark, she figured it must be serious.

"Pauline, thanks for coming up," Colonel Nightingale said. "There's no easy way to put this, so I'm just going to say it: the colonels promotion list is coming out tomorrow and you are not on it. I'm so sorry."

Then he was Mark again. He came around from behind his desk, sat in the chair next to Pauline and put his hand on her shoulder.

"I really am so sorry," he said. "And pissed. You should be on that list—I know some of the knuckleheads who are, and it really pisses me off!"

Pauline recovered her senses that had escaped her initially and told him that it was not his fault, that she appreciated that he was the one who told her, that she was fine. At least that's what she hoped she told him. She was pretty much in shock. Not that she had necessarily expected to be promoted, but she hadn't expected to be passed over either.

"Listen, Pauline, I was so surprised not to see your name on the list that I pulled all your efficiency reports to see if I could find out what the hell," Mark told her.

"And?" Pauline asked.

"An awful lot of them describe you as "candid"—and I mean a lot of them," Mark told her.

"Really?" Pauline said. "You think I'm being passed over for being candid?"

"Well," Mark said, "I'm not sure how to say this, but I think it might also be your third file."

"My third file?" Pauline asked. "What does that mean?"

"I'm just saying, Pauline, you used to date a lot. And you're pretty tight with Tim. And you've never married. That kind of stuff can make people talk."

"Oh, I see, because I used to—emphasis on 'used to'—date a lot and I hang out with a guy who happens to be a first class slut, I must be a slut too. And the Corps can't be promoting sluts. Of course, being a slut doesn't seem to have held Tim back much. Or is it just a combination of 'slut' and 'uterus' that the Corps can't tolerate?"

"Pauline," Mark said, "I know you're upset, but hysterics won't help. You're in a great job now and if you don't screw up, you'll be a great candidate for an above-the-zone selection."

"Colonel Nightingale," Pauline answered, "with all due respect, Sir, you can screw that."

Pauline had been telling herself that her job in the Pentagon kept her too busy to even think about Arden, the Alphas, or getting away for the Weekend. But after her encounter with Mark, Pauline decided that it was time for her to take some control back over her life. So she fed her Courage and called Angela.

"Martelli," she said when Angela answered the phone. "Why the hell haven't I heard from you guys?"

"Vickers," Angela answered, "where the hell are you? We thought you were moving to Florida after Kansas and we never heard from you."

"I'm in Washington, DC."

"What the hell are you doing in Washington?"

It had not occurred to Pauline that the Alphas would not know about her accident, her brief assignment at SOCOM, or her move to the Pentagon.

Pauline filled Angela in on all that had happened since they had been at the beach together and then asked.

"Have you talked to Arden lately?"

"Not recently," Angela answered. "Why do you ask?"

Pauline paused, and then gave another bite to Courage and told Angela everything. Oak. The pregnancy and ending it. Her conversation with Arden and how badly it went. Even about her mother at the hospital after her accident.

"Oh shit, Pauline," Angela finally said. "I don't know what I can do about your crazy mother, but we can figure this thing out with Arden. Let me make some calls."

"Thanks, Ange," Pauline said. "I love you."

"Yeah, well, none of this would have happened if you two hadn't been sleeping with men."

A couple of days later, Jeanne called Pauline.

"Listen," Jeanne said, "Ange and I have talked to Arden. Things aren't as bad as you think. I think she feels as bad as you do about how things went down. She downplayed it at the beach, but she and the man really wanted that baby. You walked right into a minefield. You figure something out for Columbus Day Weekend and we'll see you then."

When Pauline told one of her JAG friends in DC that she was looking for somewhere to go for a girls weekend, her friend congratulated her for getting away and told her about a "to die for" bed and breakfast in Luray, Virginia, in the Shenandoah Valley. Pauline called the innkeepers at the Molasses Hill B&B and booked four rooms in the main house (the only rooms in the main house). She left the office at noon on the second Friday in October and picked up the Alphas at the Dulles Northwest baggage claim. Angela and Jeanne hugged Pauline hard. Pauline and Arden embraced lightly, but Pauline felt a chill where their hearts touched. They squeezed their bags into Sven's miniscule trunk and Angela and Arden squeezed into the miniscule backseat. At least the weather was fine, so they could drive with the top down.

Once they left 66W, the drive into the Valley was spectacular. By the time they reached Route 340, the sun was setting and the sky over the trees on the mountains filled the women with their colors and shadows. They drove past the entrance to the world-famous Luray caverns and drove through downtown Luray.

"One stoplight–a sure sign of a perfect Alpha Weekend town," Jeanne noted.

A marquee outside the local performing art center announced the Shenandoah Valley Acoustics Blues Bash, Friday and Saturday nights.

"We are so there," said Angela.

When they arrived at the B&B, Henry and Karl, the innkeepers, had the porch light on for them and a tray with four wine glasses and a plate of cookies waiting on the console by the front door. The women dumped their bags in their rooms, dug out a few bottles of wine and four corkscrews, and settled in the rockers on the wrap-around porch to watch night fall over the hills and farms. They listened to the crickets and the night birds and watched for fireflies. Winter was creeping in and it was cool and refreshing on the porch after the oppressive atmosphere of Washington. The quiet was perfect. Pauline wondered if it could all be real. The other Alphas seemed to feel it too.

"This is the best," Angela said. "Henry and Karl are too wonderful. We roll in late, take every room in the house, and they have cookies waiting for us! If they weren't gay, I'd fall in love with them both."

"But if you're gay too, Ange, aren't you allowed to fall in love with them?" said Jeanne.

"How can they be so nice?" Angela said, ignoring Jeanne.

"I think it's because they are happy," Arden said.

Pauline realized those were the first words Arden had spoken since they left the airport.

The next morning, Pauline woke up early, as was her habit. She pulled on some sweats and crept down the stairs to the front door. Molasses Hill was settled in the hills of the Shenandoah and a fog had settled there too. It was not a fine, misty sort of fog; it was a heavy, suspended rain sort of fog. Pauline could see the water droplets hanging on the air and feel the damp on her face. The grounds around the B&B were fenced and Pauline decided to walk around the perimeter. As she reached the far corner of the fence, she sensed that she was not alone and looked over her shoulder to find a small, dirt-colored cat following in her path. She knelt down and held out her hand, but the cat stopped and stared. Pauline took a slow step toward her, and the cat turned as if to run away. Pauline turned back around and resumed her perimeter march. It was very quiet. On the other side of the fence, a herd of dairy cows were having their breakfast. One of the cows looked up at her and came over to the fence to see what sort of creature Pauline was. The cow walked along its side of the fence with her for a short distance before spotting a particularly tasty-looking clump of grass and letting Pauline walk on alone. Not really alone; the stalker cat was back and kept her distance behind Pauline, but not too far back. The grass was wet and Pauline could feel the wet seeping in through her sneakers. She passed behind the Lilac, Honeysuckle, and Rose Cottages—small cottages that were part of the B&B. She came to another out building that appeared to be used for storage and sat down on its concrete stoop. She had only been there a couple of minutes when another cat, this one with only three legs, sauntered over to her and made herself comfortable on Pauline's lap. The absence of one of her front legs did not appear to have any adverse impact on the cat; she was huge. It was like holding a soft, furry radiator, except this lap warmer purred loudly. She snuggled with Pauline and allowed Pauline to stoke her fur until the cat was sufficiently warmed, then she stretched, purred her thanks for the cuddle, and went on her way. When the warmth of the cat left her, Pauline realized that she was cold and started to walk back to the house. As she approached, Henry waved to her from the back door and signaled that he had the coffee on. Pauline changed her trajectory and made for the back door. Just as she was opening the door, the dirt-colored cat scooted in before her, something small and brown and furry hanging from its mouth.

"For heavens' sake, Alan Kittymain, get that out of the house," Henry said as he scruffed the cat until it dropped its lifeless prey onto a pile of newspaper. Henry wadded up the paper and took the bundle outside to the bin. Alan Kittymain, nonplussed, followed Henry out to continue his hunt.

"He's a great mouser, but he tends to leave his prizes in the most inconvenient places," Henry told Pauline. "Last week, the couple staying in the Lilac Cottage were greeted by a dead mouse on the threshold when they opened the door for their breakfast tray. I saw Tripod schmoozing you out there. Did you come across Eartha Kitten too?"

Breakfast was served in the main house. Pauline sat in the kitchen with Henry and Karl, luxuriating in the aroma of sizzling bacon, baking cinnamon rolls, and brewing coffee, until the other women filtered downstairs. Since breakfast was delivered to the cottages, and the Alphas were the only guests in the main house, they had the dining room to themselves. The wonderfully decorated room was just what one would expect in a wonderfully rural Virginia farmhouse-turned-inn. Dark wood. Heavy dining table. Tchotchkes on every horizontal surface, except the dining table, which supported only a centerpiece of fresh, autumn flowers. A wonderfully elaborate chandelier with glass fruit and flowers and leaves reflected colored light all over the room.

"What are you girls going to do today," asked Henry, as he put a carafe of hot coffee on the table.

"I think we have to do the Caverns. We can't come to Luray without seeing the Luray Caverns, the 'largest and most popular caverns in Eastern America,'" Jeanne said, reading from a brochure.

"There are a number of antique shops on Main Street, and the Acoustics Blues Bash should be pretty good," said Henry, as he brought in plates of bacon, rolls, fruit, and slices of Spanish frittata. "We have a gem of a blues guy here in Luray who will be playing tonight."

"I think we should do it all—who knows when we'll be back in this neck of the woods?" Angela said.

"You girls have fun," Karl said as he entered the dining room with more coffee, the deliveries complete. "I'll call the box office and have them hold tickets for you for the show tonight, and I'll call and make dinner reservations for you at the Artisan Grill, the best restaurant in town. It also happens to be across the street from the performing arts center."

The Alphas had a wonderful day in Luray. After paying their tourist dues at the Luray Caverns, which, they had to admit, were pretty spectacular, they took a leisurely pedestrian cruise of the antique shops along Main Street, notwithstanding Angela's declaration that antiques were really just "overpriced, old, used stuff." Arden found a plastic bracelet and earrings, which, she insisted in a whisper behind her hand, were in fact Bakelite and worth several times more than what the shopkeeper was asking for them. Jeanne found an old advertising poster for Standard Oil that she intended to frame and hang in her office. "Exxon Mobil is Standard Oil's direct descendent in corporate existence," she explained to the others.

"Pauline, why don't we find a coffee shop and have a coffee while they continue shopping," Arden asked as they left one shop, heading for another.

Angela caught Pauline's eye and smiled.

"That sounds great," Pauline answered. "I think I saw one around the last corner."

Arden put her arm though Pauline's and they turned, backtracked to the previous corner, and found the Java Jolt. They ordered coffees and found a table near a window.

"Pauline," Arden said.

"Arden," Pauline said.

They laughed.

"Let me go first," Arden said.

Pauline nodded.

"I am so sorry," Arden said. "I said horrible things to you and I am so sorry."

"No, I'm sorry," Pauline said. "I was so wrapped up in myself that I was arrogant enough to think I knew how you were feeling."

"And I thought you were trying to minimize my grief, or worse make a competition of our sadnesses."

"Oh, Arden. I hope I wasn't. I really am sorry you lost your baby."

"And I am so sorry that you went through all that alone."

They both had tears in their eyes and when they made eye contact, they both laughed.

"Now, we better get our acts together before Angela sees us," Aden said. "We're supposed to be crusty old bitches by now, not whining little puppies."

They finished their coffees about the same time Angela and Jeanne found them and declared themselves shopped out. They took their booty back to the B&B and honored the cocktail hour with Kamikazes. "Why Kamikazes, Jeanne?" they had asked. "Why not Kamikazes?" was the answer. Then they walked back to town for a delicious dinner at the Artisans Grill and then to the performing arts center.

Just as Karl had promised, four tickets were waiting at the box office for them. The "concert hall" at the performing arts center was a big room with a stage and a number of round tables with metal folding chairs pushed up to them. The Alphas claimed a table, and Angela and Arden went to the bar. Pauline and Jeanne held the table and surveyed the gathering crowd. It was clear from the conversations that they overheard that everyone knew everyone else, with an occasional "we've never met but I'm a friend of . . ." thrown in.

"Well, nothing beats a home crowd for an appreciative audience," Pauline said.

"You just might like it too, Lieutenant Colonel Vickers, ma'am," said a voice from over Pauline's shoulder.

"Oh for heavens' sakes," Pauline said. "You're not the "gem of a blues guy" someone told us about, are you, Cappy?"

Pauline stood and shared a bear hug with man with clear blue eyes and an army-holdover haircut under a well-worn cowboy hat.

"How did a wave-making JAG Girl like you get past security?" he said, and smiled.

"I just can't believe it. Cappy Morgan," Pauline said. "Jeanne, this is Sergeant First Class John 'Cappy' Morgan. We served together a million years ago when I was at the Litigation Division. How long have you been retired, Cappy?"

"Five years, give or take."

"And how are you here?" Pauline asked.

"Well, you know I used to play at all the JAG Corps picnics and parties," Cappy said. "And then JAGs started hiring me to play at promotion parties and family reunions and birthday bashes. And then I started thinking to myself, 'I'm pretty good at this. This could pay the bills.' So, when I was assigned at the JAG headquarters in DC, I started hanging out up here on the weekends, playing gigs on leave, and finally, I cut a CD. I figured that when I retired, my retirement check would keep me solvent until I started making a decent living in the music biz. And it did and I am."

He handed Pauline one of the Acoustics Blues Bash programs piled in the center of the table. "I'm a headliner," he said.

And he was. And he was really, really good.

The Alphas returned to Molasses Hill after the concert. Karl had left a tray with glasses and cookies in the parlor. The Alphas had moved them onto the front porch and were basking in the twilight stillness.

"That was really fun," Jeanne said. "Your friend is really good, Paul."

"Do you know why he is so good?" Arden asked.

"Why, Arden?" Jeanne asked.

"He's good because he found his passion at just the time in his life that he was meant to," Arden responded. "He writes and sings about things that he knows and has experienced. A twenty-something American Idol can write about things he has read about or heard about in another song. He can regurgitate someone else's song, like 'Let It Be,' but you'd be hard-pressed to find a twenty-something who has lived a song like that. What makes Cappy's music so good is that he's lived–he's been around and can write and sing about what he has seen and felt. He has a passion for what he's doing and yet isn't so driven that he can't see the humor in life. The innkeepers here are so good because, I think, they found a passion–making people welcome and taking care of them–and have lived enough to know how to do it right."

"I need a passion," Pauline said.

"You have a passion, Pauline" Arden told her. "Everyone has a passion. You just need to identify yours, and you will when the time is right for you to do so."

"Why do you need to find a passion, Paul?" Angela asked.

"Because next October I will have twenty years in the army and can retire," Pauline told them. "And I'm going to. Ever since I first joined the JAG Corps, I told myself that I would only stay in as long as I was having fun. For almost twenty years, I've kept an updated resume in my desk drawer, ready for the day that I wasn't having fun anymore. And I'm not having fun anymore. I thought at first that it was because of the nature of my current job. Dealing with political hacks who are more interested in their personal advancement and sucking up than in doing what is right. Commanders who are more worried about covering their asses than taking care of their troops and who will only ever tell the political leadership what it wants to hear. But it's more than just this job. I'm becoming disillusioned and I'm afraid I'm becoming bitter, so I think it's time for me to throw in the towel. Besides, I wasn't picked up for colonel, and I really do believe in 'up or out.' I'll hang on until my retirement vests, so, in the next year, I need to find my passion so I can figure out what I am going to do for the next twenty years."

"Come on, Pauline," Jeanne said. "The army can't really be your whole life. Surely there is something out there you're interested in, even if not passionately."

"Well," Pauline said, "I have been tinkering with an idea . . ."

"Do tell," Jeanne said, "we're all ears."

Pauline paused.

"Lately, I've been thinking a lot about when I lived in Monterey a million years ago. My favorite restaurant there was in an old converted Victorian mansion. Upstairs, in the turret, there was this huge monstrosity of a chandelier–dripping with colored glass fruit, flowers, and leaves. Probably weighed a ton. At night, when it was lit up, you could see it from every direction, and it was the most outrageously beautiful thing you've ever seen. I used to go there a lot, and I can still feel how happy it made me to see it from the sidewalk and being, I don't know, young and excited about life."

She paused again.

"That was such a remarkable time in my life, my time there," she finally continued. "And this might sound crazy, but I've been thinking, what if I could make something like that? That would be so cool. What if I could learn how to do that? I would like to do something creative and it makes me happy to think about creating something from my time in Monterey."

"Can you be satisfied to put that on hold for another year while you gut it out in the army?" Arden asked.

"Any better suggestions?" Pauline answered with a question.

"Yes, find you a man and get some really good sex to get you through it," Angela said, lightening the mood.

"You're a pig, Martelli," Pauline said, laughing.

"Hey," Angela responded, "to quote Suzanne Sugarbaker, if we can put a man on the moon, we can put a man on you."

Arden and Pauline turned in early, at least, earlier than the others. They shared a Jack and Jill bathroom as they washed their faces and brushed their teeth.

"I would say, be wary of passion, Pauline," Arden said, picking up the thread of the earlier conversation.

"Why do you say that," Pauline asked.

"Passion can be like a maelstrom," Arden answered. "It can exhilarate and thrill you and then it sucks you down and drowns you. You remember when my marriage was going through a rough patch and that handsome litigator joined our firm? I thought I had run out of passion for my husband and that we were old, tired, and too accustomed to each other. It was exciting that this new guy–this new, handsome, exciting guy–tested the waters with me and made me feel beautiful and exciting and desirable. All those things that my husband hadn't made me feel in a long time. I realized–almost too late–that

Handsome Litigator was good at lighting those kinds of fires but that my husband was great at caring for the embers that kept, and continue to keep, me warm and wrapped in love. Maybe whenever I look my husband I don't feel my blood boil, but I still feel the heat. I'm just saying, don't look too hard for the 'on fire' kind passion; I think you'll be happier in the long run with a slow burn than with a mad conflagration."

CHAPTER 14

A few weeks after Pauline returned from Luray, Tim took his mid-tour leave in DC. It was not a true "mid-tour" leave; Tim had arrived in Baghdad the previous August and did not take leave until April. When Pauline asked about the timing, Tim told her that a very wise man advised him to take his mid-tour as late as possible because after a break, like the grinding wheels of justice, the clock moves exceedingly slowly to the end of the tour. Pauline offered to put him up on her sofa, but he declined. He'd met a guy from State Department in Baghdad who had an empty apartment in Foggy Bottom and Tim came back to the States with the key to it in his pocket. He flew into DC, found the apartment, and slept for sixteen hours. Twenty hours after hitting the ground, he called Pauline and convinced her to go out with him that night.

"Georgetown is calling our names, Vickers," he'd told her. "Even you should be able to find a date there."

For once, he was right.

Doctor Colin Majors was originally from South Africa. He had been educated in the United Kingdom, enlisted as a private soldier in the British Army, served two years, got more education, and finally went to medical school in London. He did his first mission for Doctors Without Borders in

1999, providing medical care for refugees in the Northern Caucasus. Since then, he had worked on missions in Haiti, providing care for victims of violence at a trauma center in Haiti, and in a project in Bangladesh. When Pauline met him that Friday in a Georgetown bar, he had recently returned from the Palestinian Territories where he had been collecting data on the Palestinian health services crisis there. He was in Washington as part of a delegation of representatives of nongovernmental aid organizations meeting with State Department officials to discuss aid to the Palestinians. Like Tim and Pauline, he had ventured into Georgetown to be with people in general and maybe meet someone to be with in particular. Tim, Pauline, and Colin were crowded at the same bar, trying to catch the eye of the same bartender when Colin caught Pauline's eye instead and held it. Cautiously hopeful introductions were made and the necessary and minimal bar pleasantries were exchanged. The rest of Colin's story Pauline learned later over dinner.

"Tim," Pauline told Tim, "Colin and I are going to find some dinner. Can you manage your way back to Foggy Bottom without me?"

"Vickers, you minx," Tim said. "Has the world turned itself completely inside out since I've been gone? You're leaving me in a bar? By the way, thanks for asking, but I wouldn't dream of joining you. I'll call you in the morning to make sure you got home okay." This last, Tim's words directed toward Pauline, but his eyes fixed on Colin.

Colin and Pauline left Tim leaning over a woman too young for him, telling who knows what fantastic stories about his exploits in Iraq. Pauline was happy to see it. She had been worried about Tim. She was just now beginning to appreciate his capacity for compartmentalizing. Where darkness would prey on her mind and weigh down her entire being, Tim could look into the dark, either discard or lock it away, and move back into the light. Pauline had imprisoned herself in shadows for years; she was just beginning to see the sun again.

Over their table at the restaurant, Colin asked Pauline the classic conversation starter: "Tell me about yourself." Pauline told him she was an Army JAG. She was worried that the revelation might be off-putting, but Colin was nonplussed. Lady soldiers did not intimidate him. Instead, Colin asked about her career and her work. Pauline flooded him with her travels and anecdotes from her nearly nineteen years in the army. She told him about the Alphas and the Three Date Rule. She told him about how she loved the beach and that the ocean spoke to her soul. She shared with him her frustrations in her current job and how hard it sometimes was for a lawyer to serve in the government in the current times. Pauline was very aware that she worked for the Department of Defense and that Colin worked for an aid organization that was held in contempt by many in the department as festering nest of naïve, uber-liberal do-gooders. So although she told him where she worked and the general nature of issues that she worked on, she began to feel uncomfortable about talking about her job, and Colin sensed it. She thought that maybe he thought she was ashamed of her work, but hoped he realized that there was simply so much about her work that she couldn't talk about. Nearly everything that crossed her desk was classified. Some of the Pentagon knuckleheads would probably accuse her of a security violation for even having dinner with a Doctor Without Borders doctor.

In the back of her mind Pauline thought that Colin was probably calculating her age—four years of college, three years of law school, nineteen years on the job—but she told herself to put it out of her mind; that she didn't care. No one had ever asked her about herself and seemed so genuinely interested in hearing her talk. So what if Colin seemed younger than she was? She was surprised that she noticed. That was something a woman notices when she is attracted to a man. That she felt like a woman jarred her. That she was attracted to Colin startled her like a splash of cold water in her face and the realization caused her to momentarily lose her words. She didn't

110

know what to say any more and she had already said too much. He was too good a listener. She seemed to have told him everything about herself that mattered before they even had dessert. She had to stop.

"How do you happen to be working for Doctors Without Borders?" she asked Colin, knowing that she had been talking too much.

"I was working in a very posh consulting office off Harley Street," Colin answered, "and one morning I realized that I could be doing something better. I felt like I had gone to all this school and learned how to save life or make life better for people, and all I was doing was making a boatload of money to spend on things—a bigger flat with a better view, a weekend cottage in Cornwall, holidays in Spain, a new Land Rover. It seemed so, well, I'm sorry, but it seemed so American. Have you noticed that everything over here is newer and faster and shinier? Anyway, some Doctors Without Borders chaps were recruiting at the medical school at King's College and I signed up. I was still working in the consulting office when I did three six-month gigs for Doctors. Then, about a year and a half ago, I moved to New York, got privileges at a couple of hospitals there, and I now work for Doctors in the US, recruiting, fundraising, and showing the Doctors Without Borders face as required."

It was Colin's turn to talk too much. He told her about life in South Africa. Colin told her about growing up in the white elitist society and being aware that it was doomed but living the life that it was because it was his life. Formal introductions and tea time and cricket played in whites. It all sounded very romantic to Pauline.

"Have you been to Tallahassee?" Colin asked Pauline, out of the blue, and bringing her back to earth.

"Yes," she answered. "Why do you ask?"

"The weather there is exactly like where I lived as a boy," Colin told her. "The whole time I lived in the UK, I felt like I would never feel the sun again.

I liked living in London, but I feel like I was beginning to rust on that damp little island. I like New York much better."

"Tell me about New York," Pauline asked him.

"I love it," he said. "New York is so alive. There were people out and around all the time. The energy is tangible in the air. London is the Thames, gray and stagnant, and New York is the Hudson and the East Rivers, moving and living—do you see what I mean?"

Pauline nodded, and let him continue.

He told her about living near Battery Park and playing cricket in the Municipal Parks city cricket league. He talked about the heat in the summer and the rain in the fall and the winter and how snow, when they were lucky enough to have it, made Central Park clean and fresh and friendly. Yes, it all sounded very romantic and Pauline was ready for romance.

Pauline loved listening to him talk. His accent was softer than a Brit's and it soothed her ear. Colin's face lit up when he talked about his life in New York and his work with Doctors. His talk about war and conflict from the non-military end of the spectrum made Pauline think. And here was a doctor who was passionate about something other than money!

When they left the restaurant, he held her chair and guided her to the door with a light hand on her back. Of course, he opened the door for her and purposefully walked on the curb side of the sidewalk. Maybe what she loved was not so much his manners, but how he treated her like a woman. At work, in camouflage fatigues, she was only ever treated as a Lieutenant Colonel. Men didn't stand when she entered the room. No man ever offered her a seat on the Metro. None of the other officers would think twice about swearing in front of her. Not that she expected men to stand up or offer her a seat or stop swearing. But it was so nice in Georgetown on that Friday night to be treated like a woman by a man with a pleasant accent who loved life and who felt he had a purpose in his life. *Maybe he isn't so much younger than me after all,* she thought.

They left the restaurant and walked aimlessly around Georgetown. When they reached the corner of M Street and 35th, they stopped to consider their options. Colin was staying near Georgetown University and could easily walk to his hotel from where they were. Pauline thought she should say good night, find the nearest Metro stop, and go home. Colin did not press her to stay or go back to his hotel with him. He expressed concern, though, that there was no Metro stop in Georgetown.

"Let me call you a cab," Colin said.

"No," Pauline told him, "that's not necessary. It's an easy walk across the Key Bridge and I can catch the Metro at the Rosslyn stop on the other side of the river."

Pauline assured Colin, that she would be fine on her own, hoping that he would not believe her. Fortunately, he didn't.

It was a nice night for a not-very-long walk across the bridge and through the tangled mess of streets in Rosslyn with a South African doctor. Colin bought a Metro card and waited on the platform with her. Because of the late hour, they had to wait for almost half an hour for a train to come. They didn't mind. When it did come, the doors opened and Pauline stepped in and Colin followed her.

"I decided that at this time of night," Colin said, "I really ought to see you to your door."

They shared the Metro car with a sleeping homeless woman and some teenagers in basketball jerseys and shorts that drooped almost to their ankles. When they got to Pauline's stop Colin walked Pauline to her building, a couple of blocks from the station. Most of the restaurants and all of the bars were still open. There were all kinds of people everywhere.

Standing outside Pauline's building, they found that they had joined hands somewhere between the station and the stoop. Then came that awkward moment when a man and a woman think, but they aren't sure, that they should kiss.

"I'm going to kiss you now," Pauline ended the awkwardness and pulled Colin toward her by the collar of his button down shirt and they kissed. Perfect.

"Would you like to come up for a cup of coffee?" Pauline asked when their lips parted, "It's a long way back to Georgetown. You could spend the night on my sofa if you like."

"No, I better not," Colin answered. "After all, if you talk in your sleep and reveal military secrets, you'll have to kill me in the morning. Besides, what would your boyfriend from the bar say if I were here when he calls in the morning?"

Tim stopped by Pauline's cubicle in the Pentagon first thing Monday morning. In the old days, Monday mornings at the office meant coffee and Tim's tales of outrageous exploits over the weekend. When he came by this morning, he had no stories to tell, having gone straight from the bar to the borrowed apartment and slept for twenty hours straight. He looked at Pauline with expectant eyes, waiting for her to fill the void.

"So," Tim said, taking up what little space there was in Pauline's cubicle, "tell me all about your weekend with Gunga Din."

"Kipling's Gunga Din was Indian, not South African," Pauline told him. "And there's nothing to tell. We left you in the bar, had dinner, he saw me home, we kissed goodnight, he took the train back to New York Saturday morning, and I spent the weekend in the office dealing with Somali pirates one of our Navy vessels came across."

"He didn't spend the night?" Tim asked. "What–did you leave all your feminine wiles in your other purse? At least you got some tongue, didn't you?"

"Go away, Tim."

"Yeah, yeah, yeah," Tim said. "I've got people to see anyway." On his way out he turned to add, "Hey, get Gerry on the phone and we'll get together this week. How's he doing anyway?"

"All right," Pauline said. "He works like a fiend. I haven't seen him much since Jill's funeral last August. He's working in the Military Commissions for the guys at Gitmo, poor thing. Nadia graduates from high school this summer and apparently plans to start college on time in the fall. Don't know where she's planning on going."

"Sucks to be him," Tim said. "See you around, Paul."

Pauline didn't think it was any of Tim's business that Colin had called from Union Station early Saturday morning and explained, with regret in his voice, why he had to leave that day.

"There's a fundraiser in the city tonight I must attend," he had told her. "I'll probably be back in DC in the next month or so. May I call you? Maybe you will have business in the city sometime? And I can show you around?"

After his call, Pauline had found it difficult to concentrate on Somali pirates when she was called into work that Saturday. Did the rules of engagement permit the Navy to fire a shot across the pirate ship bow? Could the Navy board the pirate ship and seize contraband? It took all of Pauline's mental self-discipline to focus on crimes on the high seas and not a particular South African.

It was weird to think that she may have a "love interest" in her story. She wished that she had met Colin before the Alpha Weekend; it would be good to talk to them about it. Jeanne and Angela would be positively giddy that she might have a man in her life. But even as she was thinking these thoughts she knew that she was reading too far ahead in the book. She forced her mind back to Chapter 1. *Girl meets Boy. Girl likes Boy. Boy goes back to New York. Will Boy call Girl? Will Boy come back to DC? Will Girl please get on with her business and stop thinking about Boy!*

Tim stopped back by Pauline's cubicle after making the rounds to the various legal offices in the Pentagon. While he was there, they got a hold of Richard and arranged to meet for dinner the following night. Tim was looking forward to going for a run, having a hot shower, and getting more sleep. "I don't know if it's jetlag or if it's that I am entirely spent after eight months in Baghdad, but all I can think about is going to bed—wanna come, Paul?" Tim had asked, only half joking. As he was about to leave, Pauline's phone rang. It was security at the Pentagon's Metro entrance. Someone was trying to deliver something to her. She left the office with Tim, and together they navigated the corridors of the Pentagon to the escalators down to the Metro entrance. Before she reached the glass-enclosed security desk, Pauline could see her delivery: a field of lilies seemed to fill the security booth. Sunshine in a vase. The note read, *These are native to my home in SA. To commemorate date #1. Colin.*

"Damn!" Tim said. "Think of what he would have sent if you had put out!"

"Go away!" Pauline told Tim for the second time that day.

The next night, Pauline, Tim, and Richard met for dinner after work.

"So, tell me all about what's cooking in the Pentagon," Tim said. "I want to know all the gouge."

"Tim," Richard said, "if you are going to talk shop, Pauline and I can find another table."

"Okay," Tim replied, "let's talk about Paul's new boyfriend."

"Funny," Pauline said, "that's what he called you."

It was like old times but it wasn't. Pauline, Richard, and Tim had walked across South Parking and through the tunnel to Pauline's favorite Thai restaurant in Pentagon Row. They sat outside. It was a little cool, but after breathing the recycled atmosphere in the Pentagon all day, they craved the fresh air. Despite pinging Tim for talking shop, that was what they were all interested in, and Richard asked Tim about Iraq.

"Just between us, it sucks," Tim said. "Most of Iraq was third-world before we invaded and it is not any better now, and in Baghdad it is worse. It pisses me off every time a soldier or Marine dies in Iraq. If you asked me, they made up reasons to invade Iraq this time, and in the meantime, Afghanistan, where we should have really taken it to al Qaeda before it migrated to Iraq, is going to hell. But, on the up side, Halliburton and the rest of the defense industrial complex are making billions and billions of dollars and everyone's next job is secure when they leave government."

"Do you really think they made up a reason to invade Iraq?" Richard asked Tim. Tim was usually so happy-go-lucky that Richard was surprised and a little impressed that Tim was thinking deeper thoughts.

"Listen," Tim answered, "why did we invade Grenada in 1983? Because weeks earlier, terrorists bombed the Marine Barracks in Beirut and killed 241 U.S. personnel. Reagan needed to flex some muscle and taking down Grenada, a country with no military, was a hellava lot easier than trying to take down the terrorists in the Middle East. We got hit on 9/11. Even Bush and Cheney and Rumsfeld could figure out that taking down al Qaeda was going to be really hard, so what did they do? Invade Iraq. Should be easy—we almost finished the job ten years or so ago and Saddam is such a really bad guy that they thought the Iraqi people would meet us waving the Stars and Stripes and throwing flowers. What a bunch of knuckleheads!"

"Tim, buddy, that's pretty bleak," Pauline said. "You were always the happy one among us. You're making me very, very sad."

"Then come home with me tonight, Paul," Tim said, returning to his old self. "That will put a smile on your face."

The mood lightened as Tim became his old self, complaining about the damper General Order #1, and the ban on fraternization, was having on his quality of life in Baghdad.

"Unlike you, Paul," he said, "I'm not used to living like a monk. I don't know how you have survived all these years."

This was the quality of Tim's character that would prevent Richard and Tim from ever becoming "hanging out" buddies. Were it not for Pauline, they would probably never have exchanged more than the most perfunctory exchanges of pleasantries. But thrown together by their separate friendships with Pauline, they found aspects of each other's characters that they could appreciate. Richard begrudgingly admired Tim's optimism, his easy ability to make friends, and his comfortable nature. Tim secretly envied Richard's skills as an attorney and his certainty of his place in the world. Tim wondered why Pauline was not attracted to Richard; he seemed to be just her type–serious, responsible, dutiful–just like her. He wondered if Richard didn't have some passion buried inside him, as he knew Pauline did. Maybe Richard was more like Pauline than anyone knew.

"Are you going to Savannah before you head back down range?" Pauline asked Tim.

"No, I don't think so," he answered. "Mandy is apparently getting serious about some guy down there and I know that if she thinks she still has a shot at me, she'll lose him like a bad habit. I don't want to screw up her chances for happily ever after, so I think I'll keep my distance. What about you, Paul, are you looking at happily ever after?"

"Well, let me see," Pauline said, "I've had one date in the past ten years. The date in question lives in New York and I live in Washington. He works for a bleeding heart liberal humanitarian aid organization and I work for the

Department of Defense. He's from South Africa and I'm mostly from northern Minnesota. We've shared exactly one dinner and a couple of phone calls. I think 'happily ever after' is a little premature."

What Pauline didn't tell Tim and Richard that evening was that Colin had invited her up to New York and she was going in two weeks. She didn't know why she didn't tell them. She would have thought that following Tim's divorce, he would once again be her best friend and she would tell him all the things that a woman shares with such a friend. After all, Tim was part of a defining moment in her life. But something inside her was keeping her relationship, or more accurately, her potential for a relationship, with Colin to herself. She still loved Tim, but the nature of that loved had changed with his marriage and had changed again with his divorce. Strangely, she didn't feel inhibited from talking about her relationship with Colin to Richard. In fact, the week after the three met for dinner, Pauline and Richard went to lunch and she told Richard all about it.

Having lunch with Richard was much different from having lunch with Tim, or with Tim and Richard. It was calmer. They walked back over to Pentagon Row, this time going to Pauline's favorite pseudo-pub restaurant there. It was a pleasant afternoon and there were tables outside, but they sat inside anyway—*it is pub-ier to sit in the bar than on the patio,* she thought. She told Richard about meeting Colin when he was in town for meetings at the State Department. She told him how about his exotic background and how nice it was to be treated like a lady for a change. She told Richard about Colin's work and his commitment to it. She told him how it made her wonder if she couldn't better be serving God and country as something other than an officer in the JAG Corps. She wondered if Richard, Mr. Army, ever had doubts about his vocation in the Corps.

"Have I had doubts?" Richard answered. "In the early years, before Jill's illness, I really believed that being in the army was the most important thing that I could do. I know Tim laughs at me, but I believed in the army and all its regulations, rituals, and traditions. When Jill became ill, my focus changed from serving the nation to keeping her well. I know you may not understand this, but I truly felt that I was sacrificing not only my career, but my ability to serve to my full potential by seeking and taking assignments that accommodated her treatment and care, rather than assignments that would have put me where I could best serve the Corps and the army. Then 9/11 happened. I felt like we–me, you, the JAG Corps, the army–failed on 9/11 and three thousand innocent civilians lost their lives because of our failure. Our one mission was and is to protect the United States and we utterly failed to do that on 9/11. After 9/11, all I wanted to do was get in the fight and go after the bastards who did 9/11 and help restore our honor. But, by late 2001, Jill's condition was worsening and it was no longer about keeping her well, it was about not letting her die. I failed in that too. Now, I'm losing Nadia and I'm working on the Commissions, which are fraught with problems like secret evidence and coerced statements and about which I have real concerns, but I don't know a better route given the position the terrorists have put us in. So, I guess to answer your question, 'do I have any doubts?' I'd have to say hell yeah, only about everything that I have believed in and been motivated by for the past twenty years."

CHAPTER 15

Pauline wasn't thinking about Richard or Tim the following Friday afternoon when she got on the Amtrak at Union Station en route to Penn Station in New York. She liked to travel by train, especially in the designated quiet cars. Less hassle than at the airport and it was slightly less frantic at Union Station than at Reagan National on a Friday afternoon. Although she would only be gone from Friday afternoon to Sunday night, she took leave so she could tell the guys in her office not to call her.

"Listen to me," she had told them sternly, "when I'm on leave, think of me as dead. Don't even think about calling me."

Just before she left the office after lunchtime, she sent Tim, who was back in Iraq, an email telling him that she was getting away for the weekend, but not where or with whom. She left before he would have a chance to read it and send back some wise-guy response. Although she took her government cell phone with her, she turned it off with a clear conscious, and promised herself that she would not check her email until the train ride back on Sunday night.

She had labored a long time over packing the night before. Colin had told her that his was a studio apartment and she wasn't sure what he expected the sleeping arrangements to be or how much privacy she would have. It was so different from packing to go to Club Nightingale with Tim all those years ago. She thought about things that she never would have thought about then, such as what sort of pajamas or nightgown should she bring? Or should she sleep in shorts and a T-shirt like she did at home? Should she take her make-up off at night and reapply it in the morning, or leave it on overnight and risk leaving mascara tracks on the pillowcase? Should she leave her contacts in all weekend or take her soda-bottle glasses to wear like she did at home when she was in for the night? Pack her wear-anywhere little black dress just in case? Should she pick up a host gift for him at the station? If so, what?

It was late when the train pulled into Penn Station. There Colin was, waiting behind the security gate with a bunch of flowers. As she walked up the linoleum incline toward him, she had an "oh crap–do we kiss?" moment, but it dissolved when she reached him and he took her by the arm and kissed her on both cheeks in the European, and apparently South African, way. All perceived awkwardness evaporated into vapor. He took her bag and gave her the flowers, commenting that although he had gotten them for her, he was glad that he had the foresight to pick stems that weren't too feminine since they would be residing on the table in his flat for the next few days. Pauline was charmed by his use of the word "flat" and let herself be guided to the taxi queue outside.

"I thought we'd take a taxi rather than the subway since it's late and I thought you might be tired," Colin told her. "I thought we'd stay in tonight and have something for dinner at home. Tomorrow we have to go over to Canarsie Park in Brooklyn–my cricket team is playing. You know what cricket is, right? I play with the Indians and Pakistanis and Bangladeshi expats. We have a match tomorrow against a West Indies team. Very fun. The wives bring the greatest Indian and Pakistani food and you'll love them."

Colin was talking fast, and Pauline realized that he was as nervous as she was.

"Can you believe it—Indians and Pakistanis playing cricket on the same team?" Colin couldn't seem to stop himself. "I've told them that I'm bringing a lady friend, but don't let them overwhelm you—their culture abhors a single man over thirty like nature abhors a Hoover, so they may be a little pushy if you know what I mean. But they are lovely people. I can explain the game to you tonight so you won't feel like a fish out of water tomorrow. Also, tomorrow night I thought we'd go to a Doctors Without Borders reception, marking the opening of a photograph exhibition of Doctors Without Borders in Afghanistan, all taken before we had to shut down operations there in 2004. It's at the New York Public Library."

By the time they flagged down a taxi, Colin had run out of steam.

Colin didn't need to explain cricket to Pauline. She had lived in England as a girl in high school when her father was stationed north of London. She remembered the English cricket team getting thoroughly routed by the Australians in test match in late '79-early '80 and had jumped on the English national cricket bandwagon. She had been an enthusiast ever since. She didn't tell Colin that that night. She was too enchanted by his non-stop commentary in the taxi to interrupt, and when she saw his apartment, she was stunned into silence. It was breathtaking.

Breathtaking. When Colin opened the door of his apartment she could see across the room and across the island of Manhattan. The front door opened into a hallway that widened almost into a foyer. Two doors on the right. She later learned that they opened into a walk-in closet and the bathroom. The foyer widened into a room with a sofa on one side and an armoire facing it. The wall at the end of the hallway/foyer/room was not a wall at all but panoramic picture of Manhattan behind seventeen-foot tall sheets of glass. As Pauline walked to the windows, she did not notice another doorway into a small kitchen on the right or the twelve-foot tall pocket doors just beyond it. All she saw as she passed the sofa were the lights of the city of Manhattan. She looked back at Colin who had followed her into the room, but she couldn't say anything. There was no word that was big enough to describe the scene in front of her. But then, she knew he knew that.

"You'll sleep in here if that's okay," he said as he pushed back the sliding pocket door to reveal a queen-sized bed nestled into the short leg of the L-shaped room. She saw that the window continued into the bedroom and around the corner of the room. The East River and the lights of Brooklyn served as the headboard. "The sofa pulls out and I'll be very comfortable there. So, do you like it?"

That Saturday was a lovely day. When Pauline awoke that morning, the sun was flooding through the windows, basking her in its warmth and clear, undistorted light. Colin must have come in during the night because there was a flannel robe lying across the foot of the bed. She got up and put it on. It smelled like Colin although, until that moment, she hadn't noticed that he had a particular scent to him. Colin was sitting at the table, drinking coffee from what looked like a bowl. They had coffee together and then Colin announced that he was going for a run and would be gone about an hour. After he left, Pauline drank another bowl of coffee, did the dishes, showered, and got dressed. When he returned home, he changed into his cricket whites and they headed off to Brooklyn.

Pauline discovered that cricket in Brooklyn was remarkably like cricket in England. All the players wore white. Family and friends were in folding chairs alongside the pitch, socializing with each other and the batting team players. Unlike baseball where the batting team sits on the bench, segregated from the spectators as well as the other team, in cricket, the batting team players sit with their family and friends in chairs along the pitch while they wait for their turn at bat. Alcohol was in good supply, even though it was only ten o'clock when they started play. Children were playing in the grass behind the folding chairs. They broke for lunch and later for tea in the afternoon. Periodically, conversation along the pitch would break for polite applause at some action, with occasional cheers for a batsman who hit the ball to the boundary or bowler who bowled a batsman out. The wives were particularly friendly and interested in her. Colin had warned her about that.

"Surely a good-looking boy like you and a doctor, too, should be able to find a wife," he said, imitating a clipped colonial accent.

"Be careful what you say, Pauline," he had warned, "or they will be planning our wedding by tea time."

Colin had been right. During the course of the day, Pauline was pumped for information, in the very friendliest way:

"How long have you known our Colin?"

"A lawyer? Oh, a doctor and a lawyer is always a fine match."

"Washington, DC? But there are plenty of jobs for lawyers in New York."

"You're how old? And you've never been married? Well, a woman doesn't want to wait too long to start a family."

"One can tell a lot about a man by how he plays cricket. Colin is such a fine cricket player, don't you think?"

When they got back to Colin's apartment late that afternoon, Pauline told Colin about the grilling and they laughed together as they got ready to go the Doctors Without Borders reception and exhibit.

That was an entirely different event for Pauline. Champagne in plastic flutes and Costco-quality canapés. The photographs in the exhibit had been taken by non-professional photographers and were stunning for it. They lacked the slickness of most National Geographic pictures and their realness gave them power. As a Doctors Without Borders event, it was largely attended by people with similar political views, ranging from liberal to ultraliberal. When the posh set met Pauline and learned that she was an army officer and a lawyer, they reacted in one of two ways: some looked at her with either pity or contempt and quickly sought out more desirable company, that is, people who thought like them, and others very politely patronized her.

"It must be so hard to work for a war-mongering government."

"I'm sure you personally have nothing to do with torture and disappearing people, but it must be horrible to work with people who do that."

"I have such respect and sympathy for our men and women in uniform; it must be so hard for you."

Colin stayed by Pauline's side through it all and although he did not defend the United States, he did not pile on the criticism. Pauline knew that their scorn would not have been so thinly veiled had he not been there, holding her arm. After the reception was finally over, Pauline, Colin, and some of Colin's co-workers from Doctors found a pub that had a Quiz Night going on.

"We will kick butt tonight, Pauline," Colin told her, as they settled into a booth. "One of us is a sports fanatic, so we have sports covered. His girlfriend works for a music company so we have music. One's husband teaches Renaissance history at NYU, and another has forgotten more about plants and gardening than I'll ever know. With a lawyer cum soldier, we have the board covered –we can't lose."

Colin was wrong. Pop culture did them in.

It was as much like an authentic English Quiz Night as a bunch of Americans could make it. Unfortunately, they played Quiz Night like Americans–to win–not like the British who play for fun. And unlike in most English village pubs, here the winners' tab was not covered by the other teams and the losers were not awarded a wooden spoon.

Just as she had been at the cricket match and the reception, Pauline was very conscious of being "with" Colin at the pub. None of them would remember her as Pauline, but only as Colin's date/friend/girlfriend. It was odd and oddly pleasing for Pauline to think that she was not just Pauline for a day, but somebody else's something.

When they had returned to Colin's apartment, they were too tired and too sated with the day to worry about sleeping together. So they did. Sleep together. A kiss goodnight, a comfortable spooning—*Thank God I brought real pajamas*, Pauline thought—and the glow of the nightlights of Brooklyn above the pillows. A perfect recipe for a good night's sleep. Pauline slept like a stone. Sunday morning, they shared bowls of coffee and Colin took Pauline to Penn Station.

"How are you going to tell your boyfriend that we slept together?" Colin asked as they waited for her train.

Pauline knew that fully explaining her twenty-year relationship with Tim would take more time than waiting for the train would allow. She wasn't even sure that she could explain her relationship with Tim to Colin, or anyone for that matter, or if she even fully understood it herself. She hoped Colin was teasing her. Surely he didn't think that she and Tim had ever been with each other as she had been with him all weekend? Surely he didn't think that she and Tim slept together any differently than she and Colin had slept together the night before? She wanted to tell him, "Listen, Tim is my friend. I love him, but not like a woman loves a man. Even though I'm a woman and he's a man. It's more like how I would love a cocker spaniel." But it was more complicated than that so she said nothing. When the train pulled in, Colin kissed her goodbye on both cheeks—very European-style and very safe—and she boarded a quiet car and turned on her government cell.

One day later that week, Pauline received a package in the mail from New York. A wooden spoon and a note reading: *A step toward authenticity. To commemorate date #2. With great affection, Colin.*

CHAPTER 16

When Pauline returned from the weekend in New York with Colin, the annual JAG Corps Ball was right around the corner. The JAG Corps Ball was their social event of the year. Every member of the Corps stationed in or near Washington, DC, was unofficially expected to attend. The junior officers debated about whether they should invest in Dress Mess uniforms for the occasion, or whether their Blues will do. They looked forward to dressing up, playing grown-up officer, and schmoozing with the senior leadership of the Corps. The senior officers cut out the carbs and ran an extra mile in the morning so that they could squeeze into their Dress Mess uniforms and concerned themselves with the seating chart. For some, their proximity to The Judge Advocate General will make or break the evening. The mid-grade officers fall into two classes—those who look for reasons to be out of town over the Ball weekend, and those who resign themselves to an evening of mandatory fun. The resigned spend the weeks leading up to the Ball trying to convince at least seven of their friends to go so that they can fill a table and have a fighting chance of having good time.

Pauline and Richard fell firmly into the mid-grade officer sensibilities.

"I heard some crazy talk that you're not going to the Ball," Pauline told Richard, over lunch in the Pentagon food court one afternoon. "Say it ain't so."

"It is so," he responded. "I'm not going this year. Everyone I'd want to see there I see every day anyway, and there will be too many people there I don't feel like seeing, let alone have to make nice to."

"But, Richard, you can't not go," Pauline said. "You are in a very high-vis job, everyone knows you never take leave and will be in the area, and a lot of people will view your absence as a snub to the Corps."

"Thanks for your concern, Pauline," he replied, "but I really don't want to go. You're going to think this is stupid, but on top of everything else, I don't think I can face a social event stag. I know you're used to going to these things alone, but I've always had Jill in the past. With her, I always had someone to talk to and was never left standing around alone looking pathetic. I have lost the gift of small talk since she's died, and I think I'd rather poke myself in the eye with a pointy stick than go to the ball alone."

"All right, look," Pauline said. "I was debating whether to ask Colin to come down to go, but instead of inflicting the ball on him, you and I will go. I'll dig up six fun people to go with us and we can get a table so you won't have to talk to anyone you don't want to. We'll get you liquored up over dinner so that when the dancing starts, you'll be loosened up and can go with the flow. I bet with the number of young captains there, and you being such a young, charming, handsome widower, your dance card will be full and you'll have no time to stand around looking pathetic."

"I'm not young or charming or handsome, but if you promise not to leave me nursing a drink in a corner, I'll go," Richard said.

The night of the ball, Pauline threw her Mess uniform and her black pumps with the highest heels and the deepest toe cleavage in the back of her car and drove out to the Gerard house in McLean. Pauline was surprised not to find Nadia at home.

"She's spending the weekend with a friend from the volleyball team," Richard told her. "I don't see much of her these days. She's still so angry about her mother's death. I've talked to the school psychologist and she seems to think that Nadia's grieving process just needs to run its course."

Pauline changed in a spare bedroom, and when she and Richard met in the foyer to leave, she had to admit, they looked good in their fanciest uniforms with the gold braid, cummerbunds, and medals.

"I have to say, Richard, we clean up pretty good," she said, looking Richard up and down.

The ball was held at the Officers' Club at Fort Belvoir and Pauline insisted on taking her car.

"It's not that I think you'll pull a Kennedy and leave me there," she said. "I just think that you may need more lubrication to get through the evening than I will so it's better if we take my car."

Richard agreed, but only if he could drive.

"After all, Pauline," he told her, "what would it do to my manhood to be driven to an official function by a girl? Besides, didn't you once say that you liked being treated like a lady?"

As Richard pulled Pauline's car under the porte-cochere in front of the Fort Belvoir Officers' Club, she saw Gloria Nightingale alight from the vehicle in front of them.

"Perfect timing," Pauline said to Richard, as she got out of the car. "Gloria and I will grab a table while you and Mark park the cars."

"OMG, you look fabulous," Gloria said as she and Pauline met and gave each other a heart-felt hug. "I'm always jealous of you military women in your fancy uniforms."

"Well, you look pretty specular yourself," Pauline said, "I'm always jealous of you civilian women who get to wear such beautiful ball gowns. We never get to play 'Princess.'"

They both laughed and entered the Club, arm in arm. They checked in with the Captain at the reception table and picked up place cards with their names and coded menu selections and made their way into the club's large ballroom. The room was arranged with about thirty-five tables of eight crowded around a large dance floor. Pauline and Gloria found an unclaimed table next to a set of French doors leading to the large veranda that spanned the length of an exterior wall.

"Let's put Richard between us," Pauline said as she put her and Richard's place cards on the table. "I think he's feeling a little melancholy about being at his first big JAG event stag. This way, we can keep an eye on him and his wine glass full if necessary. Who else is joining us?"

"A couple of majors who work for Mark and General and Mrs. Andrews," Gloria answered.

"General Andrews?" Pauline repeated. "Are you kidding me? We all worked for him at Ord when I was a young captain, and it was not fun."

"Pauline," Mark said from behind her.

Pauline turned and saw Mark and Richard had joined them at the table.

"Pauline," Mark continued, "before you say anything, let me explain."

Pauline didn't say anything and Mark continued.

"I asked General Andrews to sit at our table, first, because even though he just retired a couple of months ago, none of the leadership thought to ask him; and second, even if you don't care about your career, it will be good for Majors Thorpe and Clay to get some exposure. Ord was a long time ago and although he might not have been the most enlightened guy about women in the army back then, he really did come around. Really."

Pauline hoped Mark could see the skepticism in her eyes.

"Besides," Mark continued, "he tells the best stories about the JAG Corps from back in the day. It'll be fun, trust me."

"Yeah, he's a good guy, Pauline," Richard added. "Come on – let's get a drink before the 'festivities' begin."

The four made their way to the bar and pushed their way through the pack of junior officers clustered there. Having secured libations, Pauline, Richard, and the Nightingales mingled with crowd. It was good to see some of the old faces that Pauline had served with over the years and it was good to catch up with old colleagues. She smiled to hear the young captains and majors making post-ball plans, the lieutenant colonels gossiping about their absent peers, and the colonels sizing each other up as competition for Brigadier General Andrews' yet-to-be-filled general officer billet. Eventually, the lights flickered, the signal to be seated, and Pauline and Gloria made their way to the ladies' lounge to freshen up before dinner.

As they were leaving the bar, Pauline felt her elbow jogged and turned to find a lieutenant colonel she had served with for a short time at Special Operations Command clutching her arm with one hand and a glass of wine with the other.

"So," the lieutenant colonel said, "I see you and Colonel Gerard are together. Does that mean he's off the market?"

"Gee, Allison, it's nice to see you, too," Pauline said. "It's been a few years, hasn't it? No, Colonel Gerard and I are not 'together.' We're just friends from way back. And I really can't say if he's in the market – maybe you should ask him."

"Kind of defensive there, Vickers," Allison responded. "Are you sure you aren't together? Or maybe you just want to be?"

Pauline pulled her arm free and as she turned away she said, "well, it's been great catching up. Maybe you should get some food in you before you top that up again," nodding to Allison's glass.

Allison smirked, raised her glass to Pauline in a mock salute, and then turned and made her way, a little unsteadily, toward the tables.

132

"Wow, retract claws, Pauline," Gloria said. "What was that all about?"

"Oh, that's Allison Ellis," Pauline said. "We served together at SOCOM and were among the few women assigned there at the time. It would have been great if we could have been friends, but she's one of those women who thinks we are always in competition with one another, you know what I mean? And I was recovering from the accident and probably wasn't the most fun to be around. Anyway, she just has a knack for getting under my skin."

"She's right about one thing – you and Richard do make a nice couple."

"Now come on," Gloria said quickly before Pauline could respond, "forget about her. Let's just enjoy the evening, deal?"

"Deal."

By the time Pauline and Gloria found their way to their table, Richard, Mark, the Andrews, and the majors were already seated. As they approached all the men stood. Pauline nodded at General Andrews and his wife, who was seated almost directly across from her, and Mark introduced her to Major John Thorpe, sitting on Pauline's left, and Major Penelope Clay, next to him. As soon as she and Gloria were seated, a waiter appeared with two bottles of wine, one red and one white. *Good service – one of the perks of having a G O at your table*, Pauline thought. Salads had been prepositioned at their places and as soon as the general put down his fork, more waiters appeared and their salad plates were whisked away and their main courses promptly served. Gloria kept Richard entertained with stories of their growing brood of children and Pauline struggled to make small talk with Major Thorpe. Pauline kept catching glimpses of General Andrews out of the corner of her eye and she could see that, like many of his peers, he was displaying symptoms of "Retired General Officer Center of Attention Deficit Disorder" and was holding court. Giving up on Thorpe, Pauline listened.

Fortunately, Mark was right – Andrews did tell some really good stories:

"When I first got to Ord, back in the day, before you lot got there, the Staff Judge Advocate completely lost it. He was going down to clubs in Santa Cruz and picking up male prostitutes. JAG headquarters found out about it when the commanding general called and told them he had fired his 'fairy' lawyer and what was JAG going to do about it? The JAG leadership was so pissed off that someone telephoned the SJA and told him that he was being reassigned. When the SJA asked where he was being reassigned to, he was told to get in his car and start driving east. He was to stop at every military installation that he came within 50 miles of, call JAG headquarters, and ask if he was at his new assignment yet. As I recall, he got as far as Fort Rucker, Alabama, before someone told him "you're there.""

"I never heard that story before," Mark said.

"Like I said," Andrews responded, "it happened before you all got there. Did you ever hear about those captains in Saudi Arabia?"

They all shook their heads, and Andrews began:

"During Gulf War I, I was deployed in Saudi Arabia. I had a married couple of captains with me. She was adjudicating claims and he was doing contracting. After she had been to one of the local villages to assess some damage caused by some of our tanks, the local sheik came to see me. He had been so taken by my captain that he wanted to buy her and make her his third wife. I told him that I would discuss it with her husband. I called the couple in and relayed the Sheik's proposition. 'What's he offering?' the husband asked. 'Camels, sacks of gold, barrels of oil – you know, the usual,' I replied. 'Get me driving privileges on Saturdays and we've got a deal,' the wife responded. As you know, women are not allowed to drive in Saudi and that turned out to be a deal breaker. Best young officers who ever worked for me – other than you guys, of course."

They were good stories, and Pauline found herself liking Andrews, in spite of herself. He spoke about the women JAGs who had served with him with respect and, in some cases, genuine affection. Maybe he had evolved from the guy who had called her 'little lady' and asked her if she weren't really in the Army 'just to land a husband' when she had worked for him. And she had to admit, he and his wife had been married for many, many years, and as she watched them over the course of the meal, they seemed to genuinely like each other.

Pauline wasn't sure of what to make of Mark's majors; Thorpe was drinking way too much and starting to pay sloppy attention to Clay, who was drinking only water. Pauline tried to distract Thorpe by asking him about his job and his previous assignments, but Thorpe was persistent in his tipsy attentions to Clay. Pauline was relieved when The Judge Advocate General of the Army, a three-star general, rose from his seat to make his remarks and lead the traditional toasts.

After his remarks, which Pauline forgot as soon as she heard them, the JAG began the toasts.

"To the United States of America."

Everyone stood and repeated, "to the United States," and everyone sat down.

"To the President of the United States."

Everyone again stood and repeated, "to the President," and everyone sat down.

"To the ladies."

The men stood and repeated, "to the ladies," and the men sat down.

"To our fallen comrades in arms."

Everyone stood and repeated, "to our fallen comrades," and everyone sat down. Everyone except Major Thorpe.

"John, what are you doing?" Major Clay asked in a loud whisper.

"Maybe I want to make a toast of my own," Thorpe loudly replied.

"Sit down, John," Clay said. "You're drunk."

"So what if I am drunk?" he said. "A guy would have to be drunk to get through all of this mandatory fun bullshit."

"Alright," Pauline said, standing up. "I'm feeling a bit woozy and need some air. Major Thorpe, please take my arm."

Thorpe looked at Pauline with surprise and before he could say anything, Pauline took his arm and firmly guided him to the French doors behind their table. With her other hand she opened the door and propelled Thorpe onto the veranda. She followed and closed the door behind her.

"Come on," she said, again taking his arm, "we don't need to put on a show for those knuckleheads."

With her arm tightly through his, Pauline led Thorpe down the length of the veranda and around the corner of the building, out of sight of the ballroom. In the dark it took her a few moments to get her bearings, but when her pupils were sufficiently dilated, she could see the club was situated near the 18th hole of the Fort Belvoir Golf Course, and she could see a couple of benches near the green. She led Thorpe down to one of the benches and told him, "take a seat, Major." Thorpe was either sufficiently drunk, or sufficiently surprised, or both, that he obeyed Pauline's order without protest and sat. After a moment, Pauline sat down next to him. They were quiet for a long time.

"What do they know about fallen comrades?" Thorpe finally spoke.

"I don't know," Pauline replied.

After a long pause, Thorpe said, "I'm prior service, you know."

"No, I didn't know that. But I thought you looked kind of old to be a major."

Pauline could see Thorpe trying not to smile.

"I was enlisted in the Navy, got out, went to law school, and then downgraded to Army and applied for a commission," Thorpe said.

"Navy JAG wouldn't have you, huh?" Pauline asked.

"No, I didn't apply with the Navy. Too much baggage."

They sat in silence and Pauline tried to figure out where Thorpe was going with this. Finally, he spoke again.

"It was all that crap about 'here's to our fallen comrades,'" he said. "I was at Punta Paitilla."

Pauline had heard about Punta Paitilla when she was part of the invasion force in Panama in 1989. Some Navy SEALs on a mission at the Punta Paitilla Airfield in Panama City were in a firefight with the Panamanian Defense Forces and four SEALs were killed.

"Hearing all these lawyers talk about our 'fallen comrades' and none of them have probably ever heard shots fired in anger," Thorpe said. "And all they know about are Iraq and Afghanistan. We lost four good men at Punta Paitilla and I bet no one in that room even knows that. Four good men and no one even remembers their names or that they died in service of their country. I just couldn't take it."

"And it probably didn't help that you're three sheets to the wind," Pauline said. "But, you were pretty trashed before the toasts even started."

Thorpe didn't say anything.

"What's going on with you and Clay?" Pauline finally asked.

"I don't know what you mean."

"Yes, you do," Pauline said. "You were all over her in there. You work together. She's a pretty woman. You're not exactly repulsive. You're getting hammered and she's drinking water. I think you're either freaked out that you're going to be a dad or ticked off because she cheated on you."

Thorpe's back stiffened, and Pauline was afraid she had gone too far.

"I've heard about you, you know," Thorpe said.

"And what have you heard about me?"

"We were wondering what had happened to you two," Major Clay's voice broke the pane of silence that followed Pauline's question.

"I didn't hear you coming," Pauline said. "we're just getting some air, but I'm feeling better now, so I think I'll head back."

Pauline stood up but before she could get away, Thorpe said, "she thinks you're knocked up, Penny."

"Oh, god," Major Clay said, and slumped down on the bench next to Thorpe.

"She thinks I'm losing my shit because either I'm the dad or I'm pissed that I'm not."

"John," Major Clay said.

"It's alright," Pauline said. "It's none of my business. Clay, will you be okay if I leave you two alone."

"Oh, for crying out loud," Thorpe said. "what do you think I'm going to do?"

"It's all right," Major Clay said. "You don't have to go, ma'am. Can you just sit with us for a minute?"

"Sure."

Pauline sat back down on the bench next to Major Clay and after a moment, Clay took her hand and held it in her lap.

"Listen, you two," Pauline said, "Penny is not the first woman to get pregnant ahead of when she might otherwise have planned. It's not the end of the world."

"So, you agree," John said, "we should get married as soon as possible to minimize gossip and any possible adverse effect on her career."

"No, I didn't say that," Pauline responded. "I just meant that women get pregnant all the time and the world doesn't stop turning. Penny has some decisions to make and we will support her in any way we can."

"Thank you, ma'am," Penny said.

"What do you mean 'decisions to make?'" John asked. "you mean like to marry me or not to marry me?"

"I mean decisions that are *her* decisions," Pauline said.

"So she can end up like you?" Thorpe said.

"Pardon me?" Pauline said.

"John, be quiet," Penny said. "He didn't mean anything, ma'am."

"That's all right, Penny," Pauline said, and then turned to face Thorpe.

"You better listen up, Thorpe. I don't know if you love this woman or, more importantly, if she loves you. But you better get your shit together if you want to be worthy of her or any other woman."

"You were gone a long time," Richard said when Pauline entered the ballroom from the veranda. "Major Clay volunteered to check on you guys and now she's gone, too."

"No worries," Pauline said. "She found me and Thorpe and now they're sitting on a bench on the golf course looking at the stars."

"You all right?" Richard asked. "Thorpe all right? He was pretty hammered."

"I'm fine. He's fine. We both just needed some air. Did you save me a dance? Or has Allison Ellis filled up your dance card?"

"What?"

"Never mind."

"Where are Mark and Gloria?" Pauline asked.

"On the dance floor," Richard answered. "Hey—you missed it—Mark says Tim is likely to come to DC after Iraq."

"Does Tim want to come to DC?" Pauline asked.

"Yeah, when he was here on his mid-tour he mentioned that he was going to talk to the assignments officer," Richard said. "He asked me about what I thought might be good jobs to lobby for in the area. I'm surprised that he didn't talk to you about it."

Well he didn't, Pauline thought. It surprised her that Tim had discussed his next assignment with Richard and not her. Why would he seek Richard's judgment and not hers? Tim didn't even like Richard that much. Yet in his emails to Pauline, Tim had never raised his next assignment. When he was in the area during his mid-tour, he had not said anything to her about coming to DC after Iraq. As a matter of fact, once when they were walking through the halls of the Pentagon together, Tim had stopped and grabbed Pauline's arm.

"Listen," he had whispered.

"What?" she had asked.

"When it is really quiet like this you can hear the building suck," Tim had answered.

Pauline could not imagine that Tim was seriously seeking an assignment in DC.

As it turned out, Pauline had more to drink at the ball than Richard did, and he wound up driving back to his house. In addition to the Thorpe-Clay drama, one of the retired generals at the ball had commented to Pauline that it was good to see Richard getting out and what a handsome pair they made. "I'm not with Richard," she wanted to quietly shout at the time. "I know what it means to be with someone, and Richard and I are not with each other." The off-handed comment had caused Pauline to gulp down her glass of wine and reach for another. Now, as she leaned her head against the back of the seat, she closed her eyes and her mind raced.

Being with Richard at the ball only meant that they knew each other, had come in the same car, sat at the same table, danced a couple of dances, and spent most of the evening in the same circle of people. Surely being with Richard at the ball was not like being with Colin in New York. In New York, she was linked to Colin by all his friends and co-workers: Colin's lady friend.

Colin's date. That was much different from being with Richard. No one thought of her as Richard's lady friend or Richard's date or Richard's anything. Yet she knew Richard, and Tim too for that matter, longer and better than she knew Colin. Maybe it was the wine and the swimming motion of the car, but the more she thought about it, the more confused her relationships seemed to her. She pressed her head more firmly against the seat and tried to stop the flow of feelings from her heart that were overwhelming her. It was as if she had jettisoned her feelings when she left Fort Ord almost twenty years ago and now they were coming back in a flood. She was struggling to navigate in those waters.

"Pauline, are you awake?" Richard's question brought her back to reality. "We're home. I don't think you are in any condition to drive back to your apartment. You'd better spend the night here."

"I'm not drunk, Richard, I'm just tired." Pauline said, almost believing it. "But, maybe I will stay here tonight, if you don't mind."

"My casa is your casa," Richard told her. "You can sleep it off in the spare room."

Richard opened her car door for her and took Pauline's shoes when she handed them out to him. She silently followed him barefoot him into the house. Although it was the end of April, there was a chill in the air and it smelled like rain.

"Should I put some coffee on?" Richard asked.

"That would be great," Pauline answered.

Richard put the pot on and took Pauline upstairs. While he found her a towel and a toothbrush, she changed back into the sweats she had worn to his house earlier that evening. They reconnected in the kitchen where Richard was putting slices of bread in the toaster and the old-fashioned percolator was burping way.

"I'd give you a hard time about getting a twenty-first or even twentieth century coffee maker if I didn't use the broiler for a toaster," Pauline said as she sat down on a stool at the kitchen island.

"Well, Pauline, I guess that just shows that we both know to go with what we're comfortable with," Richard responded.

"Do you think that's true? That we should stick to what we are comfortable with? Not venture out, not stretch ourselves?" Pauline asked.

"Are you asking me about toasters or about 'Gunga Din'?" Richard responded, as if he had been reading her mind in the car.

"Not you too," Pauline said. "And unlike Tim, I bet you know that Kipling's 'Gunga Din' was not South African. But yes, he is a 'venture out' for me,'" Pauline said, trying to explain. "The first twenty years of my life I spent mostly with my dad's Air Force friends and families and when I went to law school, with good solid Minnesotans. Then I joined the army and the next twenty years of my life, I spent in the company of clean cut young hard bodies who talk about God and Country and mean it. And now, into my third twenty years, I meet Colin. Exotic, elegant. Passionate about righting the inevitable consequences of war. Interesting and interested."

"Did you listen tonight?" Pauline continued. "All anyone could talk about was the army –what it has done, what it is doing, who's in it. Some of those people are absolutely incapable of a non-army related conversation. It was great to spend a weekend in New York with a decidedly unmilitary man and not talk about, or have to listen to, anything army-related. There's a big non-military world out there and, yes, maybe it is time for me to venture out into it."

"So, are you going to put in your retirement papers and run off to the big city?" Richard said, challenging her.

"What if I am?" Pauline answered with a question.

"Then maybe I will too," Richard said, surprising both of them.

It was a surprise, but it shouldn't have been. After all, in a few months, both Pauline and Richard would complete twenty years of service and be eligible to retire. As for Pauline, when she was assigned at the Special Operations Command at MacDill Air Force Base in Tampa, before she knew she'd be there for less than a year, she had purchased a condo with bay views and had held onto it, renting it out to keep up with the mortgage. She could easily go back to Florida to live with the fifty million other retirees there. Or, she could sell the condo and move to any place that she wanted to live. Even New York, if she wanted to. She wouldn't practice law in the Real World; she was only licensed in Minnesota and didn't want to go back there. She didn't want to take another bar exam and have to plan another conditional suicide. Besides, she could not picture herself chasing an ambulance, reviewing a commercial lease agreement, or defending some guy on his third DUI.

But what was Richard thinking? Pauline could not imagine that he would retire at twenty. He was, and had always been, a thirty-year man, serving as long as they would let him. Could it really be that the army was no longer Richard's entire life, but only a part of his life? Still, it was very unsettling for Pauline to think that Richard was thinking about getting out.

Pauline spent a restless night in Richard's spare room. She had mentioned retiring to the Alphas, but thinking about retiring during an Alpha Weekend was different from thinking about it in the Real World. Talking about it out loud with Richard was unsettling—it made the possibility so much more real. Why not retire when the time comes? Before this assignment, Pauline had never felt any burning desire to leave the army. It had always been interesting, meaningful, sometimes exciting work. The pay was good. Most of the people that she worked with and for were honorable, intelligent people. Sure, many of them lived the army and some of them were political get-aheaders, but she had other friends and people to hang out with—the Alphas, neighbors, her book club, friends from church. Being in the army as a junior officer had been fun—being with commanders and soldiers, not working with other lawyers all the time, having a mission and accomplishing it, and moving on to the next mission. But as she had advanced in rank and responsibility, being in the army had grown less and less fun. She knew that many of the more senior officers enjoyed the politicking and gamesmanship of serving higher up the chain of command. But Pauline found the closer she got to the senior leadership of the military, the less fun it was. She knew the longer she stayed in the army, the further she would find herself from the fun of being in the army.

CHAPTER 17

Pauline and Colin had not seen each other since their weekend together in New York. It had only been a few weeks, but Pauline was starting to feel an ache to be with him again. She was no good at email conversation. She read his words too hard and too carefully crafted her responses. Email lacked spontaneity and honest, unfiltered reactions. Even emails with Tim, still in Baghdad, had the same filtered quality, especially when they were discussing non-work related matters. Pauline found herself limiting the flow of information about her day-to-day life with Tim. She had told him that she had seen Colin in New York, but because her visit had happened to coincide with Fleet Week, it was easy to let Tim think that she had been to the city on business and that she and Colin had just gotten together for dinner or drinks. When Tim pinged her for more details--"tell me you finally got some, Paul"–she simply didn't respond. That was one of the beauties of email. She told Tim that she and Richard had driven to the Ball together–Tim had referred to it as "the prom," and asked her if Richard had given her a corsage– but she did not tell him that she had spent the night at Richard's house. In email, it was easy to be evasive or to simply ignore questions that she did not want to answer.

Likewise, Pauline hated to talk on the phone and Colin must either have felt the same or sensed Pauline's shortness the few times that he did call.

Spoken words were just sound without eyes and hands to fill out their complete meaning. Where email exchanges were filtered conversations, phone conversations were incomplete conversations.

Pauline wanted to see Colin. So when he called a few weeks after the ball, and told her that he had tickets to the semi-finals of the Cricket World Cup in the West Indies, her happiness at the thought of seeing him again momentarily trumped her incredulousness at being asked to go to the Caribbean.

"We can meet in Miami and fly down to Saint Lucia together," Colin told her, like it was nothing out of the ordinary. "South Africa is playing Australia in the semi-finals and getting tickets was a lot easier than I thought it would be. Have you ever been to the Caribbean? You've got a valid passport, right?"

Later, when Pauline thought back on the four days she spent in the islands with Colin it was a blur. Although they went down for the cricket, looking back, the cricket was just a footnote in the island getaway chapter of her story. They had met in Miami, as planned, and flew down together. It was too beautiful to be real. Colin had found them adjoining rooms with a shared balcony in an upscale hotel on the sea. After living in and being accustomed to Washington and New York air, the atmosphere was blindingly clear. Blue sky, bluer water, whiter sand, greener landscape. Pauline was overwhelmed by the purity and vibrancy of the colors. The island had been teeming with cricket fans from all over the world. Partying Australians were everywhere. The South African team was determined to shake their reputation as "chokers" and South African fans were talking big all over the West Indies.

Sadly, the South Africans did not win, and even though Colin and Pauline had come to the island for the cricket, the disappointing play did not dampen their spirits. The day after the South African loss, they spent browsing the shops, walking on the sand, drinking fruity drinks at tables outside cafes, and enjoying life in a tropical paradise. That night, after an exhausting day of absolute leisure, Pauline soaked in a steamy tub of bath oils and flower petals and then wrapped herself up in one of the luxurious snow white robes provided by the hotel.

She was trying to decide if nine o'clock was too early to go to bed when she heard "tap, tap, tap" on the door.

"Yes?" she asked.

"Room service, madam," said a voice.

Pauline opened the door to find a clean cut young man pushing a cart laden with champagne in a bucket and two crystal glasses.

"Are you sure you have the right room?" Pauline asked. "I didn't order this."

"Quite sure, madam," he answered.

Puzzled, Pauline thanked the young man and closed the door behind him as he left.

"Tap, tap, tap," she heard on the connecting door between her room and Colin's.

"Yes?" she asked.

"I'm parched," a voice said from behind the door. "You don't happen to have anything for my present relief, do you?"

Pauline opened the connecting door. Colin was smiling and Pauline felt her heart melting. He popped the cork and filled the glasses. They took their glasses to the balcony and sat looking out over the blackness that was the sea. Colin turned off the lights in Pauline's room, leaving only the moon and the stars to illuminate their silent togetherness.

"Where are you, Pauline?" Colin asked quietly.

"Oh, I don't know," Pauline answered. "I was just thinking. What am I doing here? This is not my life or how I live. I get up early, do PT, work hard, worry about friends in unfriendly places, and engage in periodic mandatory fun events with the army. I go to work, book club, and church and occasionally go out for drinks and/or dinner with those same people.

"I don't jet off to the Caribbean to watch cricket with glamorous, elegant men that I meet in bars," she continued. "I don't know what I am doing here, in a fancy hotel on Saint Lucia, in a bathrobe, drinking champagne with you. It scares me a little that right now I feel only peace and contentment. I don't trust my feelings."

"But you are here, in a fancy hotel in a bathrobe on a balcony drinking champagne with me," Colin responded. "This is how you are living right now. Why mistrust it? I sit here by the sea under the stars drinking champagne with an unfathomable woman in a bathrobe. It is the life that I am living right now, for these moments."

Colin paused and continued. "These days, most of my days are spent grinding money out of people who want to feel good about themselves with the least possible inconvenience, and cajoling arrogant young doctors to spend six months of their lives treating patients with illnesses and infirmities they will only otherwise read about in obscure medical journals. I don't mistrust the peace and contentment that I have right now simply because it is not what I have in my 'real life.' It is my life right at this moment. And right at this moment, it's your life, too."

The next moment Pauline was in his arms and they were kissing. And the next moment she was in her bed alone, letting herself feel peaceful and contented.

A week later, back in Washington, Pauline received a package in the mail. A champagne cork in a jar of sand and a note that read, "*I couldn't figure out how to package sun and sea breezes. To commemorate date #3. Love, Colin.*"

CHAPTER 18

A few days after she returned from Saint Lucia, Pauline and Richard met for coffee at the café in the courtyard in the center of the Pentagon. It had been called "Ground Zero" before 9/11, because during the Cold War, everyone assumed the Pentagon would be the primary target of a Soviet nuclear attack. But after 9/11, that wasn't funny anymore.

"Richard," Pauline asked, "if someone describes a person as 'unfathomable,' what does that mean?"

"I don't know," Richard answered, "but it is unfathomable to me why a professional woman would go away for a few days and not turn her 'out of office' email response on."

"I'm serious," Pauline said.

"So am I," Richard said. "Tim called. He didn't get a reply after sending you a couple of 'urgent' emails so he called your office. When he asked where you were, one of the knuckleheads you work with told him, 'we think of her as dead.' He was so desperate that he called me and I told him that you had gone to the Caribbean for a few days with your boyfriend."

"Jeez, Richard!" Pauline said. "Why did you tell him that? Now he'll think we were doing something that we weren't. Did you have to call him 'my boyfriend'?"

"Pauline, dear," Richard said, "if you jet off to the islands with a man and if that man is not your father or your brother or gay, he is your boyfriend by definition. You and Tim have been playing the 'he/she is not my boyfriend/girlfriend game' for almost twenty years. So now you have a real boyfriend and you think by saying 'oh, he's not my boyfriend' you can make it so. Well, you can't. The words 'he's not by boyfriend' are meaningless if you are running off to Berkeley or New York or Saint Lucia with a man. So get used to it–you have a boyfriend. For almost twenty years, Tim was your boyfriend and everyone has known it except, apparently, you two. He never should have married Mandy when it has always been so obvious to everyone– again, except to you and Tim–that you belong together. If you don't want people to think you are doing something that you aren't, then I suggest that you either stop running off with men or that you marry Tim or the South African or somebody ASAP."

"That shows what you know, Richard Gerard," Pauline responded, as she felt her anger rise. "For your information, I do love Tim *like a puppy*, but I cannot imagine being married to him! It just so happens, I love you too–or I did until a few minutes ago–but that doesn't mean that I want to marry you either. And, just for the record, Colin and I have only been on three dates and, as Tim would say, they were not meaningful dates. So he is not my boyfriend, and he has not asked me to marry him, but maybe someday if he does, I just might say 'yes.' What do you say to that?"

"I'd say going from three dates to married is a hell of a leap," Richard said, sounding pleased he had gotten a rise out of Pauline.

"Why don't you go take a leap, Colonel Gerard?"

It was a hell of a leap.

Pauline didn't sleep well the next few nights. Her mind was still churning when she drove to Rock Creek Park the next Saturday morning to go for a run. Rock Creek Park is a bit of cool heaven in the concrete and marble hell of DC. Quiet in the early mornings, especially on Saturdays. It was a typical Potomac spring morning, which meant cool but extremely humid. The grass was saturated with dew and the branches and bushes that encroached on the running paths dampened Pauline's t-shirt when she brushed against them. It was a Saturday morning creek– slow running, quietly caressing the rocks in its path, barely murmuring a greeting as it poured along its way. Although the sun was up, the new leaves on the trees blocked its direct effect and the path was shadowy and cool. Pauline never ran with headphones and all she could hear was the sound of her shoes finding the ground and the sound of the air being pushed in and out of her lungs. It was a good place to run and to think.

Pauline was almost forty-five years old. Never married. She had loved and did love, but had never believed that she, or anyone for that matter, was predestined to find their One True Love and live happily ever after. She tried not to indulge in the What Might Have Been game, but a flicker of a thought had seeped into her heart some years ago, and as her life moved forward, the flicker had grown brighter. That morning in Rock Creek Park, Pauline feared that she was beginning to see a flame and it lit a place in her heart that she wasn't sure still existed. What if twenty years ago, when she had ended the potential life in her, she also ended a certain capacity in her to love? She loved her family, she loved Tim and Richard, she loved the Alphas, she loved the Creator. She didn't think that she loved Colin, but that story was not complete yet. She knew about heroic love, the kind of love that makes a soldier fall on a grenade to save his buddies. She had never had to demonstrate that kind of love, but she believed that she had the capacity for it if ever tested. But there was another kind of love that would drive someone to give her life for another's. Loving in such a way that she would suffocate in the world if that other person were not there to provide breath. As she was running that morning, she tried to imagine loving someone so much that if that person left the world, she would choose to end her life, too, rather grieve until death at the gods' convenience. She feared that was the kind of love that she extinguished before it fully took hold in her heart. Maybe she was no longer capable of the kind of love that connects one person's soul to another's. Forty-five years old and she had never experienced it. Maybe the way that she loved Tim, or Richard, or maybe one day Colin, was the biggest love she would know. She wondered that if ever she did, whether it would be big enough.

When Pauline adopted the Three Date Rule, it had been part joke, part defense mechanism, and part acknowledgement that she was not ready to love. Then, and now, she was certain that love had to come before sex. Movies like *Pretty Woman* and television shows like *Sex in the City*–promoting the idea that if a woman sleeps with enough people, she will find love –made her crazy. But everything had clicked when Pauline and Oak had been together, and she loved that weekend. Maybe Tim had been right. Maybe she should have tracked him down and given them a chance to walk on the same path for a while. Maybe she was wrong, and maybe he was predestined to be her One True Love, and she had blown it. These years later it made her a little sad that she could not remember exactly what he looked like. When she remembered their weekend, she thought to herself, *taller than me, blond crew cut, blue eyes, buff,* but when she tried to picture him in her mind all she could see was a young Val Kilmer. It wasn't that Oak looked anything like Val–he didn't–but he had the same way of looking. Pauline wondered if Oak remembered what she looked like, her name, or if he ever even thought about her at all. She wondered how long Colin would remember what she looked like if they did not see each other again. On the plane back to Miami, they had talked about him coming down to DC for some meetings at the U.S. Institute of Peace on the Palestinian situation in June. He invited Pauline to come up to New York and they could take in a show. In light of the cards that he had sent, commemorating their dates by number, she knew that he was mindful of the Rule, but she didn't know the nature of his mindfulness. Was he being funny or clever with his "Date #s?" Would a Date #4 be more than just a fourth date to him? To her? Would it give rise to expectations from either of them?

That damn Richard! He just had to over-think everything and make sure that she did too. All his talk about boyfriends and "jetting off" and marriage. Weren't people just allowed to live in his world? Go with the flow and see where it takes them? Did he have to put words to everything and make everything more complicated than it was? Trying to describe something that was beyond words just resulted in everything being wound up into knots. Pauline did not think of herself as a navel-gazer and tended to view most self-examination as self-indulgent. One year, the Alphas had gone to see the *Vagina Monologues* and, unlike most of the theater critics, Pauline found the show embarrassingly self-absorbed and patently pandering to the female audience. She hated that kind of thing. Now here was Richard, making her examine her feelings and think too much about twenty-year relationships she had never given two thoughts to before, and about where a new relationship was going after the Third Date. She knew that when she talked to Colin again she would be thinking too hard about every word they said. Damn that Richard!

CHAPTER 19

B ack in her apartment, Pauline needed to talk to someone. *Where is an Alpha when I need one*, she thought, as she dialed number after number, getting no response. She finally got an answer at Angela's number, but before she could say a word, Angela jumped in.

"Listen, Vickers, you know I'm coming to town for the National Association of Women Judges annual conference, right? Well, I'm coming a few days early and I'm not shelling out for a hotel on my own dime, so get the red carpet ready."

Angela had been a trial judge in the Cities for more than ten years and had earned a name for herself in Minnesota judicial circles and beyond. There was talk, heard and reported to Pauline by Jeanne and Arden, that Angela was considering a run for the Minnesota Supreme Court. Pauline would have thought that Angela was too candid and politically incorrect to run for office. And, although the Alphas, and probably everyone else who knew Angela well, knew that she was gay, she had never ceremonially "come out." Pauline thought the conference might be a "testing the waters" for a run; Angela was not just attending the Judges Conference, she was moderating a panel on cross-cultural issues in the courtroom. That looked to Pauline like a run-up to an announcement. So although not a member of the organization, Pauline had registered to attend the morning of Angela's panel discussion.

Pauline was looking forward to seeing one of the Alphas out of The Weekend setting. Pauline almost never got to see her friends with their game faces on, and she was looking forward to seeing one of her posse doing her professional thing. Angela planned to come to town the Friday before the Monday start of the conference and spend the weekend with Pauline. At about eight that Friday evening, there was a knock on Pauline's door.

"Really, Paul," a familiar voice called through the door, "if you'd just give me a key to your place, I wouldn't have to dance with the doorman to get up here."

"Tim Kennedy, what the heck are you doing here?" Pauline said as she threw back the bolt and opened the door to her apartment.

"What—have your fingers fallen off the pulse of the Corps?" Tim asked as he dragged his bag into Pauline's place. "I'm going to be a military judge and they sent me home early to go to the judges' course that starts next week. I thought I'd crash at your place for the weekend and conquer jetlag before heading down to Charlottesville, bright and early Monday morning."

So it was true. Tim's next assignment was in fact in the National Capital Region. He was being assigned as military judge at Fort Myer, just south of DC. Before taking his seat on the bench, Tim, like all newly assigned army judges, was required to attend the two-week Military Judges Course at the JAG School in Charlottesville. Tim had flown back for the course and after it was done, he would drive down to Fort Stewart and arrange to have his things shipped up to DC. In the meantime, he would have to buy a car, and find a place to live in DC so that he would have an address to have his things shipped. Pauline did not have time to find out why Tim had not mentioned all this in the torrent of emails that he and Pauline had exchanged in the months before his appearance on her doorstep. As Tim was foraging in her fridge for a cold beer that was not there, the phone rang.

"Paul, I'm at National," Angela's voice came across the line. "Come and get me, baby."

"Collect your bag and I'll be right there to escort Your Honor to my place," Pauline responded.

Pauline and Angela had arranged for Angela to call Pauline when her plane landed at Reagan National Airport and Pauline would jump on the metro and bring her back to her apartment.

"Great, I'll come too," Tim said, after Pauline explained what was happening. By the time they arrived at the airport, Tim had filled Pauline in on his assignment kabuki dance:

"I don't know why they have a moron doing assignments. First they told me that they're sending me to Fort Bragg so I can turn right around and go back to Iraq in the fall. When I told them what they could do with that assignment, they told me that I was going to Guantanamo Bay to prosecute at the Military Commissions there. Not only would I have to advocate for the use of coerced statements and secret evidence at trial, I'd have to have pretty regular contact with your boyfriend, Gerry, so I gave that one a 'hell no' too. Then they offered me a seat on the bench at Myer, and I figured, what the hell, I can beef up my rep as an intellectual and hang out with you."

"Who's the babe we are going to meet?" Tim asked as the train pulled into the airport station. "Good Minnesotan gal–tall, blond, and liberal?"

"We're going to meet Judge Angela Martelli, petite, dark, and trust me, not your type," Pauline told him. "She's coming to DC for a women judges' conference and is spending the weekend with me until she checks into the conference hotel on Monday."

"Great," Tim replied. "She can have the sofa and I guess I'll just have to bunk in with you."

Back at Pauline's apartment, after a late supper at a restaurant down the street and a couple of bottles of wine at her place, Pauline and Angela were sharing the bed while Tim made himself comfortable on the pullout sofa in the front room.

"Tim seems like a good guy, but you're the one who has known him for twenty years," Angela said. "Is he real or is it all a façade?"

"I think it is all real," Pauline answered. "He's the only person I know like him. It's like he got in line twice when they were handing out 'happy.' He's— I don't know—he's *buoyant*. He's had some pretty hard knocks professionally, I think a pretty painful breakup of his marriage, and he saw some pretty horrible things in the Gulf War. This past year in the Green Zone couldn't have been much of a picnic, either. Stuff that would weigh down someone else like an anchor, and yet he always seems to bounce back up. He used to tease me about being a water walker, but in fact, he's the real hero. He was recently promoted to colonel, which is more than I can say."

"Sounds to me like you have a thing for this guy," Angela said. "You're not thinking about throwing yourself away and getting hitched are you?"

"You know, I wish everyone would just back off with this marriage talk!" Pauline said, over-reacting, much to Angela's surprise. "No one has asked me to marry him. I don't know if I even love or can love anyone in the marrying way. You're lucky—no one bugs you about this stuff."

"Hold on there, sister!" Angela said. "All I know is that you talk about this guy Tim like he's your best friend in the whole world and the greatest thing since the push-up bra. I don't care if you do or don't ever get married. And don't tell me that I'm lucky—love is hard for everyone. I'm not romantically alone because I want to be. Although I have to say, loving a woman has to be easier than loving a man, but I digress. I think you and I both know that we are the kind of people who find it harder to love and to accept being loved than most. But, that's the way it is, and if you found someone you can love and who can love you, I'm happy for you and I say take it while you can get it."

"I'm sorry," Pauline said. "Another old friend of mine has been harassing me about getting married. It's starting to make me tired, that's all. That and being in the army. I'll have twenty years in this autumn, and I've been thinking a lot more seriously about retiring since the last Alpha Weekend."

"Holy smokes!" Angela replied. "We've been out of school for twenty years? Damn! We are way too young to be this old. Now I'm depressed. You can tell me all about your retirement plans tomorrow. I'm going to cry myself to sleep now."

The next morning, Pauline rose early, as was her habit, left Angela and Tim sleeping in the apartment, and went for a run. When she got back, Angela and Tim were drinking coffee on the small patio.

"Your other boyfriends called while you were out," Tim told her.

"What? Who?" Pauline was momentary confused.

"Gunga Din," Tim said. "Got into town late last night. Said he called, but must have been while we were out."

"By the way," Tim continued, "he sounded a little surprised when I answered the phone. Haven't you told him about us? Anyway, we decided to drive up to Annapolis today to look around. Then Gerry called so I had to invite him, so he's coming too. They should be here in," Tim looked at his watch, "about thirty minutes. You better get moving."

"Kennedy, there is no 'us,' so knock that crap off," Pauline said. "Angela, what . . ."

"Don't look at me," Angela interrupted. "Tim did all the talking. I just sat here, drank coffee, and minded my own business. Sounds like a fun day, though, don't you think?"

158

"Well, Tim darling, my car is only a four-seater," Pauline said. "Did you think of that when you were making all these fun plans?"

"That's why Gerry's driving," Tim replied. "I told him he had to if he was coming. We'll give Gunga Din shotgun and the three of us can take turns necking in the backseat. Maybe later we can shop for a grown-up car for you."

If Colin found it awkward to spend the day with Pauline, two old Army buddies, and one of her dearest girlfriends, it didn't show. It was, in fact, a wonderful day. Richard drove, which was a blessing for Pauline who hated city driving. Colin did ride shotgun and he and Richard engaged in an intense discussion about rendition, forced disappearance, and extra-judicial detention. Pauline enjoyed listening to them debate the issues. She addressed those issues all week at work, and it was a treat to be able to listen to two informed, intelligent people's views without having to offer her own. It became obvious, at least to Pauline, that had he been given a choice, Richard would have taken Colin's position. As it was, he couldn't bring himself to agree with criticism of his country, particularly criticism from a foreigner and particularly from a foreigner who worked for a liberal aid organization. Tim had insisted on riding in the middle in the backseat and after some obligatory "take you hand off my knee" exchanges, he grilled Angela for insight and advice on being a judge. Pauline just listened, leaned against her window, and let the sun warm her from the aggressive chill of the Richard's SUV's air conditioning.

The weather was fine in Annapolis. Because Richard's vehicle had a DOD decal, they were able to drive onto the grounds of the Naval Academy and park there. Before leaving the Academy grounds, they paid their respects to Revolutionary War naval hero John Paul Jones and absorbed some of the cool peacefulness and grandeur of the Academy Chapel. From the Academy, they walked into town and toured the State House where they marveled at its stained glass marvels. They elbowed their way through the crowd to a table at Chick and Ruth's Deli for classic and fabulous diner food. They walked down to the waterfront and soaked in the sea breezes and salt air and seagull cries. As evening fell, they found a pub and as fate would have it, a Quiz Night. The five strangers soundly beat the regulars, but they paid their own tab. No one was surprised that Tim proved to be a Pop Culture king, but who would have suspected that Angela was Sailing subject matter expert?

It was a quiet drive back to Washington. Richard was the designated driver and Pauline took shotgun home. Angela and Colin discussed the pros and cons of woven versus laminate sailing fabric in the backseat. Tim slept off jetlag, so he was revived and himself by the time they got back to Pauline's apartment.

"So, how long are you in town for, GD?" Tim asked Colin.

"Just until Tuesday night,' Colin answered. "I've got meetings at the Institute of Peace on Monday and Tuesday. Then back to New York. But tell me, why do you call me GD?"

"Ignore him, Colin," Pauline told Colin, "he thinks he's being funny."

"Yes, well, Tim's a very funny man," Colin replied. He looked Pauline in the eyes. "I don't know that anyone would take him too seriously."

"The world is a very serious place," Tim said, ready to spar. "If we take ourselves too seriously, we just add to Atlas' burden. I'm serious when gravity is called for, but on a beautiful day, playing tourist in a charming town with good friends, I think a little levity can be forgiven. Sometimes a person has to lighten up and enjoy life; a person's brow does not always have to be knit."

"I'm sorry, you guys are getting much too heavy for me," Angela said, sensing things were getting a little testy. "Colin, it was very nice meeting you. Richard, thanks so much for driving. Tim, you're something else. Pauline, I'm going to bed. Come in quietly. I'm going to Mass in the morning, if you or Tim want to come. I hope to see the rest of you tomorrow. Did we plan on meeting for brunch somewhere?"

"Bistro Francais on M Street at eleven?" Tim said.

"Sounds lovely," Angela responded. "Good night all."

"Goodnight, Your Honor," Colin said. "I guess it is getting late. I'd better head back to the hotel."

"Where are you staying, Colin?" Richard asked.

"Foggy Bottom–same place I always stay when I'm in town."

"Too bad Pauline's got a full house this weekend, what with me and the Judge staying here," Tim said.

"Yes, it is too bad you're crashing at my place, and so uninvitedly too," Pauline told Tim. Her lips said the words, but her eyes told Tim, "*back off.*"

Pauline walked Colin and Richard to the door of her apartment. Richard offered Colin a ride to his hotel, but Colin declined, saying that it was just a short metro ride and walk away. Richard left to un-double park his car before it got towed.

"Let me walk you to the metro," Pauline said.

"No, that's not necessary," Colin told her, "and besides, if you do, who will see you back home? Not Sir Galahad there," nodding his head toward Tim who was already taking the cushions off the sofa, preparing to open up his bed.

Pauline and Colin rode the elevator down in silence. Once at street level, they stopped on the stoop to watch the people who were still out on the street, wondering how those night owls' lives brought them to Dupont Circle in the early Sunday morning hours.

"I've known Tim for twenty years–my whole army life," Pauline told him, wanting to explain, even though Colin had not asked her to. "He's been a good friend, and in spite of appearances sometimes, he's a good officer and lawyer. I think he thinks of me as his little sister sometimes."

"Don't kid yourself, Pauline," Colin said. "Tim does not think of you as a sister. I can't imagine why he would let you walk me down alone. He must know that I'm going kiss you."

"I don't think he would care," Pauline replied, not knowing if it were true.

"I guarantee you that you are wrong about that."

And he kissed her. Not on both cheeks, European-style. Not like a father or a brother or how a schoolboy crush would kiss a school girl. But like a man kisses a woman and it took her breath.

"Well that was quite a day," Angela said, after Pauline had returned to the apartment and was getting ready for bed. "You, me, and three men in love with you. This is great material for the next Alpha Weekend."

"Oh, don't you start, Angela," Pauline told her. "I hardly know Colin, and Tim and Richard and I are old friends. You shouldn't listen to Tim's malarkey—he loves life and all the women who enter into his. He can't help flirting with women, me included—it's reflexive for him, like drawing breath. He has talked the same trash for the twenty years that I have known him. And Richard has always been inclined to be serious and he's become even more taciturn since his wife died last year. He is still grieving and trying to help his daughter through her grief. He has no room in his heart for anything else right now."

"Well, sometimes a person knows when he's found the person who completes his heart the moment he meets her," continued Angela. "And sometimes it takes a person a while to know what his heart needs—twenty years sometimes. And sometimes the only cure for a heart with a hole in it is something to fill it up again. Pauline, my friend, you might want to be careful how you brook this river; you're liable to get washed away in the current if you're not paying attention."

Other than with Angela, and a kiss on the stoop with Colin, Pauline did not have two minutes alone with anyone that weekend. Saturday had been one big group date and on Sunday, Tim, Angela, and Pauline met Colin at Bistro Francais for brunch. They had a wonderful meal and anyone observing them would have thought that they were two happy couples, couples who didn't have a chance to get together very often. Afterward, they walked around Georgetown, sometimes arm in arm, whose arms interchangeable. Angela and Pauline linked elbows, standing in front of a shoe store, gazing at the goods with want in their eyes. Colin guided Angela across the street with his hand in the small of her back. Tim dragged Pauline away by the arm when she stopped in front of an antique shop and looked as if she were going to go in ("it's just old, used, overpriced stuff, Paul"). When they found a shady bench in the little park near 35th Street, Tim sat with his arms across the backs of Colin and Pauline, while Angela schmoozed a pair of bulldogs and their people. There was a casual friendliness about Tim's gesture that warmed Pauline. Men could be so funny sometimes about even inadvertently touching each other that Tim's arm on the bench behind Colin's shoulders seemed so civilized to Pauline. She was glad the men with her were so at ease with themselves and each other, even though she knew they weren't particularly fond of one another. They leisurely made their way back to Pauline's apartment and spent the rest of the afternoon drinking coffee and reading the newspapers on the patio—Pauline had the Washington Post delivered and Colin insisted on purchasing a New York Times. Pauline and Colin were almost alone for a few minutes when Angela retired to the bedroom to review her notes for her panel discussion the following morning and Tim fell asleep on the sofa. They sat on the patio exchanging sections of the papers, commenting on an article or exclaiming about an upcoming performance or exhibition at the Kennedy

Center or the Met. Pauline was happy. She liked having Tim and Angela in her home. She liked sharing newspapers with Colin. She liked the quiet of the apartment against the backdrop of the muted Sunday afternoon noise on the street. No worries about love or hearts. Peace.

Sunday evening, Colin went back to his hotel, after making plans to have dinner with Pauline the following night. He and Angela left together. For all her apparent ease, Pauline could tell that Angela was nervous about her presentation the following morning. It was Angela's first foray into the national scene and she was understandably a little tense about it. To help calm her nerves, she had decided to check into the conference hotel that evening, so she could review her notes and get a good night's sleep without worrying about having to find the hotel and being in the right place at the right time in the morning. Colin insisted on escorting her to her hotel before heading off to his own, helping her with her bag and seeing that she found her hotel and got checked in okay.

"How are you getting down to Charlottesville, Tim?" Pauline asked after Colin and Angela were gone.

"I'm getting a ride with someone else going to the course," answered Tim. "He's going to pick me up here early tomorrow morning. My plan is to buy a car next weekend. What do you think you'd look good riding in, Paul?"

"You just can't help yourself, can you? You always have to throw in a little flirt when you are talking to a woman—even me. I don't even think you mean it most of the time," Pauline responded, remembering the earlier exchange between Colin and Tim, and how she was annoyed by it.

"I am what I am," Tim said. "Your problem is that you overthink everything. You and I may be buddies, but you're still a woman and I'm still a man."

"So you've been hitting on me for twenty years just because I've got a uterus and because I might have said 'yes?'" Pauline said, her annoyance growing.

"Listen, Pauline," Tim said, annoyance in his voice as well, "when I asked you to marry me, back at Club Nightingale, I probably meant it. And had you said 'yes' like 99.9% of all women in your situation at the time would have done, we might have made it work. But you didn't, and you did what you thought you had to do, and I married Mandy and learned the hard way that I wasn't cut out for marriage."

"Well, it's pretty easy for you to say you're not cut out for marriage, and continue to sleep your way through the female population, but that doesn't work for me," Pauline said.

Pauline began pulling the cushions off the sofa, but Tim grabbed them from her and threw them to the side.

"I can manage, thanks," Tim told her. "And where the hell did that come from? 'Sleep my way through the female population?' Is that what you think of me?"

Tim and pulled the out the mattress of the sofa bed so forcefully, the sofa moved forward a couple of inches.

"No, that's not what I meant."

"Well, that's what you said."

"All I know is that according to Mark Nightingale, I was probably penalized by the Corps for being *perceived* to be a slut, and you made colonel when everyone knew–and joked!–about your sex life."

"So it's my fault you got passed over? Or maybe you'd prefer that I got passed over, too?"

"No, that's not what I said," Pauline said.

Pauline retrieved the bedding from the trunk/coffee table, and shook out the sheets to make the bed.

"*I said* I can manage," Tim said and tried to take the sheets from Pauline, but she pulled them out of his reach and after some tussling, they found themselves standing on either side of the sofa, begrudgingly working together to make it a bed.

"Don't you find it at all frustrating that we are held to two totally different standards," Pauline asked.

"I wouldn't say *totally* different standards," Tim answered.

"What do you mean by that?" Pauline asked.

"You know exactly what I mean."

"No, you're just going to have to spell it out for me," Pauline said.

"Fine," Tim said. He stopped tucking in a blanket and stood with his hands on his hips, glaring at Pauline across the bed. "You say I'm a slut. Maybe I am. But it's always–*always*– mutual and I never take advantage of the tipsy or a woman on the rebound. I never force myself on anyone–hell, half the time they come onto me, and I've prosecuted enough date rape cases to know 'no' means 'no.' And the whole time I was married to Mandy, I never cheated on her, *never*, not once. However, you . . ."

"I what?"

"You never even told the guy you were pregnant."

"Oh, and you be thrilled to hear from one of your floozies that you knocked her up? Really?"

"I would expect to be informed and given an opportunity to weigh in. You didn't even give Galahad a chance."

"A chance to what? To tell me what to do with my body? My life? You think you would have that right if you got that call from one of the women you slept with?"

"Pauline, it was a baby."

"No, it was a fertilized egg," Pauline said.

"And, yes," Tim said, ignoring her. "If I ever got a call like that, I would do the right thing."

"'Do the right thing?'" Pauline responded. "What does that mean? Force her to marry you? Have a baby? And I didn't 'do the right thing?' Is that what you're saying? That I was wrong? Immoral? Evil?"

"Now you sound like some worn out women's libber."

"And you sound like some privileged patriarchal know-it-all."

They were quiet. Pauline could hear them breathing, and she was afraid they were reaching a point of no return, but she couldn't let it go.

"Anyway," she finally said, "do you think it was easy for me? The decision I made? To deal with that alone?"

"You didn't have to be alone. You could have told Galahad. You could have taken me up on my offer. You had a choice."

"Right," Pauline said. "I could have married a guy I didn't love and who *just said* he wasn't cut out for marriage. That's a great idea. We could have made each other miserable for who knows how long and then divorced and there would have been a kid to fight over. That would have been *great*.

"Yes, you're right," she continued. "I had a choice, and it was *my* choice, not yours, not Galahad's. And I exercised my right to choose and I chose what I thought was best."

They finished making the bed in silence and sat on either side, with their backs to each other. Time seemed to stop.

"We good?" Tim finally asked.

"I don't know," Pauline answered. "What do you think?"

She didn't wait for an answer. "I think I'll turn in."

The next morning, Pauline and Tim avoided each other as best they could in the small apartment. They made no plans to get together when he returned from Charlottesville. Tim caught his ride to Charlottesville and he was gone.

Pauline spent the next day at the conference and sat in on Angela's panel discussion. Although her boss hadn't wanted to give her the day off to attend, Pauline played the "CLE Card" and he couldn't say no. Pauline was still licensed to practice law in Minnesota, and Minnesota has a mandatory Continuing Legal Education requirement that she had to fulfill to remain a member of the bar in good standing. Consequently, Pauline's boss could not have not let her go. Although Pauline could not stay for the entire four-day conference, that evening, she and Angela met for a glass of wine before Angela went to dinner with some of her fellow jurists. Pauline had plans to have a quiet dinner with Colin, just the two of them.

"Ange, who knew you had it in you?" Pauline said. "You were great this morning."

"Well, I know that Minnesota comes across as pretty beige," Angela said, "but we have our share of issues. For every *what if* someone managed to think up, I had a real-life courtroom situation with which to analogize it. Makes for easy panel-moderating. Also, knowing when to nod and say, 'how interesting,' or 'what do you think?' helps too."

They paused their conversation while their server topped up their waters. As they waited, Pauline saw a glint in Angela's eye and Pauline suspected Angela was not going to be content to talk about the conference.

"I want to know, what's going on with you and Colin?" Angela said, to Pauline's relief she didn't ask about Tim. "He was charming, but not obnoxiously charming, when he saw me to the hotel last night. Very pleasant, very tall, very Gucci accent. He really believes in what he is doing with Doctors Without Borders, which is kind of refreshing–to meet someone who believes in his or her work. Since Jeanne isn't here, I'll ask for her–have you gotten to know him yet, in the Biblical sense?"

"You can tell Jeanne to mind her own business," Pauline said, and laughed. "He is very charming. And smart and interesting and gentlemanlike. And passionate about what he is doing. That's all very attractive and also a little overwhelming. I feel so purposeless and out of my league around him. It seems like all I want these days is some peace–no conflict, no controversy, no 24/7 on call, no rushes of adrenalin. I think if he knew how boring I want to be, he'd drop me like the wet rag that I am."

"Baloney," Angela responded. "You're not a wet rag. It could be that people who are always consumed with an 'on fire' sort of passion need the balance of someone with a calm, quiet sort of passion. No one can burn all the time."

"So you're saying he needs a wet rag," said Pauline.

"I'm saying you better figure out want your own heart needs and go for it."

Pauline and Colin met for dinner at an Indian place near Pauline's apartment. It was crowded and hot. Colin told her about his meetings at the Institute of Peace that day. He had found it refreshing that the meetings had focused on practical matters, like how the various governmental and nongovernmental agencies could work together to minimize the suffering of the innocent civilians in the Palestinian areas, rather than on the theoretical.

"Most meetings that involve nongovernmental humanitarian agencies and U.S. government agencies to discuss how to help the victims of conflict get wound around the axle about which side was right, rather than focusing on helping people," Colin said.

"Are there really any innocent Palestinian civilians, Colin?" Pauline asked. "After all, didn't they elect a terrorist organization to lead their government?"

"That's my point," Colin responded. "When it comes to treating the sick and wounded, I don't really care about whose side is right or wrong. I'm more interested, for example, in providing prenatal care to impoverished pregnant women and treating kids who otherwise would die or suffer permanent disabilities. That's what I like and don't like about Doctors Without Borders—we do provide desperately needed care to the most desperate people. But sometimes the organization gets too political—too involved in who is right and who is wrong. Unfortunately, most of our biggest contributors have political agendas they want to press and the Doctors' leadership constantly has to be vigilant not to pander to them. We don't always do a very good job at that. That aspect of the organization makes me crazy."

"What aspect of your organization makes you crazy?" he asked Pauline, pausing to take a sip of wine.

"It makes me insane that so many intelligent people in DOD can be so oblivious; too often we seem to think that because we want things to be a certain way, they will be that certain way," she responded. "It seems like we get so enamored of our plans that when things don't go according to plan, we can't see it and then get bogged down in years—decades—of trying to force reality into what we want it to be."

"What else makes you insane, Pauline?" Colin asked trying to lighten the mood.

"Oh, I don't know," Pauline responded, "man's infinite capacity for cruelty, people who think that making money is actually making something, people confusing sex for love, tamper-resistant packaging that renders a package un-openable."

Their conversation waned as their meals were delivered and they tucked in.

"On a related note," Pauline resumed the conversation, "in October, I will have twenty years in the army, my retirement will vest, and I am going to jump ship."

"And then what will you do?" Colin asked.

"I don't know, Colin," she answered. "Any ideas?"

"Yes, I have an idea—why don't we finish our dinners, go back to your place and discuss it?" Colin answered.

At that moment, it hit Pauline—this was their fourth date.

"I'm not going to sleep with you tonight, Colin," Pauline said.

"Well, damn, there goes my reason for living," Colin responded.

Back at Pauline's apartment, the conversation lost some of its seriousness. Colin opened a bottle of wine and they settled on the sofa. In the coolness of the apartment, they talked about other important things: Whether Colin should buy a car. Where the Alphas would meet this year. The advantages of wearing a camouflage uniform and combat boots to work. "It's like wearing pajamas and boots to the office," Pauline said. How Colin's cricket team was doing. The *Post* or the *Times* or the *Wall Street Journal?* CNN or Fox?

It was cool that night, and Pauline went down the hall to adjust the thermostat. When she returned, Colin was looking at some papers on Pauline's small desk near the patio doors.

"What are these?" he asked.

"What?" Pauline said. "Oh, those. Those are some sketches I did of some of the stained-glass windows that we saw in the Maryland State House on Saturday. I love stained-glass and goof around with designs and colors when I'm just lying around."

"I can't imagine that you are ever 'just lying around,'" Colin said. "Nevertheless, these are very good. Have you ever tried to make anything?"

"No," Pauline said. "Don't know how. I've read a lot about it and I've looked into classes at a couple of places—there are a couple of places in the area that offer classes. I've thought about signing up, but haven't found the time to do it yet."

"Based on these sketches, I think you might have a talent for this," Colin said. "I suggest you find the time and take a class and find out if you have a gift for it. Maybe it will help you find what you want to do, post-army."

"You think?" she asked.

"I do," he answered. "And I also think that if we aren't going to sleep together—even though it is our fourth date and all!—I'd better go. I'm leaving for New York right after the meetings conclude tomorrow. I'll give you a call."

Another breathtaking kiss. Pauline was glad she had already told him she wasn't going to sleep with him because at that moment, had she not already committed not to, she would have asked him to stay.

CHAPTER 20

Several weeks later, Nadia graduated from high school. Richard asked Pauline to attend the ceremony with them.

"Why are you here?' Nadia asked. "My dad bribe you or something?"

"I'm here because your dad asked me to come, and he didn't have to bribe me," Pauline told her. "He's so proud of you that I think he couldn't stand the thought of not sharing this afternoon with someone else who loves you. And I do. And I am proud of you too."

"Well, thanks, Pauline," Nadia said. "I'm glad you're here."

Pauline and Richard left Nadia at the locker room door, where she and 260 of her closest friends would gown up before the procession into the gymnasium for the graduation ceremony. While they were waiting for the ceremony to begin, Richard made some adjustments to his camera and Pauline fished an air horn out of her handbag.

"You are not going to use that!" Richard said.

"I sure as hell am!" Pauline answered.

"She'll kill you," Richard responded.

"She'll love it," Pauline said with confidence.

Pauline squirmed on the bleachers, trying to find a comfortable position for the long ceremony.

"You know, she's graduating with honors and an invitation to play volleyball at St. John's in New York," Richard said.

Pauline smiled—he just couldn't help bragging.

"Jill was an athlete too, wasn't she?" she asked.

"Yes, Richard answered. "I think that made her disability that much more difficult for her."

They were quiet, lost in their thoughts.

"But I don't want to talk about Jill right now," Richard said, breaking the silence. "Today is about Nadia. I'm really glad that you came with us, Pauline. You'll come back to the house this afternoon? Nadia is going to a party at a friend's house later so I thought I'd put some steaks on the grill for a few people. Tim's back in town, and I've invited him as well."

So, Tim hasn't told Richard about our dust up, Pauline thought.

"Sounds great," she said. "How long until Nadia heads up to St. John's?"

"Almost immediately. Volleyball practice starts in a couple of weeks. I'm taking her up next weekend to get her settled in."

"This is the life," Pauline said as she reclined on a chaise in Richard's backyard, sipping a margarita. The other cookout guests were long gone and only Pauline, Richard, and Tim were still in the backyard, enjoying the quiet twilight of the day. Tim had returned from the Judges Course driving a new BMW Crossover and ready to put a down payment on a row house in Old Town Alexandria. "I made a mint in Iraq," he told them, "combat pay and tax free and nothing to spend it on over there." He had been staying at the BOQ on Meyer until the closing and had driven out to Richard's house after the graduation ceremony. Although Richard's house was only a stone's throw from Washington, his backyard was worlds away. Mature trees and privacy fences separated his yard from the neighbors. He had dumped the coals from the grill into a firepit in the back of the yard and added some wood, making an amiable fire. The moon was rising over the trees and the evening was quiet, save for the occasional buzz of a mosquito.

"This is the life," Tim said. "I'm thinking about chucking it all in, retiring, and living a life of leisure."

"Baloney," Richard said. "I bet you do thirty and then they will have to pry your fingernails out of the desk to get you to leave."

"I, myself, am not waiting that long," Pauline said. "I've got my paperwork typed, ready to sign and submit. I'm waiting to drop it on Branch until after the Fourth of July. Six months from now, the army will just be a fading memory."

"And what are you going to do then to pay the rent and avoid a slow death from boredom?" Tim asked.

"I don't know," she answered. "I've been planning this finance-wise for a while, so I've got enough in the bank so I won't be homeless for about a year. I haven't decided what I want to do yet. I read, or rather re-read, Kathleen Norris' *The Cloister Walk* about once a year, and I'm thinking that I might go live in a monastery for a year or so."

"Now who is full of baloney?" Tim said. "You don't need to join a monastery to live like a monk–look at Gerry here. Besides, I hear those robes are really itchy. I think you need to do something more productive than contemplative. Why don't you go work for Halliburton or Booz Allen or somebody like that? With your experience and security clearance, I'm sure they'd love to have you, and you'd make a bucket of money."

"There you go, Pauline," Richard weighed in, "you can either be a monk or a prostitute. We all should take career advice from Tim!"

"What about you, Gerry?" Tim said, not rising to the bait. "You'll have twenty too. Going to put your paperwork as well?"

"I've been thinking about it," Richard replied. "One of my great-aunts died a couple of months ago and she had a house in Montauk on Long Island.

Now that Nadia has graduated and will be in New York for at least the next four years, I'm thinking about retiring, selling this place, buying my aunt's house from her estate, and living a life of leisure. Do you think I could cut it as a contemplative?"

"I think you're both nuts," was Tim's reply.

Maybe this is how it will be now with Tim and me," Pauline thought. "*Polite conversation in the company of friends.*

"Well, Richard, it's done," Pauline said over dinner on Pentagon Row the Friday after the Fourth of July holiday. They'd individually decided to submit their retirement paper that week and had agreed to meet that evening to celebrate the start of the next phase of their lives.

"I took my paperwork down to Branch on my way out of the building this afternoon," she continued. "They asked me to take it back and think about it over the weekend, but I told them that I'd been thinking about it for weeks and I'm done. I can't believe it! After thinking about it and struggling over it, it is such a relief to have made the decision and to have done it. I feel a hundred pounds lighter! You must feel the same. When did you turn yours in?"

"I went down to Branch and talked to them yesterday," he answered.

"What do you mean you 'talked to them'?" Pauline asked. "Did you submit your paperwork or not?"

"Well, Pauline, I had it with me and fully intended to turn it in," Richard said. "But when I got down there and got to talking to them and they told me that they really needed me to stay in and to go to Iraq for a year, I told them that I would."

"Iraq?" Pauline said. "You're staying in to go to Iraq? Have you lost your mind? What about Nadia? What about 'buying my aunt's place and living a life of leisure?'"

"Pauline, after talking to them and doing some soul searching, I just felt that it's my duty to do a tour in Iraq before I get out."

"Duty?" Pauline said, unable to contain herself. "You've done your duty for twenty years! Deployments, crappy jobs, working for assholes. How much time have any of those desk jockeys at Branch spent in Iraq? And they talk to you about duty and guilt you into going. Oh, Richard!"

"Pauline, I respect your opinion, but the fact is that we are there, our troops are there, and they need JAGs there," Richard said. "I don't think that I could live with myself in retirement if I don't go now that I've been asked to. I know you think that makes me a sucker, but that's the way I feel."

"I don't think you are a sucker," Pauline told him. "But I do think you feel some guilt about the fact that when Jill was ill, you tended to put your family above the 'needs of the army' when negotiating assignments, and I think maybe you feel like going to Iraq now is in some way paying your debt for that. But, Richard, you served the army well and honorably in all those assignments and you were needed in all those billets too. There is nothing dishonorable about retiring, after twenty years of good and faithful service, just because we are involved in Iraq. You have paid your dues."

"Thank you." Richard said, leaning across the table and kissing Pauline lightly on the cheek. "But I'm going. Don't worry, I plan on taking the advice Tim gave me when I told him and try not to get my ass blown off."

"Well, that's good–you'd look pretty funny ass-less," Pauline said, trying to make light. "When are you going over? Have you told Nadia?"

"They are going to cut me orders with a 1 October report date," Richard said. "I haven't told Nadia yet. I'll probably go up next weekend to talk to her. Why don't you come up with me? You've had a good rapport with her since Jill died."

"Not for all the salt in the ocean!" Pauline responded. "You are on your own with this, Mr. War Hero."

When Pauline got back to her apartment that night, there was a message from Tim on her machine.

"Paul, this is Tim. We're good, right? Okay. . . okay, listen, I need to furnish my place before I start on the bench. I don't hate your place, so I was wondering, you know, if you'd give me a hand? Tomorrow morning. My place, I'll buy you a coffee. Thanks."

Pauline did not return his call. But the next morning she drove to Tim's new place.

Tim had spent a mini-fortune on an historic row house in Old Town Alexandria. "Thank God the housing market sucks or I could never have afforded this place, even with all my tax-free deployment loot!" he had told her. Pauline loved it: old wood floors, small rooms, narrow stairwells, drafty windows, closet-sized bathrooms that probably were closets at one time, and almost no hallways. The stoop was two steps from the sidewalk and when Pauline opened the front door, she was in the living room. Immediately behind the living room was the dining room, behind that, the kitchen and a powder room that looked like it originally had been a sort of lean-to on the back of the house. Out the back door was a concrete slab, and a small garden separated from identical gardens on either side by privacy fences. Upstairs, there were two bedrooms and a tiny bathroom and upstairs from there, a finished attic with pitched ceilings, a skylight, and a window overlooking the street. Tim told Pauline that he was going to use the attic as an office and there were boxes of papers, notebooks, military manuals, and files waiting to be unpacked and put away in a desk, bookshelf, or credenza that was not there yet. In one of the bedrooms, there was a mattress on a metal frame. In the dining room, there was a small maple table that had belonged to Tim's dad. He told Pauline that his dad had it in his first bachelor pad and Tim had it since he graduated from college. No chairs. In the living room there was only an old battered recliner and a brand spanking new large screen plasma TV.

"Mandy took most of the stuff when we split and she was welcome to it," Tim told Pauline. "But now I'm thinking I need to start living like a grown-up and that's where you come in. Like I said in my message, I really like your apartment and since you furnished that, I figured you could help me deck this place out and I won't hate it."

So, that morning after a coffee at a local coffee shop, Pauline and Tim looked in all the home furnishing and décor stores in Alexandria for furniture to turn Tim's bare row house into a comfortably habitable space. Later, they stopped at a little bistro for lunch.

"I'm sure you think it's none of my business, but I really think you should reconsider your decision to retire," Tim told Pauline.

"No," she told him, "it is time for me to go. My time with the army is up and I know it, and to tell you the truth, it is quite a relief. I'm looking forward to piling all my uniforms in a box and dropping them off at the nearest Thrift Shop."

"When is your last day on the job?" Tim asked.

"I think I'll take about thirty days terminal leave, so my last day will be on or about 1 September," she answered.

"Damn!" Tim said. "That is right around the corner. What are you going to do with yourself then?"

"I'm not sure," she answered.

"Going to stay in the area?" Tim asked.

"For the time being," Pauline answered. "I'm a little sick of DC, but I like my apartment okay and I can ponder the future here as well as anywhere. I've still got the condo down in Tampa that I bought when I was stationed there, but I have no burning desire to move down to Florida. I guess eventually I'll have to find a place to call home. Some place quiet and the close to the water. That's my dream anyway."

"Want hang out this afternoon and then grab an early dinner?" Tim asked.

"No," Pauline answered. "I'm a little tired. I think I'll just head home."

"Oh," Tim said, "well, thanks for your help today. See you around?"

"Sure."

CHAPTER 21

"Can you meet me in Baltimore next weekend?" said an exotically accented voice over the phone. "I have to come down for a Recruitment Information Session Friday evening and there is something in town there that I want to show you."

Pauline knew that part of Colin's job was recruitment for Doctors Without Borders workers. He periodically hosted presentations for prospective medical and medical services-related aid workers in cities along the eastern seaboard. Pauline was glad that he asked her to meet him in Baltimore and was glad for the reason to get away from Washington, even if it was only forty miles away. It had been a long hot summer. Life in the office was frustrating. All of her co-workers and clients knew that she had put in her retirement paperwork and that this would be her last summer in uniform. Although she was determined that she would not have a short-timers attitude, many of the people she worked with assumed that she was RIP, "retired in place," and either failed to consult her on matters upon which she should have been consulted, or assumed that she no longer cared about the mission and treated her opinions accordingly. It drove her crazy, but Richard repeatedly counseled her to relax.

"After all," he had told her recently, "you should be thinking about your future—where you're going to live, what you're going to do, how you're going to pay the rent. If your clients don't get your opinion when they should, that's their problem, not yours. You're the one always telling people to think of you as dead when you're on leave. Go with that."

"But I'm not on leave and I'm not dead," Pauline had responded. "I'm not going to send back part of my paycheck every month, so I feel like I should be earning it."

Pauline had, in fact, been thinking about what she wanted to do after retirement. She was taking a stained glass class at the Art Institute of Washington in the evenings and was excited about the possibility of bringing some of her sketches and designs to full-color life. For a couple of years she had sketched stained glass that she saw in museums and churches, monuments and memorials; there were notebooks and loose pages full of drawings tucked in drawers and files all over her apartment. In the past year, she had focused on creating her own designs and she believed that she had discovered a hint of a style that she could call her own. She told Richard and Colin about this new passion she was finding. She had not told Tim. She was unsure where they stood after their argument in her apartment, and she wasn't sure that he would take an artistic pursuit seriously anyway. And after their argument, she didn't feel that she was ready or willing to justify the pursuit to him.

So she eagerly accepted Colin's invitation to get away and maybe not think about retirement or Tim for a few days.

Forty miles passed like four hundred. It was like Tim said about baseball—"four minutes of excitement squeezed into four hours of play." Four hundred miles of travel squeezed into forty miles of actual distance. Traffic was terrible and when Pauline finally reached Baltimore, one of the streets in her directions to the Inn was closed for construction and she drove around in circles for what seemed like hours before she finally arrived at her destination. Fortunately, once she arrived, parking was a breeze. Colin was waiting for her in the lobby and had already checked her in. *I must look like hell*, she thought as Colin carried her bag to her room. They agreed that a late supper was not in the cards, and Pauline scarcely had time to unpack her few items before she was crashed on the hotel bed and sleeping like the dead.

The next morning, Pauline met Colin in the lobby.

"I've got a cab waiting," he told her and they were off.

He wouldn't tell her where they were going and she was sufficiently unfamiliar with Baltimore to figure it out. She was surprised when the cab stopped in front of a church.

"You've got to see this," Colin told her.

He was right.

They were exquisite. In 2001-2003, eleven Tiffany Studios stained glass windows in the church had been lovingly and meticulously restored. Their beauty stunned Pauline into silence. The sun was bright, but not garish, that morning and the light poured through the windows in ribbons of color. The church was cool and otherwise dim, and all Pauline saw were Bible stories in colored light. The annunciation to the shepherds. John the visionary. The baptism of Christ. Christ blessing the children. Christ in the garden contemplating his fate. Gabriel the archangel. A young King David. *This is what it means to be to the glory of God*, thought Pauline.

She sat in a pew near a window depicting the baptism of Jesus by John the Baptist at the River Jordan. The scene was beautiful beyond Pauline's words to describe. A shaft of white from a dove shone down on Jesus and appeared to be breaking the surface of blue, enveloping Him in light. She could not imagine how Tiffany created the blues of the sky and water behind the Christ figure, done in such a way that there is no seam between sky and river and the figures appear to be supported by air and water. Jesus' foot appeared submerged in the river where the glass is fantastically mottled so that His toes appear to be under the surface. Unbelievable.

It was quiet in the church and Pauline wandered through the pews taking in all of the glory of the place. Colin sat in a pew in the back of the sanctuary and watched Pauline wander. Pauline knew that some people might say that the windows belong in a museum for all to enjoy, as if all were not welcome in a church to enjoy them. The thought made her sad. How could people feel, or worse, be made to feel unwelcome in a place calling itself "God's house?" Although the "They Should Be In A Museum" set would not agree, Pauline knew that the windows would lose some of their glory, and consequently some of their beauty, in a secular setting. Beauty and glory and peace. That was what Pauline found. She never wanted to leave and at the same time found she felt renewed and ready for the world outside.

"This—bringing me here—is the nicest present anyone has given me in a long time," she told Colin as they were leaving, and it was true.

They spent the rest of the day being tourists in Baltimore's Inner Harbor. They watched street performers, went to the aquarium that was almost as spectacular as the one in Monterey, and looked in shops. They toured the USS *Constellation*, the last all-sail warship to be built by the U.S. Navy, as they learned from the tour guide. They discussed visiting the American Visionary Art Museum but couldn't decide if the promise of "visionary art" was wacky and fun or pretentious. They had a drink at a café where they could watch the harbor and the people. Like most cities of any size, Baltimore is composed of self-contained neighborhoods, and Pauline and Colin legged it all over the neighborhood around the Inn all afternoon.

"When I was a girl," Pauline told Colin as they walked, "we used to come up to Baltimore from Andrews Air Force Base and go to dinner at a place called Haussners. It's a German place, but the food is not really the point. The restaurant is a—well, it's not really a museum—it's more of a warehouse full of sculptures and paintings and a huge ball of string made from old napkins threads. I think most of the art—the pictures and sculptures, not the ball of string —is real art, worth something. They have starched white cloth tablecloths and big cloth napkins and the wait staff are professionals, not college kids or out-of-work actors. We have to go there for dinner tonight."

But when Pauline asked the concierge at the Inn to make them a reservation, the concierge told them that Haussners had closed in 1999.

"I can recommend another German restaurant," the concierge said.

"No, thanks," replied Pauline, "the food was not why one went to Haussners."

Finding out about Haussners made Pauline a little sad. It had been a place full of happy memories for her and she had wanted to share that with someone. She knew that even if she retained those happy memories, the physical things that held those memories—the tablecloths and napkins and paintings and sculptures—were gone.

"It's just as well," Colin said, trying to lighten Pauline's feeling of losing an old friend. "I want to talk to you about something and it is better without the distraction of a fine arts warehouse."

Although he didn't mean to, Pauline was a little hurt by Colin's indifference to the past. And the words, "I want to talk to you about something," filled her with foreboding. *He's just become engaged to a supermodel. He's gay, not that there's anything wrong with that. He has a wife and seven children back in South Africa. He's moving back to London. He picked up an exotic virus when he was in Haiti and has six months to live. He's embezzled millions of dollars and is fleeing to Rio before they catch up with him. He found out and hates me too.*

"Oh for heaven's sakes," Pauline told herself, "pull yourself together, Vickers."

Instead of dining in a fine arts warehouse, the concierge recommended a little restaurant near the Inn.

Over drinks, Pauline said, "I have something to tell you too."

"Ladies first," Colin said.

"Okay," she said. "I've put in my retirement paperwork. On October 1st, I will be officially retired from active duty in the United States Army. I'm going to take about thirty days of terminal leave, so my last day in uniform will be on September 1st."

"Wow," Colin said. "Congratulations! I did not see that coming. You've mentioned that you would be retirement-eligible this fall, but I did not know you were seriously thinking about getting out. That changes things, doesn't it? That's great, right? You're happy with your decision?"

"I am," Pauline said, and was relieved that she believed herself. "Very happy. Now what did you want to tell me?"

"I've put in for a field mission," Colin told her. "I did a data collection mission in the Palestinian Territories a while back and the conditions there have been weighing heavily on my mind. I did a Doctors Without Borders recruitment tour through New England last month, and I was really discouraged by how few of the people who showed up for our information sessions seemed to have any real passion to serve as aid workers. So, when I got back from the New England trip, I requested another field mission and I'm heading over for Hebron in the West Bank in mid-September."

"Wow," it was Pauline's turn to be surprised. "Congratulations to you, too. I guess this is going to be a big autumn for both of us."

"Listen," Colin said. "I have an idea. I have been trying to figure out what I'm going to do with my apartment while I am gone. I hate to leave it empty for six months. I thought about finding a house sitter, or asking if someone at Doctors needs a place to live for a while, or knows anyone who needs a place to live for a while, but now I have a better idea. Since you are going to be out of the army and you have to live some place, why don't you come up and live in my place while I am gone?"

"Colin . . ." Pauline began.

"Wait," he interrupted, "before you say 'no.' You don't have any plans in DC, do you, and I know you don't particularly care for Washington, so you have no reason to stay there, right? You can come up, live rent free in a great apartment, take in all the city has to offer, and think about what you want to do next. Your expenses will be nil, so you won't have to find a paying gig right away, you can enjoy some down time and time to contemplate life with no worries."

"But, Colin . . ."

"It's not Tim Kennedy is it?" Colin asked.

"No," Pauline responded, "it isn't Tim, Colin. I just don't know . . ."

"Just think about it," Colin said. "You can come up to the city, I'll be gone, no one will be there to bother you, and you can have six months to yourself. Work on your glass. Take classes. Go to museums. Anything you want. Why not say 'yes' and I can have some peace of mind and you can have some peace?"

"All right," Pauline agreed. "I'll come up. But you have to let me pay rent—I don't want to freeload or feel indebted."

"No," Colin said, "you're not getting it. You really will be doing me a favor by staying there. Nothing would be more worrisome than an empty apartment in Manhattan. And Pauline, I can't take money from you. I just can't. And besides, after six months, when I get back, maybe you will want to stay and then taking money from you would just be, well, wrong somehow."

"Stay?" she asked quietly.

"Yes," he answered. "Stay with me."

"Oh, I see," was all she could manage.

When Pauline returned to DC from Baltimore, she found another message from Tim.

"Pauline, this is Tim. All the furniture has been delivered and I'm having a little housewarming-slash-cookout Friday night. Hope you can come."

Pauline did not return his call, but Friday after work she drove from the Pentagon to Tim's row house. When she got there, she found a nice crowd of people there–plenty to buffer her from Tim, and she was relieved that they wouldn't have to be alone together. In addition to the JAGs that were there, there were a few combat arms officers with whom Tim had served in Iraq and elsewhere, and some civilian paralegals from the Court. The only guests unconnected with the military were Tim's new neighbors and a girl from one of the home décor shops that Tim had chatted up over the purchase of some dining room chairs.

Pauline was enjoying a glass of wine and talking to some of the officers she knew from Leavenworth, when Tim asked her if he could have a word. Pauline felt a pit in her stomach, rising to her throat, but she nodded and let him lead her to a quiet corner of his backyard.

"Listen, Pauline," Tim told her, "I've been thinking. If you need a place to stay while you are living on a fixed income, you can camp out in my attic. It's quiet up there and I would leave you alone. You could think of it as your artist's garret."

Pauline was surprised by his offer and surprised that he knew about her art.

"Why would I be interested in an artist's garret?" Pauline asked.

"Gerry told me all about the classes that you've been taking," Tim answered.

"Don't you and Richard have anything better to talk about than what I'm doing?" Pauline asked. She wasn't sure why it bothered her that Richard had shared her plans with Tim. "Maybe like, life in the Green Zone or how to avoid being blown to bits by an IED?"

"Plenty of time for that before he leaves, Paul," Tim said. "I was just thinking you could save some money on rent by moving out of your Dupont Circle place. Your retirement check isn't going to go that far in DC, and you don't want to rush the 'starving' part of 'starving artist,' do you? Save a few bucks and move in here."

Pauline was unsettled by Tim's offer. She was glad she had a fallback.

"Actually," she said, "Colin has offered me his apartment in New York for six months while he's gone on a field mission in the West Bank."

"Colin?" Tim asked. "You're still seeing that guy?"

"Yes, I happen to like 'that guy,'" Pauline said. "Why do you have a problem with Colin anyway?"

"Gee, I don't know–let me think--why would I have a problem with Gunga Din?" Tim answered. "After all, he's a doctor and has that great accent and works for an uber-liberal aid organization and jets you off to the islands to watch cricket. You probably think that makes him exotic and interesting and deep. But in actuality he is just exactly what he appears to be–a rich elitist liberal who figures the best way to get you in the sack is to sweep you off your feet with his 'fine manners' and 'exotic accent.' I see him for what he is: a foreigner who looks down his nose at the U.S. and our barbaric policies from his ivory tower with the fabulous river views. People like him sit around drinking designer martinis and bashing America and telling each other that if America would just be nice and do whatever the rich elitists liberals say we should do, we would be one big happy global family. Just because we don't agree with them they think we are either stupid or evil. Why would I have a problem with a guy like that?"

"Jeez, get off the fence and tell me what you really think about the man," Pauline said. "For your information, I do think he's interesting. And I don't think that he thinks that we're stupid or evil just because we don't agree with all his views. People can disagree, you know, without one or the other being stupid or evil."

"Listen," she continued, "I better go."

"No," Tim said, "that's not necessary. Stay. It might be the last time you, Gerry, and I are in the same place at the same time for a while."

Pauline nodded her assent and left him in the corner of the yard.

Later that night, after all the others had gone, Tim, Richard, and Pauline drew their patio chairs together around the chiminea that Tim had installed on the back porch and shared the quiet that comes in the wake of the last guests to say "good night" and depart.

"So when are you moving to New York?" Tim asked, returning to the earlier conversation, without mentioning Colin or that Pauline would be moving to his apartment.

"Around Labor Day," Pauline answered. She was confused by Tim's outburst about Colin and, notwithstanding Tim's offer to stay at his place, she did not know what their relationship was anymore.

"When do you leave for Iraq?" Pauline asked Richard, to change the subject.

"Monday, October 1," Richard answered. "Fly from JFK to Frankfurt, and to Baghdad on mil air from there. Thought I'd come up to New York a few days early and spend some time with Nadia and take care of a few things before I leave. Maybe we can get together."

"That would be good," Pauline said. "What are you doing about your house?"

"I'm selling the house in McLean and buying the place in Montauk from my aunt's estate," Richard answered. "I'm going to retire sooner or later and I can't see myself coming back to the house here. And, the chance to buy a place in Montauk is just too great an opportunity to pass up. That's one of the things I need to take care of before I head out; she hadn't lived in the house during the last few of years of her life. I need to drive out to Long Island and see what sort of state that it's in. If I'm lucky it won't take much, and maybe nothing at all, to make it habitable again. By the way," he continued, "can I give Nadia your contact info in New York? Just in case she needs anything?"

"Of course," Pauline told him. "Be sure that she knows that she's welcome to come into Manhattan and stay with me anytime."

"Well," Tim said, "it sounds like you all are going to be one big happy family in New York."

"Poor Tim!" Richard said. "Should I send a note to the Chief Judge?"

He pretended to read from a piece of paper. "All of Colonel Kennedy's friends have moved away. Please make sure that someone sits at the lunch table with him until he makes some new ones."

"Jeez, and I didn't know you had 'bitch' in you, Gerry," Tim responded.

CHAPTER 22

The transition from active duty to retired life seemed to have been turned upside down. Pauline had expected the official termination from active duty to be reasonably easy. Put in her paperwork, clean out her cubicle, turn in her security badge, and walk away. She had forgotten about the curse of an organization the size of the Department of Defense: bureaucracy. Fill out these forms, make four copies of these records, go to these places and get these blocks on these forms checked by these bureaucrats. Complete a retirement physical examination—not to make sure one is well or to treat any illnesses or injuries, but rather to document how badly the army had broken the retiree—running for twenty years, sometimes in combat boots, jumping out of perfectly good airplanes, and quarterly trips to the firing range can take a toll. Apparently, no one, Pauline concluded, leaves the army with ankles, knees, and hearing intact. On the other hand, that aspect of transition that Pauline had anticipated to be difficult was easy. Give notice on the apartment. Move some furniture and boxes to storage, donate other furniture and boxes to charity, say a few brief, hopefully poignant, words at her retirement ceremony, drop her uniforms off at a thrift shop, and that was that. Twenty years done and done. She spent her last night in Washington in Richard's spare room and in the morning she gave him the keys to her car. He had sold his vehicle in anticipation of not needing it while he was in Iraq, and Pauline had insisted that he keep hers to use it to take care of his business in Washington before he left. He could drive it up to New York and use it to take care of things on Long Island as well. In the meantime, she could figure out where to garage it in the city. That last morning, Richard took her to Union Station to catch the train to New York and that was that. Lieutenant Colonel, retired, Pauline Vickers had left the building.

The few days she had in New York with Colin before he left were also easy. They went for runs (some habits are hard to break), drank coffee from bowls, read the newspapers, went to restaurants, saw some sights, and Colin played a last cricket match, soundly beating a team comprised mostly of British expats and anglophiles. One night they went to dinner with friends of Colin, one of whom was a glassblower who taught classes at a Brooklyn community center. Pauline and the glassblower spent a good part of the evening talking about their artistic aspirations and agreed to meet again to talk about Pauline renting space in the other's storefront-turned-studio in Brooklyn.

Pauline and Colin were easy and relaxed with each other. At times, Pauline felt like they were an old married couple–they seemed to want to do the same things without talking about it and much of their time was spent in amiable silence. Colin spent some time at the hospital and at the Doctors Without Borders offices, preparing for his trip. Pauline found that she was comfortable alone in his apartment and found herself feeling at home there more quickly than she would have expected. They did not talk about what would happen when he returned from the Middle East in six months, and Pauline did not think about where she would be living or what she would be doing in six months' time.

Pauline's lack of concern about the future surprised her. She had never *not* worried about the future, and the fact that she was okay with not knowing what the future held was a new feeling for her.

One morning, after an early run and a coffee, Pauline walked with Colin down to the lobby with his bags. As they waited for a taxi to take him to JFK, she thought about telling him to have a good trip, to be safe over there, or that she would be thinking of him. She thought about saying those things but didn't, because she knew that she did not need to say those words in order for Colin to hear them. She thought about telling him that she loved him, but she didn't know if she did, and if she did she was not sure what kind of love she was feeling, so how could she accurately express it in the few moments they had before he was gone? Colin, however, found words. When a taxi finally responded to his hail, he opened the cab door, kissed her, and said, "please stay." He kissed her again and Pauline was alone.

About a week after Colin left, Richard drove Pauline's car up to Long Island to close on his aunt's house. When that was done he had taken a train into the city, leaving Pauline's car in Montauk, until she figured out what she was going to do with it. That night, he was going to stay with Pauline in Colin/Pauline's apartment and Nadia took the subway into Manhattan to go to dinner with them. While Richard showered, Nadia and Pauline shared a few quiet moments.

Standing in front of the window, taking in the night cityscape, from out of the midnight blue, Nadia said, "If you and my dad want to get married, that's okay with me."

"Married?" Pauline asked. "What are you talking about?"

"Listen," Nadia said, "I know that Mother has only been gone for a few years, but if you guys want to get married, you don't have to put it off on my account. She was horrible to me and to Dad, and it's stupid if you think that you have to wait out of some sort of misplaced respect for her memory."

Pauline was too shocked to respond, and Nadia continued "My Grandparents Monroe will probably have a fit, but who cares? They didn't have to put up with her horribleness–they stayed comfortable in Seattle–never lifted a finger to help–while my dad and I took care of her, loved her, and took her hatefulness toward us. It was awful for years. If my dad can be happy with you, then I am happy for him."

Nadia was crying. Pauline could hear the water running in the shower. Pauline put her arms around the sobbing girl and led her to the sofa.

"Nadia, listen to me," Pauline told her. "Listen to me. Your mother did not hate you. She loved you. She loved you so much, and she had to live with knowing that she would not see you grown. Never see you married and happy in a life of your own. She had to live with knowing that she would not be there for you when you were hurt, or when your heart was broken, or when you suffered disappointment. I cannot imagine being blessed with a daughter, a daughter like you, intelligent and caring and gifted and beautiful, and knowing that I would not be there for such a daughter when she needed a mother. It would kill me and I know that that knowledge was like a knife through your mother's heart. I can understand that she would be angry at times and frustrated and frightened. But she loved you. There are not words to express the love that a woman feels for a child, especially the kind of love that she has for a daughter, but you must know and must not forget that your mother had that kind of love for you. And it would have been an agony for her."

Nadia had stopped crying and her shoulders were still under Pauline's arm. The water had stopped running in the shower while Pauline was talking, but neither woman noticed.

"Now," Pauline told Nadia, "I'm going to go tell your dad to stop hogging the bathroom so you can go wash your face and we can go find something to eat."

"It's all yours," Richard said from the doorway of the bathroom, his hair wet and his shirt sticking to his still damp torso.

"No hurry, honey," he told Nadia, "Pauline and I can have a drink while we wait."

Nadia looked at her father. She kissed Pauline, rose from the sofa, and kissed her father as she passed him on her way to the bathroom.

"How much did you hear?" Pauline asked him, after she heard the bathroom door close.

"Enough to know that you would have made a great mother."

"Why would you want to say something like that?" Pauline rose from the sofa. "Excuse me for a moment," and she went into the bedroom, sliding the pocket door closed behind her.

"Well, I guess I'll have that drink alone," Richard said to the lights of Manhattan.

"You would have made a great mother." The words shot through Pauline like a laser. She didn't know how she had given voice to a woman who had realized a daughter and who was taken before she was able to see the potential of that daughter fulfilled. But as she was expressing the love of that mother for her daughter, another feeling of love had burst from the place Pauline had locked away in her own heart. As soon as she felt that love burst free, she felt it pass through her and out of her and the vacuum it created sucked her breath away for a moment. Love that had run Jill's heart through with despair, was running through Pauline's with regret.

After Nadia and Pauline recovered themselves, and while Richard reminded himself that he would never understand women, not even his own daughter or a woman he'd known for twenty years, they walked around the park and found an Italian restaurant where they filled themselves with the comfort food of the gods: pasta. They attempted to walk off some of their culinary contentment, but soon found themselves back in Pauline's apartment, sleepy and sated. Rather than Richard taking Nadia back to her dorm in Queens and then coming back to Pauline's to spend the night–"I can find my way back by myself, Dad." "Not alone after ten in New York City, Sweetheart"–they decided that Nadia would spend the night at Pauline's and head back to school in the morning.

Later that night, when Nadia and Pauline were settled in next to each other in the bed and the lights were out and the apartment was still, Nadia asked softly, "Do you really think that that's how it was for my mom?"

"I know it," Pauline answered her. "It had to be really hard for her to love you so much and to deal with feeling like she was letting you down, and worse, abandoning you."

"Do you know what the really worst thing is?" Nadia asked.

"What's that?"

Nadia told Pauline what had been eating at her heart. "When they first told me that Mom had MS, when I was little, long before we knew that it was killing, not just crippling, her, my first thought was, 'oh my God–what if it's genetic and I get it too. I don't want to be crippled.'"

Nadia started to sob quietly. "Isn't that horrible? Here my mom had been diagnosed with a terrible illness and my first thought was to worry about myself. What kind of daughter am I?"

"You're a human daughter," Pauline said, trying to comfort her. "You were just a little girl. That's how kids are. Their worlds are very centered on themselves. When my dad went to Vietnam when I was in kindergarten, I remember thinking, 'who's going to take care of me if he dies?' It was all about me. Most kids–the good ones, like you–grow through that. Tragically, something bad happened to your mom while you were still in that place and everyone was naturally too worried about your mom to make sure that you understood everything that was going on and what exactly it was that was afflicting her."

Pauline continued. "I'm sure that once the shock of the diagnosis was over and you and your mom and dad were all starting to deal with it, they were able to ease your concerns and as you got older you could deal with it better."

"No, actually," Nadia said, "I thought it was hereditary until I started high school and figured out how to Google it and do some research for myself."

"Oh, Nadia!" Pauline said. "I'm so sorry. I swear, someone must have dropped your dad on his head when he was a baby! Of course, you know, that makes the fact that you have turned out to be such an extraordinary person even more amazing! We are all so proud of you! But, listen, if there's ever anything worrying you, let me know? I've always had friends I could burden with my troubles and even though they aren't particularly helpful, they mostly don't judge me and it helps just to share the load sometimes. So, you'll talk to me, okay?"

Nadia was quiet for a moment.

"Okay, but there is one thing..." Nadia began.

"What's that?" Pauline asked.

"Well . . ." Nadia said, pausing. "If my dad does ask you to marry him, you will at least think about it won't you? I mean, he's a really good guy, Pauline, but he is just no good at not being married. He really needs someone. I'm worried about him going to Iraq. I think he volunteered to go in part because he was pining away after Mom died and then I left the house. I think he thought that being in a war zone was better than being alone in McLean. I know you're really good friends and even if you don't love him, please, if he asks you, could you at least try? Please? You could learn to love him. Please, Pauline?"

"Nadia . . ."

"I know!" Nadia didn't let Pauline finish. "You've got this cool, glam boyfriend with this really great apartment, but you don't want to marry that guy, do you? Besides, I'm sure he's not the marrying kind–he definitely sounds like more Wickham than Darcy. Dad is definitely more Darcy. Well, okay, he's not elegant like Colin Firth or gorgeous like Matthew MacFadyen, but he's a good man and I bet he inherited buckets of money when Mom died."

"That's enough!" It was Pauline's turn to interrupt. "Enough! If your dad ever asks me to marry him–which he won't!–I promise that I will think about it before I say 'no.' Now go to sleep, Nadia Gerard, and put all thoughts of matchmaking out of your head."

The next morning, they all rose early and Nadia took the subway back to Queens by herself. Pauline and Richard stayed at the apartment, drinking coffee and looking out over Manhattan, watching the city wake up.

"You were wrong about what you told Nadia about Jill." Richard told Pauline.

"What do you mean?" Pauline asked.

"It wasn't like that at all when Jill got sick," Richard said. "Sure, she loved us, but she was not angry about leaving Nadia. She was angry at being sick. She was angry at being confined to a wheelchair. When she would go to one of Nadia's volleyball games, sure, she was proud of her, but she was angry that she wasn't able to do it too. You once gave me a hard time about expecting her to be graceful about her illness. Maybe I did expect too much. But Jill had never faced any sort of adversity before; everything she ever needed or wanted to do, she had or did. When she was diagnosed with MS, both she and her parents were dumbfounded–nothing like that was supposed to happen to *Monroes*. They were totally unable to deal with it. Her parents never got past 'it's not fair;' they were next to useless in helping us deal with it. They dealt with it by ignoring it–if they only talked to Jill on the phone and didn't actually see her in a wheelchair, then it was all right, wasn't it? And Jill never got past, 'why me?' and feeling sorry for herself. To tell you the truth, I don't think she gave two thoughts about no one being there to mother her daughter when she was gone. Maybe she thought I could do it. I don't know, but it was not like you told Nadia."

"I'm sorry," Pauline told him. "I'm sorry that it was so hard for all of you. And I'm sorry if you think I lied to Nadia. I was trying to help, and I just told her how I imagined Jill must have felt."

"You don't need to apologize," Richard told her. "I think in Nadia's heart, she probably knows how her mother really felt, but if she can believe what you told her, even if it's not true, it's better, don't you think? Better she thinks her mother loved her than think her mother resented her."

Pauline and Richard finished their coffee in silence, each lost in their own thoughts.

As they took their cups to the kitchen, Pauline said, "Why don't you shower first? I know you want to get out early to check on progress at the house."

"Thanks," Richard said. "By the way, are you sure you want me to leave your car out there? It sounded like a good idea over pasta and a bottle of wine last night, but are you sure you won't need it?"

"Yes," Pauline answered. "It would cost me a fortune to garage it here, and I don't drive anywhere in the city."

"Here's an idea: why don't you come out to Montauk with me–we can make a day of it," Richard said.

"Sounds like fun," Pauline answered. "Hurry up in the shower, and I'll be right behind you."

Pauline did not go to Montauk with Richard on that perfect day. Instead, she found herself on a plane to Palm Springs with a hastily packed bag and an overwhelming sense of dread.

CHAPTER 23

Pauline scanned the crowd as she exited the gate area at the Palm Springs airport. Her eyes landed on a face that looked like her brother's, only too old and much too gray. Their eyes met and her shock at his appearance must have been evident on her face because he half smiled and made his way through the throng to her. They tightly embraced, but only for a moment, before they separated and Pauline asked, "How is she?"

"We can talk in the car," Brian told her as he took her bag and led her outside to the short-term parking garage.

Pauline had been collecting her things for the trip out to Montauk with Richard when the phone rang and a voice that both sounded and didn't sound like her brother told her that their mother had collapsed on the tennis court and that Pauline should come home as soon as she could. Like all military children, she knew that 'home' was where her parents had retired in Palm Springs, notwithstanding the fact that she had never actually lived there herself.

"Well?" Pauline asked, as she fastened her seatbelt.

"Some congenital heart thing," Brian explained. "A hole in the wall between the chambers of her heart. Apparently she had it all her life and no one knew. She was playing Hepburn Rules tennis with some other old gal and collapsed."

Pauline smiled to herself. A life-long tennis player, her mother had changed the rules at age seventy after hearing Katharine Hepburn interviewed on TV. In the interview, Kate had explained that under her rules, when she hit the ball, anything inside the doubles lines counted as 'in,' but her opponent, regardless of his or her age or infirmity, was still bound by the singles lines.

"Sounds like Mother," Pauline said.

"Well, at least it proves she has a heart," Brian said, staring straight ahead out the windshield.

"Oh, Brian," Pauline responded softly.

"Have you visited her since your accident?" Brian asked, challenging Pauline.

Pauline did not respond because, of course, she hadn't.

When Pauline and her brother arrived at their mother's room, Pauline was surprised that her mother didn't look smaller. People were supposed to, weren't they? In every book Pauline had read, people arriving at a loved one's hospital bed are always surprised at how small and vulnerable their loved one looked. Yet lying in the hospital bed, her mother looked like, well, her mother. True she had an oxygen tube in her nose and an IV with a clear, unknown substance dripping into her arm. But other than that, she looked like Pauline's mother. Her eyes were closed as if she were napping and the sheet across her breasts rose and fell in a soothing rhythm, steady if not robust.

Her father sat in a chair next to her bed, holding Pauline's mother's hand. When he saw Pauline and her brother, his face might have lit up were he not watching the light of his life slowly dimming.

"Come on, Dad," Brian said as he took his father's arm and lifted him from the chair, "let's go get a cup of coffee. Paul can keep Mom company for a few minutes."

There was a time when Pauline would have shot her brother a look to kill at being left alone with her mother, but she was caught unawares and quietly took the chair her father had unwittingly warmed for her. She did not take her mother's hand. Rather, she folded her hands in her lap, crossed her legs at the ankles like her mother had taught her, and waited. She watched her hands in her lap as if they were disassociated from her and she was expecting them to do something of their own accord.

"What are you doing here?" her mother's voice asked, echoing her daughter's words from so long ago.

Pauline looked up to see her mother looking at her across the hospital bedding.

"That's a fine thing to ask your daughter," Pauline said. "How are you feeling?"

"I missed you, Pauline," her mother said.

I've missed you too," Pauline responded, wanting it to be true, but not knowing if it was.

"No," her mother's voice was weak but determined, "I don't mean since the last time I saw you. I mean I *missed* you."

Pauline's eyes began to leak salty liquid.

"Mother," Pauline began.

"Don't interrupt me, Pauline, I don't have much time and there are some things you need to know."

Pauline bowed her head.

"I love you, Pauline. You are my only daughter and I love you. I know you probably don't believe that. But what's done is done and you need to know some things."

Pauline's mother paused for a moment to take several shallow rhythmic breaths.

"Your father and I tried for many years to have children and when we finally had your brother, it wasn't easy. No, it wasn't easy to have your brother," her mother continued. "And the day he was born, I knew I had to have a *daughter*. Brian is your father's son, even if he is the way he is. I had to have a daughter. Someone to carry on my legacy, my life. And I had you. I willed myself to conceive again and to have a daughter and I did. That's not exaggeration, Pauline."

Pauline's mother stopped to breathe, and then she laughed. It was a silent, breathless laugh, but she was clearly overcome with her own amusement.

"Mother," Pauline began again, but her mother waved her to silence.

"When you were born, I took one look at you and knew you were mine. And even when you were little, before you could even talk, you were so hard, so headstrong, so sure of yourself, so sure you knew your mind and mine, too. Just like me."

Breathe.

"It frightened me that I loved you so much and I was so afraid that you would find out how much I loved you and that would be your ticket, that you would know that nothing you could do could diminish my love and so you would do anything."

Breathe.

"So I had to be strong."

Breathe.

"So you never knew the hold you had over me. I was strong and you never knew. And now it occurs to me—you never knew."

Breathe.

"So now I'm telling you so you will know."

"Mother…"

Again her mother's hand raised and she looked at Pauline and for the first time, Pauline saw it. She saw how much her mother loved her.

"Mother. . ."

"I wanted so much for you to have a child–a daughter–so you would know how much joy a daughter would bring and how much pain, too. And I wanted a granddaughter. A granddaughter I could love and not worry about loving too much."

Breathe.

"And you took that from me, Pauline."

"Mother…"

But again, that hand went up.

"That hurt me very much, Pauline," her mother said. "But, now, I've decided to forgive you. You probably thought you were doing the right thing, however selfish and misguided."

Breathe.

"I forgive you."

Pauline didn't know what to say, so she said what her mother taught her to say under such circumstances.

"Thank you, Mother."

Pauline's mother, exhausted, lay back on the pillow and closed her eyes. Breathing.

Pauline left her mother, apparently sleeping, and sought air to breathe in the wide hospital corridor. She, too, was exhausted. Her father and brother returned from the hospital cafeteria, and her father went in to sit with his wife.

"So, what's going on?" Pauline asked.

"Dad says the doctor says that they could operate to repair the hole, but she's so weak that she might not make it," Brian told her. "And Mom got it into her head that, worst case, she would have a stroke on the table and wind up a vegetable with a good heart."

"Brian!"

"I'm just telling you what she said," Brian said. "So, she said 'no surgery,' and made Dad promise."

They sat in silence until their father came out of their mother's room and told them their mother was gone.

Pauline spent the days following her mother's death helping her father go through her mother's things. The house in Palm Springs was stifling, just like her parents liked it. Her brother spent most of the days out by the pool in the one hundred plus degree sun, but at least out there, the air was circulating and although oven-like, at least it was convection oven-like. Pauline and her brother did not talk about their mother's death or life. Not talking was the Vickers way. Vickers relationships were as stifled as the air in the house, and her mother's passing did not change that.

Pauline's father moved about the house like a zombie. In their fifty-six-year marriage they had relied on each other for companionship through all the reassignments that came with a thirty-eight-year military career, and when they retired in Palm Springs it was for the weather, not for the community. They had kept themselves to themselves, and her father seemed lost with the loss of her mother's self.

One morning, her father brought Pauline her mother's large, worn multi-drawered and multi-compartmented jewelry box and told her, "Take what you want, there is no one else who will want any of it." As Pauline went through its drawers and compartments she found 1950s Bakelite bracelets and clip-on earrings; 1960s beads, bangles, and hoops; some carved ivory pieces from the 1970s and 80s before the ban on elephant ivory; opals and rubies that her father had brought back to her from Thailand; and the ropes of pearls that her mother had purchased when they were stationed in Hawaii. Her mother's engagement and wedding rings were not there; they would be buried with her. A gaudy princess ring made from opals and rubies that looked like a traditional Thai dancer's headdress caught Pauline's eye and she put it on her finger. She was surprised that it fit, and it was then she realized that she had not inherited her 'man hands' from her father.

One afternoon, Pauline found in the top of her mother's closet a box with a piece of a masking tape label that said 'Pauline.' Inside was a locket of hair in a baggie with a note in her mother's perfect cursive handwriting that said 'P's first haircut.' Another baggie held a tiny tooth with a note that said 'P's first lost tooth, kindergarten.' She found a faded photograph of a picture of a young woman and a little girl on the end of a dock on a lake with a motorboat in the background. The little girl was sitting on the edge of the dock, with her feet dangling over the water, her hands folded in her lap. The young woman was reclining on her side, legs encased in white clam diggers stretched out along the wooden planks, propped up on one elbow, with her head almost pressed to the little girl's back. Pauline held the picture close to her face and squinting, she could see that the little girl's hands were not folded, but were holding the young woman's second arm which encased the little girl around the waist. Pauline turned to picture over and saw 'Spirit Lake, 1966' was written on the back in that perfect cursive. Pauline recognized her younger self and her mother, but she had no recollection of the picture, the dock, or a vacation at a lake. Her father would have been serving his first tour in Vietnam in 1966, and Pauline had no idea who could have taken the picture, or under what circumstances. Pauline also found all of her first-day-of-school pictures and report cards, kindergarten through twelfth grade, and programs from her eighth grade, high school, college, and law school graduations. She found the copy of her first lieutenant Officer Efficiency Report that she had sent to her mother in 1988. She knew that only fools believe everything in their OERs and she knew her mother was no fool. But for some reason, Pauline had wanted her mother to know that someone had written that she was a 'tenacious advocate,' 'first among her peers,' and 'a future leader in the JAG Corps,' and that like those old report cards, it was part of her permanent record. This OER, Pauline mentally noted, said nothing about candor.

As the days passed, her father folded further in on himself and there was nothing Pauline and her brother could do but leave. Her brother drove her to the airport on his way back to his house in San Francisco. Pauline had a picture of a young woman and little girl on a dock in her carry-on bag and a gaudy opal and ruby princess ring on her finger.

"Don't worry," Brian told her, "I'll keep an eye on him."

Pauline smiled her thanks.

"Besides," Brian continued, "did you look around the neighborhood? All those blue-hairs were just waiting for us to leave so the casserole caravan could begin. He won't be lonely unless he chooses to be."

Months later, Pauline took the train from Penn Station to Union Station and met her father and brother at Arlington National Cemetery to bury their wife and mother. Other than the cemetery chaplain, no one else was there; Pauline's mother was an only child and there was no one else. At the end of the brief service, Pauline laid flowers beside the plain white cross.

On the back of the cross, in plain black letters, was printed 'Pauline Honoria MacKenzie Vickers.'

CHAPTER 24

The house was perfect. When Richard and Pauline finally made the delayed trip to the house on Long Island, Pauline fell in love with it the moment she saw it. A driveway of broken oyster shells crunched a welcome to Pauline and Richard. The front of the house was plain and gave a false impression of severity. It was a Cape Cod–*of course*, thought Pauline–one and one-half stories with dormer windows and cedar shingles. When they entered the house, Pauline realized that all the main rooms faced the back. There was a big porch on the back of the house, overlooking a marsh and, in the distance, the Atlantic. There was a ninety-foot boardwalk leading from the porch, across the marsh, to the ocean. "It doesn't have much of a beach," Richard lamented, but there was enough room between where the grasses ended and the ocean began to give the impression of a beach and room to walk on the sandy dirt sand and put one's feet in the water. When his great-aunt moved out, she had taken what little of the furniture that she wanted with her. Over the years, family members had picked over the remaining things and had taken what they wanted. Now the house was full of leftovers, just a shell holding memories of family summers and solitary winters. The house had a leaky roof, rotting windows, and 1950's electrical wiring and plumbing.

"Needless to say," Richard said as they sat on the rotting boards of the porch, "I love it." Although it was almost noon, the sun was lazy and the sunlight muted. From their place on the porch, Richard and Pauline could watch the egrets wade between the grasses, eating a leisurely bug lunch. The sky was blue and streaked with clouds and the ocean was calm and gray. Storm petrels skimmed the water, looking for more substantial luncheon fare than what satisfied the sanderlings, skittering across the beach after the foam left by the retreating waves. It was quiet save for the gulls and the sound of the ocean.

"While I'm in Iraq," Richard said, "I'm having the roof and the windows replaced and the whole place rewired. I'm also having this porch refurbished and screened in. I think that will be enough to make the place habitable, so I can move in when I get back and I can deal with the plumbing and the interior remodeling then. I'm going to meet with the contractor who is going to do the work this afternoon. Can I can give him your contact info in case of emergencies?" he asked. "Also, do you think you could sort of keep an eye on things; maybe run out to the island every few weeks or so just to make sure they are making progress?"

"'Course I can," Pauline answered. "I can see why you love this place."

"I was also thinking," Richard said, almost as if Pauline hadn't spoken, "you know, that after six months in the city, you might be looking for a place to live. By then the roof, windows, and wiring should be done. Maybe you'd like to move out here for a while. Unless, of course, you and Colin have an understanding and you are going to stay in the city or something. Which is, of course, your business and fine with me and..." his voice trailed off.

"That would be fine with you?" Pauline said. "If Colin and I shack up when he gets back from the Middle East?"

"Look, Pauline," Richard said, "Colin seems like a decent guy and if you and he have, you know, something going on, who am I to interfere? He's a doctor and everything, and interesting, and Nadia tells me that he's very, you know, attractive and if you have fallen for him, I'm not going to meddle in your business."

"I've never heard you use the phrase 'you know' so many times in one sentence in my life," Pauline interjected. "What are you trying to say without actually saying it, Richard Gerard?"

"Listen," Richard took a deep breath. "I was just thinking that when you move out of his place–whenever that may be–you are welcome to come live here for a while or until I get back or whenever."

"So I'm welcome to live in your house until you get back?" Pauline's tone became cross-examination-like.

"Damn it, Pauline," Richard said, "are you trying to misunderstand what I'm saying?"

"No, I just want you to say what you mean so that there is no confusion down the road."

"I'm just saying that I think you should live in this house," he said. "With me. That's all."

"So you want to shack up, or do you have something else in mind?"

"Damn it, Pauline!" he said. "Yes," I want you to live with me. I want you to marry me. I want you to be part of my and Nadia's family. Because I love you and when people love each other they generally get married and have a family together. But I'm not going to ask you to marry me right before I go off to Iraq for a year."

"So, yes," Richard said, letting let it all out and surprising both himself and Pauline. "I'm telling you not to shack up Colin. I'm asking you to live in my house and be at home here. I'm asking you to be a mother for my daughter. I love you, and I think you love me whether you know it or not.

I'm asking you to figure out if you want to marry me so that when I get home and ask you, you will have an answer."

"Well, I guess that's pretty clear," was all that was that left for Pauline to say.

CHAPTER 25

C olumbus Day Weekend. Twenty years after Pauline's first Alpha Weekend. Colin was in the West Bank, Richard was in Iraq, Tim was in DC, and Pauline had survived an encounter with an airline counter attendant and was in Minnesota. It was just there that she needed to be. Although Pauline was living alone in Colin's apartment, the weeks between her retirement and her twentieth Alpha Weekend had not been peaceful ones.

"Please stay."

"Figure out if you want to marry me and have an answer for me when I get home."

The words and what they meant buzzed around in her head non-stop. She found that sometimes she could focus her mind on a glass project, and so long as her hands were moving too, she could maintain her concentration. But as soon as her hands rested, her mind took off. She couldn't take her soul for a walk, read a book, or visit an exhibit in a gallery without her mind taking over. How could anyone leave her with such words and expect her to be at peace? How could she enjoy the solitude of the big city, work on her glass, and wrap herself in peace with such questions needing to be answered?

She was happy to be in Jeanne's car, riding out to Arden's cabin. There, in the company of the Alphas, she could wrap herself in the peace of old friendship, thoughtful and candid advice, and the lives of her friends.

"I think I'm going to get married," Pauline blurted out as soon as she buckled up.

"Have you got someone in mind or are you just going to play that by ear?" Jeanne asked, without missing a beat.

"Well, two men have *not* asked me to marry them, and I think I will say yes to one of them," Pauline responded.

"I can't handle this without a drink," Jeanne said. "This is going to have to wait until we are at the cabin."

When Jeanne and Pauline arrived at the cabin, they found Angela and Arden on the sofa, in their pajamas, drinking champagne.

"We're already toasting our twenty years of Alpha-ness," Arden said.

"Holy shit," Angela exclaimed when she saw Jeanne's face. "Grab some glasses, and tell us what the hell is going on!"

"Damn right," Jeanne said. "Pour us a drink and we can toast Vickers— retired from the army and finally breaking her man-fast."

"Just a minute, Jeanne," Pauline told them. "I don't want to talk about that now. It seems like a million years since we have been together—first I want to know all about what everyone is doing."

Although it had only been a year since they had been together in Luray, Pauline felt that it had been much longer since she had seen their faces. Feeling more time had passed than actually had, she was inexplicable happy to see that they had only changed in peripherals. A little more grey hair than last time. Angela had lost some weight, and it looked like Jeanne and Arden may have found it.

Arden had stopped at a supermarket on the way north and the Alphas were content to spend the first night in the cabin, wrapped in blankets on the screened porch overlooking the lake, munching on frozen hors d'oeuvres and sushi, drinking champagne and Cosmopolitans ("in honor of Pauline's move to New York," Jeanne informed them), and catching up. Arden lit the wood stove and as darkness fell over the lake, the light and warmth from the fire complemented the light and warmth from the circle of friends. There were not many lights from the other cabins around the lake. "We are too late for the summer crowd, and the winter crowd won't be up until the lake freezes over and they can drag their ice houses out," explained Arden.

"How are you digging retirement, Paul?" Jeanne asked. "Was it a hard decision to make?"

I'm loving it," she answered. "Like when Arden left the law—my time is my own. I can run out to see Nadia, my daughter from another mother who goes to college at St. John's, work on my glass, go to museums, and read non-legal, non-military books whenever I want to—it's heaven."

"I hear Justice Nordstrom is going to retire from the Minnesota Supreme Court after this term," Jeanne said, trying to provoke a reaction.

"Well, you should know, Jeanne," Arden told her. "You have your fingers on the pulse of Minnesota politics."

"That means there will be a vacancy on the Court," Jeanne continued, making deliberate eye contact with Angela.

"Clearly that is what that means," Angela said, meeting her eyes. "If you're hinting—and not very subtly I might add!—I have heard that, too, and am ninety-nine percent decided to file."

"What will it take to make up that one percent?" Pauline asked.

"Justice Nordstrom making his announcement and Jeanne agreeing to serve as my campaign advisor," Angela answered.

"Done," responded Jeanne. "Now we just wait for Justice Nordstrom to do the right thing."

By the time they decided to get some sleep—they had decided that Pauline could have the master bedroom as she was a veteran—Pauline was surprised that Jeanne hadn't exploded. Pauline had said nothing about her own quandary—it had been the night to talk about Angela's Big Decision, not hers.

She knew that some time over the course of the weekend–at her own choosing, not Jeanne's–she would tell them where her heart was and what her future might hold. She knew that Jeanne would respect her timing. The next morning, Pauline rose early, as was her habit, and when she emerged from the bedroom she found Angela, slipping on her boots.

"Let's take a walk," Angela said.

"Sounds like a plan, Your Honor," Pauline responded.

They left the cabin quietly. Arden and Jeanne were still sleeping. Pauline and Angela followed the tree-lined road that circled the lake. It was a little early, even this far north, for the autumn colors to have peaked, but many of the trees had shed their leaves and were bare, wooden infrastructures. Other trees, seemingly eager to display their wares, had allowed some of their gold to appear against the otherwise brown and grey canvas. Gold, but no orange, no red. They seemed to know that such colors would appear garish this early in the year. The women walked in silence for some time, sharing the contemplative space between them.

"Colin and I spend a lot of our time together quiet like this," Pauline broke the silence. "When we first met, we had this gush of talk and since then we seem to have fallen into a quieter, more comfortable way to be together. Sometimes we each have so much on our minds that there is no room in our brains to form words to articulate our thoughts. And sometimes, we just like the quiet and the chance to have nothing in our brains at all. Does that make sense?"

"Of course it does," Angela answered.

They walked in companionable silence for several minutes.

"This morning, my head is spinning," Angela said. "Last night was the first time that I have said I'm going to run for a position on the Supreme Court out loud. It was such a relief to have made the decision and to have announced it, like the decision wasn't really made until I said it out loud. There was nothing left in my mind but relief and calm. This morning, I know that that was the calm before the storm! Now, my head is filled with how to run a nonpartisan campaign, and what will I do if I'm actually elected. I know that Jeanne will help me with the campaign part, but right now, there is so much galloping through my brain, I don't think I could put together a coherent question to ask her. I feel like I'm drowning."

Angela took a deep breath and her whole body exhaled. "There. Now what about you? Are you drowning in all those men yet?"

"I wouldn't say that I'm drowning," Pauline replied, "but I am definitely going down for the second time. Colin has asked me to stay in New York with him when he returns from the West Bank, and Richard told me that he is going to ask me to marry him when he gets back from Iraq."

"Wow," Angela responded. "And where does that leave Tim?"

"Tim," Pauline said and paused.

"Tim is complicated," Pauline continued. "I think I may have lost Tim."

"Oh, Pauline, tell me what happened."

And Pauline told Angela the whole story, starting from a fairytale weekend in Monterey to the fight she and Tim had after Angela left Pauline's apartment those months ago.

"Oh, Pauline," Angela said. "I'm so sorry. What can I do?"

"There is nothing to be done," Pauline said. "I was stupid and reckless twenty years ago and he's a jerk and here we are. Done."

"I don't think that can be true," Angela said. "You two are like kin. So now you've seen each other's warts and imperfections, but you're still family. You'll eventually find your way home to each other."

I hope so, Ange, but I don't know."

"Trust me, I'm a lawyer," Angela said, smiling. "Now tell me about Colin and Richard. Will I soon be calling one of them 'Brother?'"

"Later," Pauline answered, smiling through tears, "I only want to have to tell it all once."

They returned to the cabin in companionable silence and found Arden emptying the refrigerator into one cooler, and Jeanne was emptying the bar into another.

"What are we doing?" Angela asked.

"Arden's husband came up last weekend and made sure the pontoon boat is seaworthy," Jeanne told them. "We're going to take a cruise around the lake. Arden is packing a picnic, and I'm packing up the liquid refreshment. You two can stand around watching us, which you seem to be pretty good at, or you can go down to the dock and start the engine."

The lake was like glass. The boat was old but seaworthy, or, at least, calm lake-worthy. It was actually more like a raft with sides and a motor from an old lawn mower strapped to the back with fishing line than a boat. It was perfect for a leisurely cruise around the lake. Angela and Pauline boarded, started the engine, and pulled the canvas covers on the seats that lined the back of the boat. After Arden and Jeanne boarded with the coolers, they puttered away from the dock, and began a leisurely cruise around the perimeter of the lake. Every now and then Arden would point to a house and tell the others:

"They own a car dealership in the Cities and the place is mostly used on the weekends by their college-aged kids."

"That place is owned by a gay couple. You should see the light display they put on at Christmas time."

"That house was gutted in a fire and the people who own it are living in a trailer parked in front while they rebuild."

"The people who live in that one are about the only year-rounders. They own and operate the best supper club in the area."

But mostly, the Alphas were quiet like the lake. Until Pauline broke the silence.

"I'm trying to decide if I should marry one guy or shack up with another," she said.

"What the hell?" Jeanne asked at the same time Angela said, "I vote for Colin."

"Sounds like you've got some 'splaining to do, Sister," Arden said.

Before Pauline could speak, Angela dived in.

"Colin is a doctor. Works for Doctors Without Borders. South African, educated in England. It's his apartment that Pauline is living in in New York while he's off doing relief work in the West Bank. Tall. Urbane. Charming. Family money. Father was a doctor for the white elite in South Africa. Mother died when he was young. Brother's a psychiatrist on Harley Street in London for ladies with too much money and 'delicate nerves.' His hope and plan is to go back to South Africa and open a clinic for the indigent in Cape Town."

Angela smiled at Pauline, "We had a nice chat that day in Annapolis."

Pauline was shocked. Not that Angela knew so much about Colin, but because she knew so many things about him that Pauline did not know herself. Pauline did not know about Colin's parents or that he had a brother in London, or anywhere else for that matter. When he talked about South Africa, he talked about life in South Africa, not necessarily *his* life there. Most unsettling, she did not know about Colin's dreams and plans. They had never talked about the upper-case Future; she had never even asked him about his dreams and plans. As she looked out at the stillness of the lake, she realized that she knew nothing about his life. She realized that most of what she knew about Colin's past, she learned in that bar the first night that they met in Georgetown. Their time together had always been confined to the present.

She looked around the boat at the Alphas. They were all purposefully not looking at her.

"And why not Richard, Ange?" Pauline finally asked.

"No, I'd say not Richard," Angela, said, shaking her head. "True, he seems to be a good man. Intelligent. Responsible. Taller than you. But he's too like you, I think. Too inclined to be introspective and serious. Too heavy with duty and responsibility to bring any lightness to your life. Wounded soul, I think. Life with him would always be like today—the sky a little overcast and the lake too still."

"Still waters can run deep." Pauline said.

"Deep maybe, but I think maybe dull too," Angela replied.

"You two are killing us!" Jeanne said. "I think we need another lap around the lake and Pauline, you need to fill Arden and me in."

So the Alphas puttered around a lake in a near-derelict pontoon boat in northern Minnesota in autumn and Pauline told the Alphas all about Colin, Richard, and wounded souls.

Later that evening, Pauline and Arden found themselves on the screened porch, waiting for the Jeanne and Angela to get ready to go to dinner.

"I don't know if I was clear this afternoon, but Colin didn't exactly ask me to marry him," Pauline said.

"What do you mean?" Arden asked.

"He asked me to stay with him in New York, but he didn't actually ask me to marry him," Pauline said.

"I see," said Arden, sensing Pauline need to talk through whatever was on her mind.

"It's very common," Pauline continued, "for couples to live as partners and not ever get married. I know a couple who have lived together for something like fifteen years, they have a couple of kids, own a house, all that, but they just aren't married. Very common."

"And you think . . . ?" Arden asked, prompting Pauline to continue.

"I don't know," Pauline said. "One part of me feels like it's a good way to begin. We could live together, get to know each other better, see if our lives are compatible, and then, if it's all good, we can get married. And, if things don't work out, I move out and move on. Might not be a bad way to go."

"How does the other part of you feel?"

"The other part of me wants, oh, I don't how to put it, a stepping off point. A point at which we commit to being with each other, like, well, like saying 'I do.' I have this picture in my mind of the two of us, in a raft at sea, bobbing along on the waves, our relationship going wherever the currents take it. But I want something a little more concrete, more terra firma, than that. I want a starting point, a this-is-a-beginning-of-our-life-together point. Something that binds us together differently than a mortgage, or his and her towels. I think I want an out-loud, affirmative commitment made in front of God and everybody."

"And Colin doesn't want that—he doesn't want to get married?"

"I have no idea," Pauline said, and shrugged. "We've never talked about it. We never really talk about the future at all. Maybe Angela knows—she seems to know more about what he wants than I do!"

"Did I hear my name?" Angela said, joining them on the porch.

"I was just saying that you seem to know more about Colin than I do," Pauline said. "I didn't know all that about his family and his long-term plan to go back to South Africa."

"That doesn't mean anything," Angela said. "Did you ask him? I did. Please don't tell me that Richard is going to win your hand just because I knew that Colin came from a family of doctors and you didn't!"

"I was just telling Arden, Colin didn't exactly ask for my hand," Pauline told her. "He wants me to live with him, but he didn't say anything about marriage."

"Tough decision for a girl who probably still thinks of it as 'living in sin,'" Angela said, teasing her.

"It's not that," Pauline answered as if Angela were serious. "It's just that I always had it in my mind that I would meet a man, fall in love, get married, and then live with him. I've not really sure that I love Colin. Of course, I'm attracted to him and sometimes I am dying to be with him in the Biblical sense, as Jeanne would say. But I think I need more than that. I might be in love with him, but I'm not sure that I love him, and I don't know he loves me in an I-want-to-spend-the-rest-of-my-life-with-this-woman way. What if he doesn't? What would I do then?"

"Well, my friend," Angela said, "you have six months to figure that out. There is no rule that says you have to decide now."

"If I have to worry over this for six months, I'll go crazy," Pauline said, wincing.

"I think we all need a drink and a decent meal," Angela said. "Jeanne, shake a leg in there! Wash those hands, gloss those lips, and let's get out of here!"

The Alphas enjoyed a delicious dinner in a supper club on the lake. When they returned to Arden's cabin, Jeanne pulled a brown cardboard box from the trunk of her car. She opened it and began unloading her loot: sparklers, Roman candles, Shoot the Moon skyrockets, and Black Cat firecrackers.

"Where did you get those?" Arden asked, "Aren't those illegal in Minnesota?"

"I'm a lawyer," Jeanne replied, "of course they're illegal in Minnesota. That's why the last time we visited family in South Dakota, I picked these up. I've been saving them to celebrate our twentieth and, as it turns out, Pauline's retirement from the army. I figure we can take the boat out into the middle of the lake and fire 'em off the deck. Perfectly safe on the water and since we are about the only ones up here this time of year, who's going to complain?"

"Jeanne, you know I love you," Arden said, "and I love your sense of fun and adventure, but, honey, I don't think this is a very good idea."

"Listen, Arden, if you're worried that we'll get in trouble, you can stay here and watch from the porch. But, I've been planning on this for almost a year and I'm doing it."

"Count me in," Pauline said.

"Me too," said Angela.

"I guess if you're all going, I'll go too," Arden caved. "But for heaven's sakes, Jeanne, be careful!"

"Jeez," Jeanne said, "how hard can it be to shoot off a few fireworks? Teenage boys have been doing it in parking lots for generations."

Everything started out fine. They launched the pontoon boat and puttered toward the center of the lake. "It's as dark as a dog's insides," commented Jeanne. They opened a box of sparklers and entertained themselves making figure eights, interlocking circles, and spinning around until they made themselves dizzy. The pitcher of Cosmos that Jeanne thought to bring helped with the dizzy part. When they got to the center of the lake, Arden stopped the motor and Jeanne set up the first Roman candle. Whoosh! Bang! The Alphas clapped their hands and laughed. And so it went. Whoosh, bang, clap, laugh, until all the Roman candles were spent. They moved onto the Black Cat firecrackers. The cracks sounded like sonic booms in the quiet of the night, the openness of lake amplifying the sound. "Too much noise, not enough show," complained Pauline, "Try a Shoot the Moon." Jeanne took one of the skyrockets out of the box, set it on the deck, lit the fuse, and stepped back. It would have been spectacular, had it not hit the boat's ragged canopy on its way skyward and set the canopy on fire. And it might not have been too bad if Jeanne had not grabbed the nearest vessel containing liquid and thrown half a pitcher of Cosmos on the blaze, trying to extinguish it. *So that's what a fireball looks like*, Pauline remembered thinking later. As Angela and Pauline struggled with the knots in the ropes tying the canopy to its frame, Arden used the empty Cosmo pitcher to scoop water from the lake and throw in on the boat deck and seats to prevent them from catching fire. After throwing the Cosmos and singeing the hair off her arm, Jeanne was too shaken to do anything at all. Finally, Angela and Pauline were able to free the canopy from its frame and guide it into the water without catching anything else on fire.

They had not realized that they were shouting at each other during the conflagration but as the flames dies, and they stopped shouting, the contrast of the silence of the lake was deafening. Once what was left of the canopy was safely in the water and they sat on the deck of the boat, looking at each other with enormous eyes, all they all heard was each other breathing hard and the thunderous pounding of their own hearts.

"Well, I never actually said I had much experience as a teenage boy," Jeanne, said, summing things up nicely.

The next morning, the Alphas took another early morning walk.

"I could see my career going up in smoke right before my eyes," Jeanne said, recalling the previous night's excitement.

"I wonder how Arden is going to explain the missing canopy to her husband," Pauline said, as if Arden weren't there.

"She'll just tell him that I set it on fire and he will understand," Jeanne offered, smiling at Arden.

"Do you really think Richard swims in dull waters, Angela?" Pauline changed the subject to what was really on her mind.

"I don't know, Paul," Angela answered. "He was just so serious."

"Maybe his seriousness suits Pauline," Arden said.

"I don't know," Pauline, said, sharing her thoughts with her friends. "I have known Richard for twenty years and for almost twenty years if you had asked me to describe him with one word, I would have chosen 'duty.' But he is more than that, and I don't think he's just serious and duty-driven. His wife was ill and crippled and bitter for a long time before she died, and he dealt with that and raised a daughter who has turned out great. I can count on Richard to give me straight answers to questions and to tell me what he's really thinking when I ask. I do love Richard, but I don't know if I love him like I want to marry him. I know that when he left for Iraq, he kissed me goodbye and it was the first time he kissed me and I did not tell him to stop. And I love his daughter and I love the idea of being part of their family, but a woman should not get married for those things, should she?"

"What about Colin?" Angela asked.

"Colin?" said Pauline. "I think life with Colin would be a life in near constant motion. Going places, meeting people, doing good deeds. But I'm not sure that a woman who married him would ever have a life with just him. Colin will always belong to belong to someone else as well as to his wife—Doctors Without Borders, his patients, his friends, his cricket team. And she would belong to those others vicariously through him—Colin's lady friend, Colin's date, Colin's partner. I imagine I could make a life for myself with him, but my point is that a life with Colin would probably not be just with Colin."

"You know, Pauline, you don't have to marry at all," Arden said, echoing their earlier conversation.

"I know," said Pauline. "I mean, sometimes I pray, 'God, if I just had someone to be with.' But most of the time, thinking about being in a romantic relationship just makes me tired. It seems to me to be so much work. I've gotten pretty good at alone, well, not alone—there are people that I love—maybe I should say 'unburdened by romantic love.'"

"And what about passion, Pauline?" Angela asked, continuing to push. "Have you given up on having a passion for someone?"

"I don't think I've given up on passion," Pauline answered. "I just think that passion changes. My twenty-something passion and where that got me is different than my forty-something passion. Not so much a fire as a smoldering."

"And do you smolder for Colin? For Richard?" Angela asked, not letting Pauline off the hook.

"Well, that's the million dollar question isn't it?" Pauline said. "I must be ready to smolder for someone! After all, if I were really happy and contented to continue living and being alone, we wouldn't even be having this conversation."

The Alphas said their good-byes back at the cabin. Arden and Angela drove back to the Cities together, and Jeanne took Pauline to airport.

"Listen, kid, don't make things too hard on yourself," Jeanne told Pauline when they were alone in the car.

"I don't know what you mean," Pauline said.

"Bullshit," Jeanne told her. "I know that you are mentally wringing your hands over what to do. I have never seen you so tied up in knots and, honey, that is not how love is supposed to work. I don't think the question that you have been asking yourself and us—should I marry Colin? should I marry Richard?—is the real question. I think the real question is—are you ready for love? I think I know the answer to that question, do you? Are you ready to love and to be loved?"

"Yes," Pauline answered quietly, but confidently.

"Good, I'm glad to hear that you know it too. Now, who?" Jeanne asked. "And don't give me all this crap about how you love these men in all these different ways. I think you are making this so difficult so that you don't have to face what's in your heart and just deal with it. It's not difficult at all—you love someone and, even if it scares you, you just need to acknowledge it, announce it, and it won't be scary any more. Like when you decided to retire, or when Arden decided to leave the law, or when Angela decided to run for the Supreme Court. Once it's been done, all will be well. Just close your eyes and say 'I love you.'"

Pauline did as she was told, shut her eyes, and said, "I love you."

"Okay," Jeanne said, "now whose face did you see?"

CHAPTER 26

I t was the same spectacular view that Pauline fell in love with over a year ago. The storm coming in ignited all of Pauline's senses. She saw the clouds rolling in, dividing the twilight sky in halves of light and dark. She felt the static electricity on her skin, the promise of lightening. She heard thunder in the distance. She smelled the impending rain and tasted the increased humidity.

Pauline looked out into her world and was happy. Tim was coming up for Thanksgiving. Pauline looked forward to seeing him. They had not seen much of each other since Richard left for Iraq, Colin for the West Bank, and Pauline for New York more than a year ago. She had spent long hours working on a piece of glass for Tim—a peace offering of sorts. She had taken some additional classes in lampworking and had learned a lot in the studio by trial and error. After long hours and many burned fingertips, she had finally completed the piece—a chandelier for Tim's Old Town dining room—and she was very pleased with how it turned out. She had modeled it after the chandelier at Pasta Mia that first ignited her passion for glass work. The piece that she made for Tim was a fraction of the size of the original and she had scoured second-hand shops for a working chandelier that she stripped to its skeleton and made into her own pleasant monstrosity with a riot of colored glass pineapples, palms fronds, and feather quills –a nod to the JAG Corps. She was anxious for Tim to see it. It was not her first completed work, but it was her most ambitious to date and she was very proud of it.

She had left her first completed work in Colin's apartment when she moved out: a stained glass window of stylized lilies. Beautiful, if she thought so herself. She had tried to duplicate the undulating colors that they had seen in the Tiffany windows at the church in Baltimore, and she was pleased with the result. She left it leaning against the windows in the living room so that it would be the first thing Colon saw when he got home. She had moved out almost eight months earlier, just before Colin returned from the West Bank.

Pauline had been filled during her six months in New York. She took classes, worked on glass in the rented studio space, went to galleries and shows. She did not meet many people and made no friends. She did not feel a part of the humanitarian assistance workers or Doctors Without Borders crowd; when she was in that crowd with Colin, she had been with Colin and had drawn her feeling of belonging from him. Without him, she felt alien and out of place. During those six months, Pauline filled herself mostly with work and it fulfilled her. When she wasn't honing her skill in the studio, she was roaming the city for inspiration for her designs. She and Colin and she and Richard communicated mostly via email. It was a good way to know what was happening in their days, but it was a bad way to know what was happening in their hearts and minds. In the city, Pauline was mostly alone, except on the occasions that she met Nadia for dinner or invited her to Manhattan for the weekend and for those six months, it was enough. When, in an email, she told Colin of her decision to move out to Long Island when he returned from the West Bank, he did not try to change her mind.

She had felt a sort of peace in the city. Her sense of peace was born with Jeanne making her stop thinking about her feelings and letting herself just feel them. She had tied herself in knots over her feelings for Colin and

Richard, instead of just letting her feelings be and taking them for what they were. Once she did, it was like a weight being lifted from her shoulders. The relief of a decision made or, more accurately, the relief of a truth acknowledged. In the sixth month in the city, the feeling of being at peace started to change into a feeling of being suffocated. She began to feel like the city was closing in on her and she longed for open sky and sea.

When Richard came home in April for his mid-tour leave, he asked her to marry him and she followed her heart and told him what she had discovered in Jeanne's car: "I love you." They celebrated with Nadia, and they moved Pauline into the house in Montauk. There wasn't much to move, mostly her glass supplies and equipment. Pauline was not a collector of stuff.

Richard wanted to convert the old detached garage into a studio for Pauline. However, on one of her trips to Montauk to check on the house before Richard came home on his mid-tour, Pauline had happened upon the Artists League of the Hamptons. The Artists League was an association of local artists, dedicated to the "promotion of the visual arts by providing a place for artists to work and exhibit their work." The League operated in an old abandoned storage terminal on a defunct railroad. The building was organized into unequal thirds; a small exhibit gallery, a middling-sized teaching and workshop hall, and a largish studio. The studio was divided into individual cubicles by corrugated plywood. The building was primitive but clean. A row of windows just beneath the roofline filled the building with natural light but left expanses of unbroken wall space for the canvas artists to display their work. Pauline joined the League and put her name on the waiting list for a cubicle. By the time she moved out to the Island, space was available and she moved her glasswork into the League facility. Most of the artists worked on canvas–oils, ink, watercolors, and pastels. There were two potters. Pauline was the only glassworker. The cubicles were as individual as the artists occupying them. Old Persian carpets, rag rugs, indoor-outdoor carpet and even artificial turf covered cubicle-sized portions of the concrete floor. All makes and models, sizes and heights of chairs, easels, and tables. The artists used the walls of their cubicles as mini-galleries for their work. Paintings in the styles of the Impressionists, Rembrandt, Rubens, and Sargent; watercolor landscapes and florals; and portraits with varying degrees of realism gave life to the studio walls. Some of the artists worked on landscape after landscape, lighthouse after lighthouse, gulls over the ocean and sandpipers on the beach after gulls over the ocean and sandpipers on the beach, to sell in the local souvenir and gift shops. Some of the artists worked on commission—portraits of people and, as often, pets, pictures of houses, and recreations in oils of photographs of patrons' childhood memories. And some of the artists, like Pauline, worked just for themselves. Pauline enjoyed the company of the other artists and she liked watching the reactions of visitors to the League who wandered through the studio section. Nadia thought Pauline was above some of the other League artists—"you're a serious artist; they paint for tourists," she would say—but Pauline explained to her that so long as they were all trying to give expression to something inside themselves, they were all treading in the same water. She had worked almost non-stop since moving out of the city and into the house in Montauk.

During those first few months on the Island, Pauline felt that she had found her life. For twenty years, the army had provided a ready-made life for her to move into from one assignment to the next. At every place, there were people like her, wearing name tags, rank insignia, and branch designation so that she knew upon first meeting a person's name, hierarchy in the food chain, and if he was a lawyer, infantryman, engineer, tinker, tailor, soldier, spy. People who, like her, knew that they had two, maybe three years, to settle in, make friends, learn the job and do it well, and then break in the new guy and move on. But now, in Montauk, Pauline felt like she was finally having to make her life herself and she was glad for it. She met other artists at the League—the landscape painter who in his prior life had been a Merrill Lynch vice-president, the animal portrait painting wife of a publishing executive in the city, the potter who left Madison Avenue to live a Martha Stewart life. Slowly, some of the people she met started to become friends. When she was in the army, she lived under the blanket of the "Army Family"—"we are all in this together so we must all be friends." True, there was something comforting about knowing wherever she was assigned, she was surrounded by people like herself, itinerant workers who viewed their job not as a just a job but as a duty or mission or even a way of life. They spoke the same language, used the same acronyms, had the same gripes about deployments, housing, and duty hours. Now, though, she found even more comfort in knowing that everyone was not like her, and she didn't have to like everyone. She liked getting to know the faces at the market or the salvage yard and those faces getting to know hers. She liked getting to know people before she knew if, and in what ways, they were like her. She found that she had more in common with the pony-tailed, tree-hugging builder who was restoring a lighthouse than the retired police commissioner who talked too loudly about love of country and waved the flag a little too franticly. For the first time in her adult life, she was making her life and not moving into a life that had been ready-made for her.

The year Pauline moved to Montauk, the Alphas pushed The Weekend back from October to the following January. Pauline was glad for the delay; she wanted to finish the chandelier before Tim came for Thanksgiving. The Weekend was bumped because Justice Nordstrom had finally retired and Angela had run his seat on the Minnesota Supreme Court. Angela asked that The Weekend be pushed back—she didn't want to take off in October right before the election —so they would be getting together in January. They had planned The Weekend deliberately after the first Monday in January, after

Angela was to take the oath and her seat on the bench should she be elected. She had been. *An Alpha on the Minnesota Supreme Court!* Pauline smiled almost to laughing every time she thought of it.

CHAPTER 27

P auline and Richard were married when he returned from Iraq.

Just before they were to exchange the "I do's," Richard told Pauline that something was weighing on his mind that he had to get resolved before they married.

"Jill is already in my plot at Arlington and I guess I'll be buried there with her," Richard told her. "I mean, I can't move her and I pretty much have to be buried at Arlington. So, where will you be buried when you're gone? Should we contact Arlington and see about getting a plot for you near where I will be?"

"I can't believe that you want to talk about where we are going to plant our remains when we are dead on the eve of getting married," Pauline responded. "However, I'm pretty sure that I could not possibly care less about what happens to my physical shell after I've died. *'Cause I'll be dead.* However, if you outlive me, make sure all my usable parts are donated and then plant my urn in that little cemetery in Pacific Grove. You know the one? I left some of myself on the Monterey peninsula—you can return my dust to the dust there."

That's how, on the eve of their wedding and after talking about dying, Pauline came to tell Richard about the decision she made in Monterey nearly twenty years before. And about Tim. And about her Mother. It didn't hurt Pauline too much to talk about any of it anymore, but she cried nonetheless and Richard cried with her, but not just for her.

They married quietly in the small church where Pauline had been attending services since she had moved to Long Island. Pauline thought she was too old for a princess-y wedding and Richard was too widowed. Nadia was there, of course. And Arden, who flew in for the occasion because an Alpha could not get married without at least one other Alpha there. Arden fell in love with Nadia and Richard and their home and immediately christened it "the Compound." She also decided that Pauline should get rid of Richard for a long weekend the October after the January Weekend. "Two Alpha Weekends in one calendar year–the very thought makes me giddy," she had said.

Pauline was looking forward to their first Thanksgiving in the Compound. Tim was coming up from Washington. He might bring a date–who knew? And Nadia and some of her friends were driving out from the city.

"I think she's bringing a boyfriend, Pauline," Richard had told her.

"Going to wait on the front porch and greet them wearing a wife-beater and cleaning your Glock?" Pauline asked and laughed.

"What's a wife-beater?" Richard asked in all seriousness.

"You don't get around much, do you?"

"That's why I married you–to expand my horizons."

Colin was coming and bringing his new girlfriend. She worked in marketing for the U.S. branch of a large British bank. When she had seen the window that Pauline had made for Colin, she had asked about its creator. One thing led to another, and one of the reasons that she was coming out with Colin was to talk to Pauline about displaying some of her work in the bank's corporate offices. "We like to exhibit local unknown artists in its buildings, in part to inspire a sense of belonging to the community and in part because it's a cheap way to 'art up' the place," she had explained on the phone. Minnesota Supreme Court Justice-elect Martelli was flying out for the weekend.

"Thanksgiving with you, your new husband, and two old boyfriends? I wouldn't miss it for the world!" Angela had joked.

"Just because you're going to sit on the Supreme Court don't think you're so smart," Pauline joked back. "One of those other guys is bringing his squeeze and the other thinks he can convince you to change religions."

Richard joined Pauline on the porch, taking in the sky and the sea, anticipating the storm. They had decided to move the dining room table out to the newly refurbished screen porch for Thanksgiving dinner.

"If you and Colin's girlfriend can work it out, are you going to let her exhibit your work?" Richard asked.

"Oh yes," Pauline responded. "It could be my next career. What could be better? Living here with you, sharing Nadia, working on my glass, exhibitions in the city, making a little pocket money?"

"Besides," she continued, "I'm not quite old enough to be really retired and sit on the porch swing in knee-highs and red sneakers, rocking, and smoking hand-rolled cigarettes. I swear, Richard, I don't deserve this life; it would be perfect if we had a dog. We need to get the extra chair out of the guest room."

"I think it's going to be too cold to eat out here, Pauline," Richard responded.

"I'm not so sure that you don't deserve to be happy," he continued, "and anyway, if we only ever got what we deserved, your friend Arden would be canonized and Tim's thing would fall off. And you sound like a ten-year-old Nadia, asking for a dog."

"We can fire up the woodstove," Pauline said, happily aware of their ability to carry on three conversations at once. "It will be great—look around—how can we not give thanks being a part of this creation?"

"And I'm not so sure deep-frying the turkey is such a great idea," Richard said, his cautious self coming through.

"If you're going to be a famous artiste," Richard picked up another conversational thread, "I guess I'd better figure out what I'm going to do. Maybe *I'll* sit on the front porch, swinging and smoking, and convince the government that I've got PTSD and collect disability."

"I thought only Southerners put their crazy relations on the front porch for the world to see," Pauline replied. "I thought you Northerners hid yours in the attic. Deep-frying the turkey will be a blast. The tide will be out and we can cook on the beach. What do you really want to do now that you've left the army life behind you? What's your passion?"

"Right now my passion is you," Richard told her, "and being with you in this place. I don't know what I want to do. Maybe I'll write a book—another *From Here to Eternity*, only set in the Iraq war. The great American novel. I really think it is going to be too cold to have dinner out here."

"Our love will keep us warm," Pauline said, singing just a little off-tune.

"You sound like a cheap romance—I won't be using that in my book," Richard responded."

"Can we go to the humane society on Monday and pick out a dog?" Pauline asked.

The house was not quite guest-ready that Thanksgiving, but because their guests were so well-known and so well-loved, it didn't matter. When Richard took possession of the house, it was filled with old—some antiques, but mostly just old – solid furniture that no one else in the family had wanted. One of the rooms on the ground floor had been converted by his aunt into an en suite bedroom so she would not have to navigate stairs as she got on in years. There were three rooms and a bathroom on the second floor. Pauline and Richard naturally claimed the ground floor room as the master bedroom and went about making the second floor rooms guest-habitable. They found a four-poster bed frame in one of the rooms, and more bed frames, chests of drawers, sideboards, and chairs–dining, side, rocking and otherwise–in the attic and in the old detached garage. With new mattresses, rearranging furniture, and generous amounts of Murphy's Oil and elbow grease, the second floor rooms were born again as comfortable and sleep-worthy, if not stylish, guest rooms.

"We can put Nadia and her girlfriends in one room, Tim in another with his squeeze if he brings one, and Angela in the third," Pauline said, having mapped it out in her mind. "Colin and his girlfriend don't plan to stay the night, and Nadia's boyfriend can have the sofa in the front room."

Their Thanksgiving did not start until dusk. Tim drove up from Washington. As it turned out, he did not bring a date. He stopped at the Newark Airport and picked up Angela. Nadia and her friends had partied until late the night before and did not leave the city until after noon. It wasn't Thanksgiving in the Middle East, and Colin had taken care of some emails from the West Bank before he and his girlfriend drove out to the island. As the sun was fading, they all gathered on the beach with jackets, bare feet, and drinks. It was the first time that Pauline had seen Colin since his return from the West Bank. Richard had invited him out for Thanksgiving when Colin had called to tell Pauline he was home and Richard had answered the phone. She was a little nervous about seeing him, but her nerves dissolved when he smiled upon seeing her, kissed her on both cheeks, and introduced his girlfriend, whom Pauline had only met by phone. Pauline had been worried that his girlfriend might not be comfortable in such an un-citified crowd–she was English and her name was Nigella for heavens' sakes!–but Pauline's worries were unrealized. Nigella and Tim were friends before they made it down to the beach, and her shoes were the first to be shed and her jeans were the first to be soaked up over her knees playing in the surf. While Richard and Tim fired up the propane tank to cook the turkey, Colin brought out a cricket bat and ball and the collegians learned-as-they-played beach cricket. Pauline, Angela, and Nigella walked on the beach.

"I should be able to do something with this," Pauline said has she picked up a piece of sea glass.

"The window that you made for Colin is stunning and the chandelier Tim showed me in the garage is spectacular," Nigella told her. "Do you think Tim will let us put it in the exhibit at the bank before he takes it home?"

"I think if a lovely woman like you asks him, it shouldn't be a problem," Pauline answered. "But, Nigella, I don't have enough done yet for an exhibition—you need to give me some time to get some pieces together."

"Take as much time as you need but not too much," Nigella responded. "I think if I lived here, the sea would swallow me up and no one would ever hear from me again. I can see it happening to you too. I think you need to stay connected with the real world or you will lose yourself out here."

"Good lord, Pauline!" Angela exclaimed. "I think she is channeling Arden! I don't know about you, but if she keeps talking like that, I think we will have to make her an honorary Alpha."

Dinner was a perfect thanks giving. The table was not really big enough for all of them, so they sat elbow to elbow which was OK because it helped keep them warm on the cold porch. Pauline and Richard's eyes met across the round table—our love is keeping us warm—and they laughed. Everyone had "it was pick-a-holiday and there I was…" stories to tell. Tim and Richard told stories about holiday meals made from MREs in the Iraq. Nigella made them laugh so hard they cried with stories of illicit boarding school feasts. Angela told "we were so poor when I was a kid" stories about turkey-shaped

Spam loafs and can-shaped slices of cranberry sauce. Pauline recounted the first time that she had real mashed potatoes during her freshman year of college, where they had served mashed potatoes in the dining hall. When she told her mother about them, she complained that they had had bits of something in them. Her mother told her that the lumps were, in fact, potato, and that the reason Pauline was surprised by them was because it was probably the first time Pauline had ever had mashed potatoes that did not come out of a box. Nadia and her friends told stories about their college firsts: sledding on dining hall trays, going commando for lack of clean underwear, grinding up No-Dozes and snorting them to stay awake all night, drinking beer through a straw ("Not me, Dad, I promise!"). Tim regaled them with stories from the old days when Tim, Richard, and Pauline were starting their army lives together at Fort Ord.

Pauline had thought that she was in heaven earlier when she and Richard were together looking out on the ocean, before anyone had arrived at the house. She knew now, at the table with these people, that she was wrong, as she had been wrong about other things too. Heaven was not one moment in time, one flash of contentment, one instant of peace. It was being alone and it was sharing the same quiet heart with the man that she loved, and it was being around a table with a crowd of family-by-choice telling stories and making each other laugh. It was working on her glass, giving expression to the colors inside her. It was telling Tim to go jump in a lake now and then, and it was wanting to have a dog. It was listening to Nadia being happy. Heaven was being where she was, wherever she was, and letting herself be at peace there. Jeanne had been right; all she had to do was accept it.

Much later that night, Pauline and Richard finished doing the dishes and walked down to the beach. Their family and friends were settled in and Colin and Nigella were on their way back to the city. The storm rolled around over the sea, hesitating to bring its power to the shore, as if it knew landfall would be the beginning of its demise.

"I meant to tell you–I saw John and Penny Thorpe when I was out-processing in DC," Richard said.

"And how are they?" Pauline asked.

"Good," Richard answered. "They told me you've agreed to be their baby's godmother."

"I have."

"They also told me what they're calling it," Richard said. "It's quite a mouthful, but I like it."

"Me too," Pauline said. "Penelope Pauline Clay Thorpe. Has a nice ring to it."

Pauline and Richard were quiet, waiting for the storm to decide its fate.

"What are you thinking about, Pauline?"

"About being here with you. Nadia. A houseful of people whom we love. Contentment. Peace. Being filled to 'runneth over.'"

"And?"

"And let's go to bed."

ACKNOWLEDGMENTS

The Army is a funny old thing: a band of itinerant workers who move every two or three years between the far corners of the country and the world. We work together, do PT together, go to the field together, deploy together, and play together. And then we are reassigned and move on. Our paths may crisscross over the years, but we decide who we keep in touch with in between such crossings. Too many heroes and sheroes to name. But, Diana Moore and Vanessa Crockford Berry, you were there at my Army beginning and are truly keepers. Godmothers to my beloved, talented, beautiful Caroline. I am everyday grateful for your friendship, camaraderie, humor, and inspiration.

Law school was not funny at all. Fortunately, I had the non-fiction Alphas with whom to study, commiserate, laugh, drink wine, stand on tables, and celebrate The Weekends. Thirty years later and we are still whooping it up! I love you and thank you, Judy Chapman, Joan Quade, Jenny Walker Jasper, Julie Wilkens-Gaardsmoe, and Laura Tubbs Booth. This fall at the beach!

When I retired from the Army after twenty years and twenty-nine days, I wrote a novel and stuck it on the electronic shelf. Years later, in the spring of 2018, at the last minute, I signed up for MilSpeak Foundation's On Point Women Warriors Writing Workshop and thus began the rebirth of the novel that would become *Cry of the Heart*. For three days on the University of Tampa, I was inspired and encouraged by remarkable women writers like

Jerri Bell, Mary Doyle, Abby E. Murray, Anne Visser Ney, Dr. Kate Hendricks Thomas, and others. There, I met Michelle Roberts and Courtney Rose who workshopped *Cry* and offered kind and thoughtful feedback that made *Cry* a better story. Ann Wicker, my wonderful editor, has made it even better. Thank you.

Thank you from the bottom of my heart, MilSpeak Foundation (and all your donors, including the Wounded Warrior Project) for helping me find my voice, and MilSpeak Books for giving *Cry* a chance.

Thank you, Wallcraft Avenue Book Group, and especially The Arranger, Mindy Taylor, who invited me to join. You have expanded my reading beyond Jane Austen, mysteries, and historical fiction and consequently have made me a better writer. Thank you for that, and for the best girls' weekends ever at Anna Maria.

Thank you, ladies of the St. John Episcopal Church's Contemporary Women's Bible Study, who pray for this wayward Lutheran and bless me every day.

Tracy Crow, president and CEO of MilSpeak Foundation and literary agent extraordinaire. Talented. Inspirational. Generous. Kind. Patient. Funny. You are the midwife who brought *Cry* into the world. Thank-you-thank you-thank you.

Good night, Vienna.

READING GUIDE

1. Why do you think Johnson chose to call her protagonist "Pauline"? What does that name conjure for you?

2. Pauline's abortion results in her spiritual descent. She apparently regretted her decision, even before she carried it out. Do you think it is possible to be pro-choice, but not pro-abortion?

3. Pauline's abortion took place in 1988 or '89. Do you think her decision would have been easier, or more difficult, today? Do you think the military has changed its view of single mothers? If Pauline's story began in 2017 instead of 1987, do you think she would have had an abortion, or would she have kept the baby?

4. Pauline observes and experiences sexual discrimination/harassment during her military career. These are problems at most male-dominated institutions. Have you ever observed or experienced sexual discrimination or harassment in your life? Do you think things have gotten better since the 1980s – '90s? What effect, if any, has the "Me Too" movement had on your life?

5. Other than a passing comment about Arden's beauty, and other very abbreviated descriptions of some of the characters, *Cry of the Heart* includes no physical descriptions of the characters, including Pauline. How important is it to know what the characters look like? Did you find yourself wondering what they look like? How did you picture the characters as you read about them?

6. What role do water and the ocean play in Pauline's life? What do they signify in life and the world more broadly? Why do you think Johnson chose to use water and water metaphors in *Cry of the Heart*? How do they help tell Pauline's story?

7. What do we learn about Pauline's family, and in particular, her relationship with her mother? How does their relationship effect Pauline's life and other relationships? Did it surprise you that Pauline's mother named Pauline after herself?

8. The Alphas' friendship is very special. It seems to be born of the strain of law school. Have you experienced shared misery resulting in friendship? What do you think sustains their friendship for twenty plus years? Arden, Jeanne, and Angela live in the Twin Cities throughout the book; do you think they get together between Weekends? Why or why not? Why do you think they held on to Pauline after she left Minnesota?

9. How unusual is the friendship between Pauline and Tim? How are women-women friendships, men-men friendships, and women-men friendships different?

10. Why do you think Tim failed to tell Pauline and Richard that he was going to get married until the day before the wedding? He must have been dating Mandy throughout the year they were all assigned at Fort Leavenworth; why do you think he hid the relationship from Pauline and Richard? Why do you think he deliberately married on a day when he knew they would be unable to attend?

11. Do you think Pauline's relationship with Tim ever returned to "normal?"

12. Were you surprised Pauline married Richard and not Colin? Or did you see that coming? If so, what were the clues? Were you disappointed she didn't wind up with Tim? Or Colin?

13. *Cry of the Heart* is, at its heart, about relationships: mothers/daughters, women/women, men/men, women/men, and husbands/wives. Do these relationships ring true with you? How do they mirror, or not, the relationships in your life?

ABOUT THE AUTHOR

RLynn Johnson is a retired member of the Judge Advocate General's Corps (JAGC), and currently works with the Department of Defense as an international law attorney. *Cry of the Heart* is her first novel.

Thank you for supporting the creative works of veterans and military family members by purchasing this book. If you enjoyed your reading experience, we're certain you'll enjoy these other great reads.

SALMON IN THE SEINE
by Norris Comer

One moment 18-year-old Norris Comer is throwing his high school graduation cap in the air and setting off for Alaska to earn money, and the next he's comforting a wounded commercial fisherman who's desperate for the mercy of a rescue helicopter. From landlubber to deckhand, Comer's harrowing adventures at sea and during a solo search in the Denali backcountry for wolves provide a transformative bridge from adolescence to adulthood.

SUB WIFE
by Samantha Otto Brown

A Navy wife's account of life within the super-secret sector of the submarine community, and of the support among spouses who often wait and worry through long stretches of silence from loved ones who are deeply submerged.

BEYOND THEIR LIMITS OF LONGING
by Jennifer Orth-Veillon

The first collection of poetry, fiction, and nonfiction to reveal the important, yet often overlooked, influence of World War One on contemporary writers and scholars—many of them post-9ll veterans. Among the contributors are Pulitzer Prize-winning and National Book Award-winning authors.

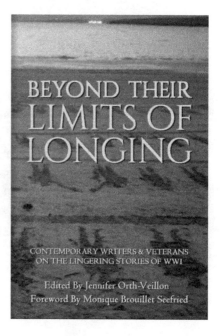

COLLATERAL DAMAGE 2ND EDITION
by Kevin C. Jones

These stories live in the real-world psychedelics of warfare, poverty, love, hate, and just trying to get by. Jones's evocative language, the high stakes, and heartfelt characters create worlds of wonder and grace. The explosions, real and psychological, have a burning effect on the reader. Nothing here is easy, but so much is gained.
—Anthony Swofford, author of Jarhead: A Marine's Chronicle of the Gulf War and Other Battles

CPSIA information can be obtained
at www.ICGtesting.com
Printed in the USA
BVHW041355120522
636877BV00003B/185